# Dead Luck

A Henry Walsh Mystery

Gregory Payette

8 Flags Publishing, Inc.

**Also by Gregory Payette**

Visit GregoryPayette.com for the complete catalog:

**HENRY WALSH MYSTERIES**

*Dead at Third*

*The Last Ride*

*The Crystal Pelican*

*The Night the Music Died*

*Dead Men Don't Smile*

*Dead in the Creek*

*Dropped Dead*

*Dead Luck*

*A Shot in the Dark*

**JOE SHELDON SERIES**

*Play It Cool*

*Play It Again*

*Play It Down*

**U.S. MARSHAL CHARLIE HARLOW**

*Shake the Trees*

*Trackdown*

**JAKE HORN MYSTERIES**

*Murder at Morrissey Motel*

**STANDALONES**

*Biscayne Boogie*

*Tell Them I'm Dead*

*Drag the Man Down*

*Half Cocked*

*Danny Womack's .38*

Sign up for the newsletter on my website:

**GregoryPayette.com**

Once or twice a month I'll send you updates and news. Plus, you'll be the first to hear about new releases with special prices. If you'd like to receive the Henry Walsh prequel (for free) use the sign-up form here:

**GregoryPayette.com/crossroad**

# Chapter 1

WHEN RAY RIVERS WALKED through the entrance into Billy's Place, heads turned. He was just as wide and tall as I remembered him. The last time I saw him was going back at least twenty years, right after he'd cracked the NFL and played linebacker for the Chicago Bears.

To most, the NFL is the National Football League. Some consider the NFL to mean Not For Long. NFL careers are short, with the average length of time spent in the league just three point three seasons.

And Ray's career had lasted, as they say, Not For Long.

At six-six and two hundred sixty-eight pounds, according to his Chicago Bears profile, he was a big man. Although he looked to still be in decent shape with a chest like a barrel and inflated arms, you could tell he'd aged, with his buzz-cut hair grayed over the ears.

He wore a diamond earring in one of those ears.

Billy's Place is the restaurant owned by my friend, Billy Wu. Although my office was upstairs on the second floor from the restaurant, I often met prospective clients downstairs at Billy's.

Most of the tables in the dining area were empty, although the bar was full. It usually was throughout the day.

I'd sat at a high-top table next to the bar, and watched all the wide eyes follow Ray as he walked toward me.

I stood from my chair and shook his hand. "Good to see you, Ray."

He nodded and looked around. "I swear I've been here before. But it looks different from what I remember."

"Long story," I said. "But the original Billy's Place burned to the ground. Actually, it exploded. So, Billy, a good friend of mine, rebuilt it."

"The building exploded?" Ray said, his eyes opened wide.

"Long story," I said, not wanting to rehash the traumatic experience for those of us involved at the time.

When Ray sat down, his body covered most of the chair beneath him, like it was too small for a man his size. He looked uncomfortable. I looked up at the bar and two customers had gotten up from their stools to leave. "We could sit up at the bar," I said. "But we won't have any privacy."

Our table was in the back corner, away from everyone else at the bar but also not within the dining area. It was my own private table, with a view of the Saint Johns River beyond the patio.

"This is fine," Ray said, shifting in his seat like he was trying to make it work. He gave me a crooked grin. "Hard to find chairs for people my size." He leaned on the table, his big hands folded together. "Thanks for meeting with me, Henry. I was surprised to hear you were a private investigator. Last time I knew, you were living up in New York, right? Working as a cop?"

"Rhode Island," I said. "I was a trooper with the Rhode Island State Police."

Funny, although I didn't talk much at all about my time in Rhode Island, most people I ran into didn't even know it was a state. Most thought it was a part of New York.

"So you're retired?" he said.

"I had what you'd call a short career."

"Oh, yeah? You get hurt?"

I shook my head. "I wish it were that simple. It's another long story I'd rather not get into right now."

It wasn't as much a long story as one I did what I could to forget. After being forced to resign from my position as detective because of my belief another officer—a superior—had gotten away with a hit-and-run accident that took a young man's life, my life had fallen apart.

And by the time I'd gotten it back together, the man I knew was guilty of manslaughter had taken his own life.

Only my closest friends understand why I willingly walked away from fighting for the truth. News of the suicide, for me, wasn't exactly closure. But I hate to admit, it felt that way.

Ray leaned back in his chair, his hands gripping the armrests like he was keeping the chair from falling apart. "So, what made you become a private investigator?" He looked out the window toward the river. "Sounds like an interesting gig."

"Interesting?" I shrugged. "I'm not sure I'd say that." I picked up my glass and nodded toward the bar. "You want a drink?" I tried to get Billy's attention. But instead, Billy's only other bartender, Chloe, caught my eye.

He looked down at my glass. "What are you drinking?"

I held up my glass. "Jack Daniels."

"Oh."

Chloe walked over to our table.

"Ray, this is Chloe. She works for the owner, Billy. Although, she practically runs the place." I looked up at Chloe, no longer the young teen and now married to Billy's head chef, Jake. I said to her, "You're probably too young to remember Ray Rivers? High school star, college star... defensive lineman for the Chicago Bears."

She looked at him, then at me with a dead stare.

Ray grinned. "That's all right. You were probably in diapers when I was balling."

Chloe had a look on her face like she didn't know what else to say. "Sorry. But it's nice to meet you." She gave him her big smile. "Would you like something to drink?"

Ray looked at Henry's glass. "I'll have what he's having."

She started to turn away and looked back at me. "I'm sorry, Henry. Did you want another?"

I waved her off, shaking my head.

Billy headed over to our table, sidestepping Chloe on her way back to the bar. He reached out and shook Ray's hand. "I'm Billy Wu," he said. "I wanted to come say hello. We met once, a long time ago. You came in here after you played the Jaguars. I think it was your first season. You bought everyone in the place a drink."

Ray laughed, nodding. "Yeah, I remember that. Would've been nice to've come back and do it again. Too bad there weren't many seasons for me after that." He looked around the restaurant. "Henry said you had the place rebuilt since then. I do remember it though."

Billy smiled. "The last thing you want is for your business to explode and burn to the ground. But it does have its benefits." He looked from me to Ray. "How do you two know each other?"

"We went to junior high together," I said. "A long, long time ago."

Ray laughed.

"But Ray's parents moved him to Douglas Williams High, because they had a real football team."

Billy pulled at his chin, narrowing his eyes. "Douglas Williams." He put his hands on his hips, shaking his head. "I heard what happened to your principal."

I gave Billy a look, and he seemed to understand he'd said enough.

He pointed toward the bar with his thumb. "You know what? I've got to get back over there. I'll let you two talk." He gave Ray a nod. "Nice to meet you."

Chloe was standing behind him with Ray's drink.

Billy took it from her tray and placed it on the table. "Here you go. On the house. You need anything else, just let us know."

I watched Billy and Chloe walk back behind the bar. "So," I said, straightening up in my chair. "You said on the phone last night you wanted to talk about—as Billy coincidentally just mentioned—Principal Hawkins?"

Ray nodded. "You know I was the football coach over there, right?"

I nodded. "Was? You're not anymore?"

"I was fired. Right after the end of the season."

"Oh," I said. "I didn't know that. I'm sorry. Some of these schools, they're so damn focused on winning. You lose a couple games and—"

"We only lost six games the whole time I was there. You're right, losing wouldn't be tolerated at Douglas Williams. But that's not what happened."

"So then, why were you fired?" I said.

Ray shrugged, shaking his head as he looked out the window. "I wish I knew the answer."

I was fairly familiar with what had happened to Barry Hawkins, although I couldn't make the full connection to what Ray had wanted to tell me. "I looked into what had happened. It's clear his death was an accident, so..."

Ray nodded. "He slipped in the shower."

"That's the part of the story that caught me off guard," I said. "What was he doing taking a shower at the school? Not to mention, during winter vacation?"

"He was working out," Ray said. "Using the weight room."

"Is that a normal thing teachers do? Use the facilities at the school for personal use? Showering in the boy's locker room?"

Ray shrugged. "I'm not sure it's that strange. The school's got state-of-the-art equipment and..." He picked up his drink and took a sip, turning again to look toward the river.

I sipped my drink and waited for Ray to tell me what our meeting was really about. I leaned forward on the table. "So, you said on the phone you needed some help. Does this have anything to do with what happened to Mr. Hawkins?"

He nodded, looking down into his drink. "There've been whispers out there." He raised his eyes to mine. "About what happened to Barry. You know what I mean?"

I shook my head. "Actually, no. I don't know what you mean. Whispers about what?"

"That Barry's death wasn't an accident."

"Oh," I said. "From what I understand, there's no question it was an accident." I picked up my glass and held it up in front of me. "But I guess I'm still not following. Did you want me to... are you looking for someone to investigate what happened?" I shook my head. "I don't understand."

It was like Ray had an idea and wanted to talk to me but was hesitant to come right out and say what it was.

He paused a moment, running his hand over his buzzed head of graying hair. "At one time, at least for the past few years, I considered Barry a friend of mine. But"—he paused, looking toward the bar—"after he fired me..."

I put down my glass and leaned back in my chair, folding my arms across my chest. "Is someone... these whispers... they have to do with you being fired?"

He nodded. "Like I said, they're just whispers. But someone's trying to spread the word around that I had something to do with it."

"That you had something to do with his death? Why? Because he fired you?"

Ray had his eyes down on his glass.

"Like who?" I said. "Students? You know how kids can be with something like this. No respect... even for a dead man."

Ray shrugged. "They don't say a word to my face, of course. But I've been hearing things."

"Saying you killed Barry Hawkins?"

Ray appeared to be sincerely bothered by the principal's death.

"So if he was your friend," I said, "why couldn't he tell you why you were fired? I guess I don't understand what—"

"A lot of people get involved in these things. These decisions."

"I'm sure they do," I said. "But I've never heard of someone being fired from a job and not given a reason why."

Ray shook his head. "High school sports, man. I loved being a coach. But it's crazy nowadays. All sports, but especially football. Parents think their kid's gonna make the NFL. Or at least get a ride for college. So they become rabid, you know? Get involved... go behind the coach's back, trying to make a change to benefit their kid."

"The school custodian found him?" I said, shifting gears.

"Yeah. Kevin Smith. He's only been there since the beginning of the school year. I think he actually knew Barry somehow, but not sure how. He went into the school that morning, found Barry on the floor of the shower. It was during the winter break, so the school was closed. Whole locker room got flooded, the way his body blocked the drain."

We both sat quiet for a moment.

I moved my glass to the side, folding my hands in front of me. "So what exactly are you asking me to do? You're not a suspect or anything. There are no suspects. The case is closed."

Ray wiped his big hand across his eyes. "Well, you know, I'm a business owner. And these rumors, I'm afraid they get out of control, it'll hurt my business."

"The sporting goods store?" I said. "In Beachwood?"

Ray nodded. He leaned as much as he could on the chair, pulled out his wallet, and handed me a business card.

I looked over the card. "RR Sporting Goods. I'm not sure I've ever been there."

"So?" Ray said. "Would you be able to help me out?"

I looked over toward the bar as I thought about what to say. I turned back to Ray. "I guess I'm not exactly sure what you want me to do?"

"Maybe just find out who's spreading the rumors? Before they get out of hand?" Ray shifted in his chair. "I'm not looking for any favors. I have money to pay whatever your rate is."

"It's not that," I said. "What I'm saying is, it's not really the kind of case..." I had to think for a moment. "I mean, what's the plan if we find out who's spreading these alleged rumors? What if it's a student? Which wouldn't surprise me. Then what? If you're really concerned, and I imagine you are... Why not go to the cops?"

Ray shook his head. "I'm afraid it'll only make things worse."

# Chapter 2

I SAT AT MY desk in my office upstairs, staring out at the sun setting over the Saint Johns. I hadn't made Ray any promises. And I hadn't accepted the case. Not without first talking to my partner, Alex.

Aside from some much-needed cash, I didn't see it as a great fit. We'd moved on to bigger cases, although the well had run dry over the past few months. We were in need of a client, at least to help us pay some bills. But taking one just for the money wasn't something either of us were ever willing to entertain unless we were desperate.

I had my laptop open in front of me, digging a little deeper into Barry Hawkins' death. There had been no suspicion or suspects or any sign of foul play.

I'd even looked into Ray's firing, which, for some reason, didn't appear to have gotten much press at all.

Barry Hawkins had also played football at Douglas Williams High. But unlike Ray, his playing days ended in high school.

There was a knock at my door.

"It's open," I said, turning toward the door from the peaceful view of the river.

Billy walked in from downstairs and sat on the couch under the window. "I wanted to come up and apologize for coming over and bothering you when you're meeting with a prospective client."

"I'm not sure he's a prospective client," I said. "Besides, it's your restaurant," I said. "You're allowed to come talk to your customers. Especially when I'm using it as my office."

Billy grinned. "Oh, don't worry. The extra fee for restaurant meetings is included in your lease." He leaned back on the couch, one arm straight out and resting on the top of the pillows behind him. "So what's the case?"

Billy was always interested in what Alex and I were working on. It was almost like a hobby for him, and he'd spend as much time as we did thinking about it.

"You know how you mentioned the principal's death," I said, nodding. "Coincidentally, that's what it's about."

Billy shook his head. "He wants you to investigate the principal's death? Did he say why?"

"Actually, I wouldn't say I'd be investigating his death." I pointed at my computer screen. "It was clearly accidental," I said. "But according to Ray, someone's been harassing him, saying he had something to do with it."

"With the man's death?"

I nodded and clicked on one of the tabs on my browser. "He's not lying either." I turned the laptop toward Billy. "I found this on Twitter. I searched for Ray Rivers, and this tweet popped up."

Billy leaned over and slipped on his reading glasses, staring at the screen. "Ray Rivers did it?" he said, reading the tweet. "That's it?" he said. "On Twitter?"

I nodded. "Hashtag RayRivers, hashtag DouglasWilliamsHigh."

"I don't use Twitter," Billy said.

"Neither do I. But you can find all the morons who do, say things, put themselves in a bind." I turned the laptop toward me. "But it's not clear what whoever it is was trying to say. I mean, no mention of Barry Hawkins." I shrugged. "I wouldn't be surprised if it's just some students messing with Ray."

Billy stepped away from my desk. "Can't you find out who the account belongs to?"

"I have no idea." I reached for my phone. "But Alex will know." I tapped her name on my phone.

She answered on the second ring. "Hey," she said. "How'd the meeting go?"

"With Ray? I don't know. I'm not even sure there's much to do. He thinks someone's trying to blame him for the death of the principal who died at Douglas Williams High."

"But wasn't it an accident?" she said.

"I wasn't able to pull up the report. I was hoping maybe you could talk to Mike?"

Alex was quiet on the other end. "I'll see what I can do."

"Okay," I said. "Now, would you mind if I ask a quick question?" I didn't wait for her response. "Is it possible to find out who's behind a Twitter account if their name isn't shown in their profile?"

"Is it possible? Sometimes."

"That doesn't help. So if I see a tweet, and I want to know who wrote it..."

"Wait, you're on Twitter?" Alex said.

"Believe me. Not for my own enjoyment," I said. "But I found a tweet, has to do with Ray Rivers." I went on and told her what Ray was worried about, and why he wanted to hire us.

"So did you tell him we'd take the case?" she said. "I thought we were supposed to—"

"No, I didn't. Of course I told him I had to talk to you about it. But I'm digging in a little deeper. I don't know if there's anything there. If I can figure out who's behind this tweet, I'm not sure I'd even charge him."

"But there's no name?" she said.

"Right. Just a bunch of random letters in the profile. Looks fake to me."

"Okay, well, when I said *sometimes*... if the person knows what he or she's doing, it's easy to create a burner account and cover his or her tracks and be undetectable."

"Isn't it a lot of work to go through just to send a cryptic tweet? The account has twenty followers. But hashtagged the school. And Ray Rivers' account. Although he doesn't appear to have ever used his. So I'm not sure what this even proves."

"Twenty? I mean, yeah, that's not much of a following to go through the trouble. But just so you know how it works... all the person would need is a Tor browser—"

"A what?" I said.

"It's a decentralized network of servers, allowing individuals to access websites anonymously. Twitter won't know the real IP address."

"Oh," I said. "That's it?"

"No, you need a burner phone. And a burner email address."

I got up from the desk. "Oh, okay. That doesn't really help, but I guess you've made it clear it's possible. At least for someone who's got a better grip on this stuff than I do." I let out a slight laugh. "Thanks. And don't worry, I'm not going to spend the day working for free. I just wanted to get a jump, see if Ray's concerns are valid. I'll show you later when I see you. Are you coming to the office?" I looked at Billy, his back to me as he looked out the window toward the river.

"In a couple of hours. I'm doing some paperwork. And I didn't want to leave Raz alone."

"How's he doing?"

She paused. "Assuming the surgery did what it was supposed to, hopefully he'll be good for the rest of his life."

"Okay, we'll talk later." I hung up, looked at Billy, and shrugged. "Seems like a lot of work for a foolish tweet without much substance."

He stepped from the window. "Isn't that what Twitter's all about?"

I nodded, agreeing with him one hundred percent. "It's a damn cesspool. Just like all of social media."

Billy said, "So why's Ray even worried about it? It looks like it could be nothing. I'd agree with you. Probably a student or some disgruntled athlete, didn't make the football team."

I stared at the screen. "I think he's worried the rumors continue to swirl. He owns a sporting goods store, said he's afraid of what rumors could do to it." I walked to the refrigerator and pulled open the door, sticking my head inside. I pulled out a glass bottle of Perrier sparkling water.

Billy pulled out his phone, tapped the screen. He kept his eyes on it for a moment and looked up. "I thought so," he said.

He turned the phone toward me so I could see it. "He's been in here before."

I looked at the picture Billy had pulled up on his phone. "That's Barry Hawkins," I said.

He nodded. "I wasn't sure this was the same guy," Billy said.

Barry appeared to be a decent-looking older man, thin face, round glasses with short gray hair. He looked like a school-teacher, if that made sense.

"Did he come in alone?" I said.

Billy turned the phone from me and peered at the photo. "Actually, I'd say he's been in a few times, for dinner or drinks." He looked up from the screen. "I'm just not sure it's been with the same woman." He tapped his phone. "You know if he's married?"

I nodded. "Don't know much about her."

Billy tapped the phone, his eyes back on the screen. He looked up, shaking his head. "Here she is," he said. "Good-looking woman." He flipped his finger on the phone's screen, raising his eyes and looking my way. "But she's not who I've seen him in here with."

I stepped closer to Billy and looked over his shoulder at the photo. "You sure? I mean, I'm not going to jump to any con-clusions, but it's worth making a note if maybe Mr. Hawkins was into any kind of, uh, extra-curricular activities."

Billy tucked his phone back in his pocket. "So what are you going to tell him? You'll take the case?" He nodded toward my laptop. "Or, you nail this person on Twitter..."

"I'm not sure I'd even call it a case," I said. I took a sip from the bottle of Perrier. "I told him I'd look into things, do some preliminary research before I could make any promises. I have a feeling Alex isn't going to want anything to do with it. Like I told her on the phone, maybe I'll do the guy a favor."

Billy laughed. "Yeah, Alex loves when you do these favors for free. Like you run some volunteer investigations service?" He shook his head. "You gotta stop doing charity work, Henry. When was the last time you had a worthwhile case?"

# Chapter 3

ALEX WAS SITTING IN a chair on her front porch, her dog, Raz, by her side, both watching me when I pulled into Alex's driveway. I parked the Mustang behind her yellow Jeep.

I'd only been driving my latest car, a nineteen sixty-eight Ford Mustang, for a little under two months. It still needed a bit of work on the body, but the engine had been rebuilt by the previous owner and ran like a top. The previous owner, a convicted drug dealer, had the car repo'd and Billy picked it up for me from the auction.

I wasn't much of a car guy, at least I hadn't been. But this model was the same one my father drove for a few months back when I was in high school. Unfortunately, my father's car was stolen one night when, as luck would have it, I was the one who had taken it out on a date. We came out from the movie theater and it was gone.

I stopped at the bottom of the stairs to the porch and Raz came down, gave me his typical greeting: a nose in the crotch.

"Raz!" Alex yelled.

"It's just what dogs do," I said, laughing. I leaned over to pet him and ran my hand down his back. He was thinner than he'd been, and appeared weaker after having a tumor removed from his stomach just a week earlier. The surgery cost Alex forty-eight hundred dollars. And she didn't take a second to decide if she'd do it. Even if it cost ten grand, she said, she would have had it done.

But after paying the unexpected bill, she was anxious for us to land a new client.

"Is he coming with us?" I said.

Alex shook her head. "He'll be better off resting inside." She slapped her thigh and started for the door. "Come on, Raz, let's go take a nap."

Raz's first two steps up the stairs appeared a bit ambitious. But he slowed and finished slower and more gingerly onto the porch and through the front door with Alex.

I hated to see poor Raz like that. Although, the truth is, dogs seem to be able to deal with pain a lot better than we do.

I stayed and turned for the car. I walked past Alex's Jeep and slipped into the driver's seat of the Mustang. I started the engine, enjoying the sound when I revved it up.

Alex came out the front door a few moments later. She had on her Jacksonville Sharks baseball cap, her long hair coming out from under it. She'd had that hat since our days running security together for the Sharks, when I was director of security and Alex was associate director.

After I left to start Walsh Investigations, Alex took over as director. But a year later my old boss, Bob Campbell, sold the team. It was moved to Tennessee and Alex was out of a job. So she came to work with me full time as my partner.

I'm not sure I'd still be in business if it weren't for her.

We'd taken Walsh Investigations to another level, mostly thanks to her being an equal partner. We'd discussed changing the name to Walsh-Jepson investigations, but Alex didn't care about her name being on the sign. And neither of us felt like dealing with the paperwork.

The thing is, it wasn't always glamorous and high-profile cases or  murder investigations. We'd take all kinds of jobs, sometimes doing investigations for a couple of major insurance companies, tracking down fraud. I didn't mind the work—or the money we'd make from it—but dealing with the corporate world and the constant emails and meetings and phone calls drove me nuts. I'm not sure how people could wake up each day and go work in some oversized building with hundreds of people crammed into cubicles... meeting after meeting after meeting.

Not my piece of cake.

Our track record was pretty good. And we'd made a name for ourselves throughout the Florida region. The thing is, just because we had a good reputation didn't mean work flowed through the door. We had to work just as hard to get business as we did to solve each case. Sometimes harder. And once a couple of contacts at the insurance agencies left, we were left out in the cold.

I backed out of the driveway and Alex fiddled with the air-conditioner. "Doesn't the A/C work?" she said.

I put my hand up in front of the vent. "You can't feel that air?"

She gave me a look, shaking her head. "It's warm air."

"Well, it is January," I said.

"Yeah, and it's eighty-two degrees today."

I laughed. "Not ninety." I rolled down my window and Alex did the same. I took off down the road.

Alex pulled off her hat, let her long hair blow behind her in the wind.

"Give it a minute," I said, tapping the temperature knob on the dashboard. It normally helped the cool air kick on. "There it is." I put my hand in front of the vent. "It works now."

Alex shrugged. "The windows are fine," she said, sniffing in the air. "What's that smell? Smells like dirty socks."

"Not me," I said, showing her my Sperry Top-Sider. "I'm not wearing socks." I adjusted the dial, slid one of the controls back and forth and changed it to outside air. "It'll clear up in a minute."

Alex covered her nose. "Just turn the A/C off. We don't need it."

I jumped onto Southside Boulevard, made a couple of quick turns, another after the IHOP, then onto Atlantic Boulevard.

Alex had her eyes down on her phone, looking at the GPS. She looked up and pointed ahead. "Next turn, onto San Marco Boulevard."

I did as she said, followed San Marco for a couple of miles until we hit the traffic circle. I turned right onto Largo Road.

I stopped in front of the two-story home, a small colonial like you'd normally see outside of Florida. With a large tree on the front lawn, most of the yard was shaded. An older-model Lexus, black, was parked in the driveway. To the right of it were shrubs along the green lawn.

We both stepped out and headed up the driveway past the car. I walked ahead of her onto the brick walkway leading to the front door. I put my foot up on the brick landing and knocked.

Not even ten seconds later, the door opened.

An older attractive woman I'd recognized from the photos online stood in the doorway, looking out and me and Alex.

"Mindy Hawkins?"

She stared back at me and nodded.

"Yes?"

"I'm Henry Walsh. This is Alex Jepson. We're with Walsh Investigations and we were hoping to—"

"Walsh Investigations?" she said, looking from me to Alex then back to me. She opened her mouth to talk, closed it, and paused for a moment. She started again. "Is there something I can do for you?"

Alex and I still hadn't officially taken the case from Ray or accepted him as a client. But I didn't want to leave him hanging with nowhere else to turn. So Alex agreed we could take a few more steps, see if we could shed some light on the finger-pointing Ray had been dealing with. And we thought Barry Hawkins' window would be a good place to start.

"Would you be willing to answer some questions about what happened with your husband?" I said. I pushed out a smile.

"What kind of questions?"

I pulled my wallet from my pocket and took out a business card, handing it out to her. "We won't take a lot of your time."

She stared back at me and slowly started to shake her head. "I... Actually... I'm busy. And I have to be somewhere soon."

I gave Alex a quick glance and she stepped forward. "Ma'am," she said. "We're very sorry for your loss. Of course, we understand it's a difficult time for you. And we hate to bother you like this, showing up out of the blue. So maybe, if there's a better time for us..."

Mindy's eyes went past me and Alex, toward my Mustang. We were in one of the nicer, although older neighborhoods in San Marco. I wondered if she saw my car as an eyesore.

"Barry had a car just like that," she said, breaking through the somber look on her face. She cracked a slight smile. "It was even the same color blue. He drove it back when we first got married." She looked out at the car, like she'd left us momentarily for another world. "He always regretted getting rid of it. I'm sure it'd be worth quite a bit of money today."

I looked back at my car. "It's being restored. A little bit at a time."

She shook her head, shifting her gaze to mine. "Barry's needed a lot of repairs, but we didn't have the money. He had no choice but to sell it." She looked down toward the bricks for a moment and held the door open wider as she stepped back. "I don't have much time, but if you'd like to come in for a few minutes?"

We followed her in the house and through the small foyer, down a narrow hall and into a dining room. A large cherry table with ten chairs surrounding it took up most of the space. Piles of papers covered the surface.

She moved the piles to one side of the table to make room. "Barry wasn't the most organized person in the world, although it was worse than I thought." She shuffled a stack of papers and leaned down, placing them on the floor with other piles pushed up against the wall. She shrugged. "I guess I'm not either." She gestured with her hand toward two of the chairs on the long side of the table, facing the window overlooking the backyard. "Please, have a seat." She sat in the chair, the one with the arms, at the end of the table to my right.

She nodded, showing a slight smile, her lips tight with a straight line between them. "It's been difficult," she said. "Barry and I have been together a long time."

"Were you together in high school?" I said.

She gave me a look, like she found it to be a strange question. "No. We were a little older, in our twenties." She looked down at her hand and the diamond on her finger. My business card was still in her hand. "So, you're private investigators. Who are you working for?"

"Well, technically," I said, "we're not working for *anybody* just yet. But, well, I'm sure you know Ray Rivers?"

"Raymond?" She nodded. "Yes. Of course. How is he doing?"

"He's okay. But, well, I went to school with him, although he left when his family moved so he could go to Douglas Williams. He went to school with your husband."

She had a confused look on her face. "Raymond hired you? I... I'm not sure I understand."

"Like I said, technically, no, we're not working for Ray. But we might."

"And it has to do with Barry?"

I was hesitant to tell her too much. "Well," I said. "Someone out there is trying to say Ray had something to do with Barry's death."

She covered her mouth with her hand. "Oh no," she said. "Raymond had something to do with—"

"No," I said. "At least, I don't believe so. According to the police report, nobody had anything to do with it. But for some reason, somebody is bothering Ray. Posting messages, trying to place blame."

Her eyes looked to be glossed over with tears. "But, the sheriff's office... they're sure it was an accident."

Alex reached out and put her hand on top of Mindy's. "Mrs. Hawkins, there's no proof it *wasn't* an accident. We just want to see if there's any reason someone might do such a thing to Ray. Or if there's anyone you can think of."

She burst into tears and excused herself from the table, leaving the dining room and turning down the hall. She stepped back into the room moments later, a box of tissues in her hand, wiping her eyes. "I have no idea who would do such a thing, or even suspect that Raymond... he would never hurt anyone. I know that." She dabbed her eyes with the tissue.

"Ray thinks maybe it has to do with the fact Barry fired him. Maybe someone suspects Ray was revengeful, could have gone after Barry?"

Mindy wiped her nose with the tissue. "Raymond was a good coach," she said. "Barry knew that."

"But did he tell you why he fired Ray?" I said.

She shook her head. "I don't know why he was fired. Barry didn't want to talk about it. And, well, we never had a chance to..." She looked down at the floor. "Barry hadn't been around much over the past few months."

The three of us sat quiet.

I shifted in my seat, moving closer toward the table with my hands down in front of me. "Mrs. Hawkins," I said.

"Please, call me Mindy." She wiped her eyes with the tissue. "Can you tell me what whoever it is has been saying about Raymond? Do you know who it is?"

"That's what we're trying to figure out," I said. "We did find something on Twitter. But it was posted by an anonymous user."

Mindy rolled her eyes. "I don't use Twitter," she said.

"It could just be a prank... a student maybe. Or maybe a former football player with something against Ray." I shrugged. "We don't know. But Ray's nervous. He's nervous it'll hurt his business... or put him in a bad position."

"Well," Mindy said. "I'm not sure his sporting goods store is doing very well to begin with. So if that's his only concern..."

Alex and I exchanged a look.

"Nobody wants rumors like this going through their own community," Alex said.

Mindy nodded. "Of course not. I understand. And I'm sorry. It's just..." She stood up from the chair and walked to the window, facing outside with her back to me and Alex. She turned from the window. "Do you mind showing me this so-called tweet?"

I pulled out my phone and tapped the page where I'd saved it in my browser. But when I clicked to view it, the tweet was gone. I looked over at Alex. "It's not here." I handed her the phone and she tapped the screen, starting to type rapidly with her thumbs.

She looked up from the phone, shaking her head. "It's gone," she said, a look on her face showing she was as confused as I was. "The profile, whoever it was. It's been removed." She handed me back the phone.

I said to Mindy, "I'm... I'm sorry." I pointed to my phone. "It was here a little while ago."

Mindy had a look on her face like she'd perhaps started to doubt what we were saying. She picked up my business card from the table. "Mr. Walsh," she said, turning her eyes toward the floor for a moment, "I'll be honest. One thing Barry used to say about Raymond was that he was a little paranoid."

"What exactly did he mean by that?" I said. "Was there something specific he—"

"It was something he said in passing," she said. "In fact, I hadn't thought of it until now."

"But we both saw the post on Twitter," Alex said. "So, we don't believe Ray is being paranoid. Maybe it's nothing, or, as Henry'd said, maybe it is just some students. But we shouldn't try to say the man is being paranoid when we don't have any answers."

"I'm sorry," Mindy said, seeming defensive.

Alex looked annoyed with the woman's implications, and perhaps that made her want to help Ray more than she had wanted to earlier. Which wasn't saying much. But Alex didn't like when people doubted someone else's story or didn't give someone a chance. She'd seen it enough over the years, where a victim or person who needed help was turned away because of disbelief. "I wish we'd taken a screenshot," she said, almost under her breath, turning toward me."

I heard the front door open and Mindy said, "Oh, that must be my sister. I'm sorry, but we're going to have to cut this off." She stepped out into the hall.

We followed her to the door, and a woman appearing much younger than Mindy stood in the foyer. She was holding a cardboard box.

Mindy said, "This is my sister, Kim. Kim, this is Henry Walsh and..." She looked at Alex. "I'm sorry, did you say your name was Alex?"

Alex gave the woman a nod. "Alex Jepson."

Kim smiled. "Are you friends of—"

"They're private investigators," Mindy said.

Kim's smile dropped from her face. "What? I don't... Are you hiring private investigators?"

Mindy shook her head. "No." She looked at her watch and held the door wide open, indicating it was time for Alex and I to leave. "I'm sorry, but we're already running late," she said. "And I'm sorry if I wasn't much help. Good luck with finding whoever it is you're looking for."

Alex and I stepped outside, and Mindy closed the door behind us without another word.

# Chapter 4

RR Sporting Goods was down in Beachwood, about three miles off Route 90 and not far from Douglas Williams High School. The bell over the glass door dinged when Alex and I walked in.

Ray was kneeling on the floor with his back to us, taking socks from a cardboard box and hanging them on a display. He looked up at us over his shoulder.

The place was small, like you'd expect at an old-school sporting goods store, the kind you didn't see around as much with the big-box sporting goods stores crushing all the little guys. As was the case in most of the retail industry.

The store had that familiar chemical smell in the air: products made of leather or rubber and plastic. Clothing made of who-knows-what materials to prevent sweating or freezing or all the natural things our bodies are meant to do on their own.

Ray grunted as he pushed his big body up from the floor, wiping his hands on his shorts. He stepped toward me and Alex, reached out and shook my hand.

"This is Alex," I said. "My partner."

He shook her hand and looked around the store. "Welcome to RR Sporting Goods." He looked Alex up and down. "You look like an athlete," he said. "You a runner?"

She shrugged. "Sometimes."

He pointed toward the sneaker display along the back wall. "You ever need running shoes, you know where to find them. I'll give you a nice deal."

Alex smiled, nodding. "Sure thing."

We followed Ray toward the back of the store, past the circular racks of clothing, although some of the racks were bare with CLEARANCE signs on top.

He walked around behind the glass display counter and turned to the register. He tapped a button, and the drawer opened with a ding. Ray pulled out a folded piece of paper and handed it to me. "This was on my door this morning, when I got in."

I unfolded the yellow, lined piece of paper. The clear tape was still stuck to the top of it, a message written in blue pen:

*I know what you did.*

I handed the note to Alex and looked across the counter at Ray. "This was on your door?"

He nodded.

Alex looked it over. "Like what we saw on Twitter."

Ray said, "What did you see on Twitter?"

"A similar message," I said. "But we went back to look at it and it was gone. We couldn't even find who posted it."

I took the note from Alex and said to Ray, "The thing I'm not sure of, is if this actually has to do with Barry? I mean, I know that's what we'll assume whoever this is, is trying to say.

But..." I paused to gather my thoughts. "Has anything you've seen or heard been more specific, using Barry's name? Or..."

Ray looked at his phone. "I've gotten a couple of phone calls."

"Oh," I said. "And they mentioned Barry?"

Ray shrugged. "I... I guess I'm not sure." He looked at me. "Are you saying you don't think this has to do with Barry's death?" He scratched his head, a perplexed look on his face. "What else could it mean?" He shook his head. "No, I know that's what it is... whoever's doing this to me is trying to—"

"But this note doesn't mention Barry," I said. I held it up. "I need you to think," I said. "Think hard, Ray. Could this have something to do with coaching? Or your business? Your wife?"

Ray swallowed and hung his shoulders, his eyes down like a scared little boy in a big man's body.

"Ray," I said. "I'm not trying to put you in a bad spot here. We just need to be sure what we're looking for here. Because if you have no idea who would be doing this to you..."

"That's why I asked for your help!" he said, his voice raised and his tone a little less friendly than it had been up to that point.

He took a deep breath and let out a sigh. "I'm sorry."

"So let's walk it through," I said. "What exactly did the caller say?"

"It was a man. But the voice was disguised. I could tell. And the phone was muffled."

"But what did he say?" I said.

Ray shrugged. "'I know it was you.'"

"Nothing specific?" Alex said.

"I guess not."

"How many calls have you gotten?" Alex said.

Ray looked at the phone on the counter. "Just a couple."

I looked around the shop, trying to understand what we were doing or what we were even looking for. I was afraid there was something Ray was holding back.

Alex walked away from us and went out the front door, the bell above it ringing.

I looked at Ray. "We stopped over at Barry's house, to talk to his wife."

Ray looked surprised. "You did? I thought you weren't sure you'd be able to help me."

"Well, we thought we should do a little legwork up front. I hoped maybe this could be easily cleared up somehow."

"Does she know I'm the one who called you?" Ray leaned with his hands on the counter, out wide from his shoulders.

"I told her why we were there. Yes."

Ray shook his head, his eyes down. "I was hoping this would have been kept quiet for now," he said.

"Keep it quiet?" I said. "I can keep it quiet, but if I can't go around asking questions, I'm not sure what you'd expect us to do."

"Okay," Ray said. "She say anything?"

I wasn't going to tell him Mindy had said Ray was someone her husband described as paranoid. "Not much," I said. "She didn't understand why anyone would want to do this to you. But otherwise, she didn't have much to add. Not yet."

Ray and I both looked toward the front of the store when the bell rang over the door.

Alex walked in and continued toward us. She pointed with her thumb over her shoulder. "Those cameras outside, do they work?"

Ray shook his head. "No. The landlord canceled the contract with the security company. I don't know if they work."

"So you don't have a security system?" I said.

"I've been meaning to get it taken care of," Ray said. "It was included with the building when I first opened. The young man who owns it doesn't like to spend money. Told me to take care of it myself if I needed security."

Alex looked at Ray. "What's his name?"

"Who? The landlord?"

Alex nodded.

"Chance Greenberg," Ray said.

"Chance?" I laughed. "What kind of name is Chance? Parents took a chance and ended up with a kid?"

Alex and Ray both looked at me without even a slight smile.

Alex pulled out her phone, tapping the screen with her thumbs. She was good about taking notes—which is what I assumed she was doing—when I preferred to rely on what I felt was at one time a strong memory.

Ray folded his arms across his chest. "Henry? Are you willing to help me out here? Because I get the feeling you don't believe me. Or you think—"

"It's not that we don't believe you," I said. "It's not crystal clear what this is all about. Maybe they are trying to say it's about Barry Hawkins' death. But you have to admit... they haven't been very specific."

"Can't you find that out?" Ray said.

I held up the note. "I know you said you didn't want to. But I think, seeing you have evidence now, maybe you should go to the sheriff's office with this. It's harassment. Whatever's going on here, it's against the law."

Ray walked around the counter and crouched down over the box he'd left on the floor. He started hanging socks on the display again, sliding each pair on the long and straight metal hooks. He seemed to be acting as if Alex and I were no longer there. Like he was pouting.

"Ray?" I said. "Listen. I'll help you as much as I can. But you have to tell me what's going on here. Something's missing."

Ray stopped what he was doing, but his eyes stayed down toward the floor. He raised his big frame from the floor, stood looking over at me and Alex. He walked toward us, slowly.

He opened his mouth for a moment, then stopped.

"Ray?" I said. "What's going on?"

He took a deep breath and exhaled. "I think Barry was having an affair with my wife. I'd questioned her about Barry just a couple of days before he... before he was found dead at the school."

I looked at Alex and twisted my neck to ease a kink. "Your wife was having an affair with him?"

Ray stared back at me, nodding. "I believe she was."

Alex and I both stood quiet.

What Ray had told us, of course, had some implications.

"Who else knows about this?" I said.

"That they may have had an affair?" Ray said. He shrugged. "I asked Shondra about it. That's it."

I walked to the front of the store, looking out through the plate-glass window toward the street. "I assume she denied it?" I turned to him.

"She told me I was a fool for thinking such a thing."

"I imagine accusing her—whether it's true or not—has perhaps caused some friction at home?"

Ray shifted his eyes toward the floor. "Shondra and I are separated. We have been for a few months."

"Before you suspected something was going on?" I said.

"Around the same time. I haven't been living at my house for a couple of months."

I walked toward him and leaned my elbow on one of the empty clothing racks. I was hesitant to say what I was about to say, but it was the only thought I had in my head. "Isn't there..." I cleared my throat and held up the note I still had in my hand. "Isn't it possible Shondra could have something to—"

"Shondra?" He shook his head emphatically. "She would never do something crazy like this. She's not like that. Shondra... she'd come right out and say it to me, ask if I killed the man."

Something slipped out of my mouth, and I wasn't exactly sure why. "Did you?" I said.

Alex looked at me, her eyes wide open. "Henry?"

"Are you serious?" Ray said, stepping toward me, the veins bulging in his neck.

"It's just a question."

Ray stopped and shook his head. "I'm not going to answer that," he said. "Why would I come to you in the first place if I did?"

I had to think for a moment. "Listen. Here's the thing. And I'm sure you already know this. But if word somehow got out she was having an affair with Barry, or even if it's just suspected, I could see how it could raise some eyebrows. I mean, losing your job is one thing. But if the same man was having an affair with your wife?" I sighed. "This looks kind of messy, Ray. I'm not saying you did it, so don't take this the wrong way. But I'd say there are a couple of motives here."

"I know," he said. "That's why I'm so concerned. Whoever's harassing me, it doesn't look good."

The three of us stood quiet, Alex and I exchanging a look.

"Where have you been staying?" Alex said.

Ray looked toward a doorway with a curtain hung across it behind the counter at the back of the store. "I sleep back there, on an air mattress."

"You sleep here?" I said. "I assume there's at least a bathroom?"

"A toilet and a sink," Ray said.

"No shower?"

Ray took a moment before he answered. He seemed hesitant to continue. "No."

"So, if you don't mind me asking, where do you shower?"

His Adam's apple jumped in his throat. "I was using the shower at the school. Up until recently."

It wasn't the answer I was expecting. "Wait," I said. "Did you just say you showered at the school? The high school where you worked? The same shower where the principal was found dead?"

Ray nodded. "I know how it looks."

"Was this before you were fired?"

"Up until Barry was killed. Of course, I stopped going."

"You still have a key?"

"Yes. Barry never took it from me. I guess maybe I was supposed to give it back."

I tried to wrap my head around everything Ray had told me in the ten minutes we'd been standing there. "This story has changed," I said, looking from Ray to Alex. "Number one, the victim was the same man who fired you. Two, he may have been sleeping with your wife." I shook my head, having a hard time believing the whole story myself. "Third, you have a key to the school and were using the same showers where Barry's body was found." I took a deep breath and exhaled, rubbing my face with both hands.

"I'm sorry," Ray said. "I should have told you all this before."

I stared back at him. "You think?"

# Chapter 5

A LEX AND I WALKED toward Friendship Fountain, the jets shooting water thirty feet in the air and growing louder as we got closer. We walked around to the other side, evading the kids running aimlessly in circles ahead of whatever adult supervision they had, or didn't have.

We stepped around to the river side and Detective Stone was already there waiting.

Mike Stone, a homicide detective in the special investigations unit of the Jacksonville Sheriff's Office, was, no doubt, one of their best. I can admit that even though we'd bumped heads more than once. My problem with Mike was the arrogance he sometimes let get in the way.

Alex had been friends with Mike from long before I met her, going back to her time as a police officer up in Virginia.

Mike was leaning on the railing across from the fountain, his back to us, facing the river. Smoke rose up from the cigarette in his right hand resting on the top rail.

"Mike," Alex said, stepping ahead of me as she reached out for him.

He turned with a take-out coffee in his hand and a manila folder tucked under his arm. He smiled at Alex, but it left his face like dripping paint when he shifted his eyes toward me. He gave me a short, quick nod with his chin and took a drag from his cigarette.

"I thought you quit," Alex said, waving her hand in front of her face to clear the smoke from the air.

"I quit all the time." He smirked. "I'm getting pretty good at it." He took another drag, dropped what was left on the ground and squashed it with the bottom of his shoe. He bent down and picked up the butt, looked it over and tapped the ash side with his finger. He tossed it into a trash can a few feet away from where we stood.

Mike was a few years older than me, somewhere into his early fifties. He had that same disheveled look most good cops were born with. I don't think I'd ever once seen the guy clean-shaven, although I wasn't one to talk. His clothes always looked like he'd taken them right off the floor each morning before work. He was tough and in decent shape, thick arms packed with muscle under the short-sleeved golf shirt he wore. His permanent expression said the job had beaten the life out of him, although I was sure it was also part of his act. Even the smoking. I swore it was a look he wanted, lung cancer or not, so he came across as the tough-guy detective you'd see on TV.

"Is that it?" I said, nodding toward the manila folder.

Mike gave me a look, his lip somewhat snarled. "Hold your panties, will you?" He huffed, shaking his head as he took a sip of his coffee. He tipped his head back and shook the cup, then tossed it in the can. He took the folder from under his arm and looked it over. "I'd like one of you to tell me why you want to see this report. Don't tell me you're sniffing around, trying to find some foolish reason this guy didn't slip and fall in the shower at that school."

Alex shook her head. "I'd rather not go into what it's for, if that's okay?"

Mike shrugged. "Sure, it's okay. But then, do I have to give you this report?"

"Not unless you have something to hide?" I said.

Mike took a step toward me. "Listen, wiseass. You want this report, then how about you show a little respect. I'm doing Alex a favor. And, technically, we haven't closed this investigation. That means I'm crossing a line sharing it with you."

Alex and I looked at each other.

"Why isn't it closed?" she said.

Mike held his eyes on her. "How about you answer my question first?" He removed his sunglasses and hung them from the neck of his collar, opening the folder in his hands. He pulled out the page on top and looked it over, tucked it back in the folder and slipped it back under his arm. "So, who hired you?" he said. "The wife?"

I shook my head. "No, she didn't. We just want to look it over. But I was hoping you'd be a little more cooperative. I'm not going to beg you to give it to me."

Mike laughed. "Oh, okay. I get it. You're bored? Is that it? No clients? So you randomly selected a man who died in a slip-and-fall accident... decided you'd like to look over the report?" He rolled his eyes. "You know, Walsh, sometimes you remind me of those ambulance-chasing lawyers, always out looking for a reason to make a case just so you can—"

"Mike!" Alex snapped. "Will you knock it off?" She looked from Mike to me. "Both of you!" She reached out for the report and yanked it from Mike's hand. "Henry's telling the truth. We're not working on a case. At least, not yet."

"Not yet?" he said. "I did you a favor. The least you could do is tell me what you want this for. Is that too much to ask?"

"We're doing some preliminary legwork," I said. "It's related to Barry Hawkins' death. But we're not exactly trying to disprove anything, if that's what you're worried about. Someone I knew a long time ago came to me for some help. There are rumors he's responsible for Barry's death. And he wants to get ahead of them. Or at least find out who's behind them."

Mike took a cigarette from a pack in his pocket and stuck it in his mouth. "Any chance this *somebody* from your past would happen to be Ray Rivers?"

Alex stared back at Mike, as surprised as I was he'd mentioned Ray's name.

Mike said, "Nine-one-one received an anonymous phone call in the middle of the night, claimed Barry Hawkins' death wasn't an accident and Ray Rivers had something to do with it." He nodded toward the folder in Alex's hand. "With the case still open, it's obviously raised some eyebrows. And we wouldn't be doing our due diligence if we didn't at least talk to him."

"Talk to Ray?" I said. "You don't know who called?"

Mike gave me one of his cocky looks. "You know what anonymous means, don't you?"

I was hesitant to talk or let on what we already knew.

He got a grin out of Alex.

But with Mike now wanting to talk to Ray, it made no sense for us to keep him in the dark. "Ray and I went to school together when we were kids. That was before his parents moved him to a school with a real football team. He called me, and I met with him. That's when he told me someone's been bothering him, floating messages out there. If I had to guess, it's the same person called nine-one-one. Honestly, I assumed it was someone trying to jerk him around. Maybe even a student, playing games. But if they've made a call to the sheriff's office, I'd say maybe it needs to be taken a little more seriously."

Mike lit the cigarette in his mouth. "Which brings up a good question: Why didn't he just come to us, instead of, uh, trying to hire a PI?"

"I asked him the same thing. He was afraid it would make matters worse for him, and spread the rumors. He owns a business. Once word gets out with something like this..."

"It opens up a can of worms," Alex said,

Mike slipped his sunglasses back on his face. "Well, looks to me that's exactly what someone's already done."

# Chapter 6

It was midafternoon when Alex and I arrived at the Duval County Public School district office off Prudential Drive. I drove around to the parking lot behind the building and could see the Main Street Bridge from where I parked.

We walked around to the front of the building and took the elevator up to the fourth floor. We stepped off and walked down the hall and stopped outside the Financial Services Department.

It's where Shondra Rivers worked.

The door was open and we stepped inside. There were two desks and a copy machine. Three green leather padded chairs were pushed up against the wall to my right. There was a lamp on top of the small corner table, the area arranged like a waiting area.

"Anybody here?" I said, standing just inside the door with Alex next to me.

A woman stepped out from what looked like a hallway toward the back left of the office. She wore a dress with a buttoned sweater over it. "May I help you?"

"Is Shondra available?"

"Shondra?" The woman slowly shook her head. "Shondra Rivers? She doesn't work in this office."

But as far as I knew, she did. "Shondra Rivers. I'm pretty sure she does."

"She's down on the second floor now. She recently transferred down there. She works in Human Resources."

"Oh," I said, glancing at Alex. "Since when?"

The woman seemed hesitant to answer. A phone rang from somewhere down the hall she'd walked from. "I'm sorry," she said, pointing with her thumb over her shoulder. "That's my phone. If you'll excuse me." She turned and disappeared around the corner. But I heard her answer the phone. "This is Linda Green."

I wasn't sure if the woman was coming back out to finish our brief conversation. But I didn't think we needed her for much else.

Alex and I left the office and turned down the hall toward the elevator. We rode it down to the second floor.

"That's odd," Alex said. "Didn't Ray tell you she worked in the Financial Services Department?"

I nodded. "She must not've told him she'd transferred."

The elevator door opened and we stepped off onto the second floor. Not knowing which way to turn, I guessed and went left. We walked down the hall and, six doors down, saw a sign with the number 208 to the right of a closed door. A sign on the door said Human Resources.

I knocked and walked into a short, gray-haired woman seated at a desk. She turned to me and slid her cat-eye glasses down her nose. "May I help you?"

"Is Shondra Rivers here?"

She paused and took her glasses off, letting them hang from the chain around her neck. "Is there something I can help you with?"

I shook my head. "We'd like to talk to Shondra. We were told she works here."

The woman's expression seemed to drop a bit, like she was trying to think of what to say. She straightened out a stack of papers on her desk. "I'll have to see if she's available." She picked up her phone, tapped a couple of buttons, and whispered into the phone before looking toward us. "May I ask what this pertains to?"

"Uh, we're friends of her husband."

The woman spoke quietly into the phone, repeating what we'd said, then hung up the receiver. "I'm sorry," she said. "She's not available right now." She got up from the desk with a yellow pad and a pen in her hand. She held them out for me. "If you'd like to leave your name and number, I'll be sure to give her the information."

I looked back at the waiting area. "How about if we just sit and wait for her, if that's all right?"

The woman shook her head. "I'm sorry. But she's going to be tied up for a while. She's in the middle of a meeting with..." She again tried to hand me the pad. "Please, sir. Write down your name and number. I assure you, she'll call as soon as she can."

I'd been blown off enough times to know when someone was clearly trying to avoid me. "I don't mind waiting."

"Sir," she said, her voice stern. "This is not the kind of office we have visitors waiting around."

I looked toward the leather chairs. "Then what are *they* for?"

The woman didn't answer. "Mrs. Rivers is not available today. Now, if you don't mind, I have work to do."

The little gray-haired woman was clearly agitated. I couldn't help but believe she was at one time a teacher, maybe moved into administration for smacking a kid on the knuckles with a ruler.

I pulled a business card from my pocket and handed it to the woman. "Please give this to her. Hopefully she'll call me."

The woman looked the card over, looked up at me and nodded. She appeared surprised by the card. "I'll be sure to give this to her."

. . . . . . . . . . .

Alex and I stood in the back parking lot, leaning against the front of the Mustang. We'd been outside, waiting, for almost an hour. I looked at my cell to see if Shondra Rivers had called, but she hadn't.

"You sure they get out at four?" Alex said.

I looked at my watch. "It's five past. But I'm surprised she hadn't even called. You'd think someone drops off a business card with something about investigations on it, you'd at least be curious enough to pick up the phone."

"Don't you think she would've called Ray?" Alex said. "And what if she..." She stood up off the car and slapped my arm.

I looked and saw a woman I knew was Shondra Rivers walk through a small door on the side of the building. It appeared like she was sneaking out. She looked back and forth and let the door close behind her before starting across the parking lot, right toward us.

I walked toward Shondra.

We were just about face-to-face when she stopped and tried to go around me. "Excuse me," she said, continuing across the lot.

"Shondra Rivers?" I said.

She stopped, mid-step, and looked back at me. "Yes?"

I walked toward her. "I'm Henry Walsh."

She stood staring at me and turned to Alex.

"Did you get my message?" I said. "I left my card."

Shondra seemed hesitant, looked at Alex again, then toward the door where she'd just come out. If she hadn't been wearing high heels, I had the feeling she was going to try to, for some reason, make a run for it.

"I just want to talk to you," I said.

Alex stepped past her and stood next to me. "This is my partner, Alex Jepson," I said.

Shondra looked around and nodded. "Would you mind telling me what this is in regard to?"

I nodded toward my car and gestured for us to keep walking away from the building.

The three of us walked.

"It's got to do with Ray," I said.

"Can you be more specific?" she said. "If this has to do with the divorce... I'm not sure why he'd hire a private investigator? I thought we had both agreed to—"

"Actually," I said. "First, I'd like to ask you some questions about Barry Hawkins."

She tried to hide it, but she swallowed hard, shaking her head. "Why would I know anything about Barry Hawkins?"

"Are you trying to say you don't know anything about him?" I said.

She held the long strap to her handbag, hung over her shoulder. "I... I know Barry. Mostly through Ray. But we're not..." Her eyes shifted across the parking lot. "I don't know what Ray told you. But he has quite the imagination, you know."

I folded my arms across my chest. "Ray has an *imagination*? What exactly is that supposed to mean?"

"It means I know what you're asking me. I already told him there was nothing between me and Barry." She shifted her stance. "You think this is the first time he's accused me of having an affair?" She shook her head. "Ray is a very jealous man. As long as we've been together, if I even spoke to another man in front of him, he'd say something about it to me. Not only is he a jealous man, I'd say he may also be paranoid." She nodded. "I'm serious."

"So you're denying you had any kind of relationship with Barry Hawkins? And telling me Ray is, for the most part, crazy?"

"For the most part?" Shondra nodded. "Yes. I don't know what else to tell you. Barry Hawkins and I were never in any kind of relationship."

I didn't want to buy a word of what Shondra was saying, but she seemed to be shooting straight.

"When was the last time you and Ray spoke?"

"I saw him at the funeral."

"Barry Hawkins' funeral?" I said.

Shondra nodded. "I believe that was the last time I saw him. Although he's called me several times. But right now, I'm not interested in talking to him. Not until he agrees to sign the divorce papers."

We stood at my car and I leaned against the passenger door. "Did you know Ray's been sleeping in the back of his store?"

She sighed and looked across the lot. "I thought, maybe he..." She fixed her eyes on mine. "So, the reason you're here is to find out if I was having an affair with a deceased man?"

I shook my head. "Actually, that's just a piece of it. I'm here because Ray came to me about someone spreading around that he had something to do with Barry's death. We came here wondering if you know anything about it?"

Shondra pointed her finger against her chest. "You think I have something to do with it? Like I have nothing better to do than play with Ray's fragile mind?"

"He's not just being paranoid," I said. "Whoever it is, actually called the sheriff's office too."

Shondra's eyes opened wide. She didn't respond.

"And you know nothing about this?" I said.

She shook her head. "I'm not going to stand here and have someone who doesn't even know me, try to accuse me of..." She walked away, continued to the back of the lot and stopped at a red Buick. She opened the driver-side door and slipped inside, slammed the door closed and took off. Her tires squealed as she left the parking lot.

# Chapter 7

After dropping Alex off at her house, I drove through rush-hour traffic to Douglas Williams High School. It was just before six thirty when I arrived, unsure there'd be anyone there.

There were no cars in front. I drove around to the back of the school, past the football stadium and tennis courts, and stopped in front of a loading dock. There was a Harley Davidson motorcycle parked by the door.

The door to the left of the loading dock was slightly open, a dozen large plastic garbage bags piled up to the side of it.

I picked up the distinct odor of industrialized school-cafeteria food. I envisioned soggy pizza... shepherd's pie... or some kind of mystery meat on top of the plastic orange trays.

I'd guessed school lunch hadn't changed much. Maybe it had gotten worse. Looking at all the overweight kids I'd seen around, I'd guessed it had.

I pulled on the slightly opened door and went inside. I walked into a kitchen and caught a strong whiff of bleach, continued through a swinging door and into the serving area where, at least during the day, you'd see the line of lunch ladies piling so-called food onto the students' trays.

It was my first time inside Douglas Williams High School, but the layout, at least the cafeteria, was like any other school. Which was, coincidentally, the same layout of your typical prison cafeteria.

The lights were off, although what was left of the sunlight outside slipped through the closed blinds. I thought I heard music on the other side of the wall and walked past the long tables with rectangular benches. I stepped out into the hallway. The lights were on, with lockers along the walls on either side. I walked toward where I believed the music was coming from and turned toward a set of double doors at the far end of the hall.

I stopped at a glass case filled with trophies and awards for state championships in, it appeared, all major high school sports. There were a handful for the boys' basketball team. Another was for the women's tennis team, and a small trophy for the golf team. There was a division championship trophy for the football team, but only one state championship, it appeared, from twenty-five years earlier.

I turned when I heard a door open.

A man about my age, wearing a bluish-green, one-piece custodial uniform, rolled a mop and bucket through the door. He looked to be a muscular man, the way the sleeves were tight on his biceps. He had a thick, dark mustache that came down into his chin, like one you'd see on someone who *wanted* to look like a biker.

I assumed the Harley outside was his.

His hair was dark and slicked back on his head.

"Can I help you find something?" he said.

"Uh, actually, I was looking for the showers."

"The showers?" he said, giving me a funny look.

I smiled. "The boys' locker room." I walked toward him. "I know that sounds a little strange. But I just wanted to take a look around." I took my business card from my wallet and handed it to him.

He studied my card. "What's this about?" he said. "Mr. Hawkins?"

I nodded.

He looked at my card again. "You're not with the sheriff's office?"

"No, I'm not." I nodded toward my card in his hand. "See where it says Private?" I grinned.

He looked at me like he didn't like my response.

"So, then, what's this about? It was an accident," he said. "Cops spent a lot of time here. I can't imagine you'd find something they couldn't. I mean, assuming you're—"

"You mind?" I said, looking down the hall toward the doors at the end of it. "Is that music coming from down there?"

He nodded. "That's the gym. I'm not sure who's in there. Students, I assume. They're supposed to be supervised. But these damn kids don't listen to me. And nobody else seems to want to put their foot down." He squinted his eyes. "Did anyone know you were coming here?" He slid his hand in his front pants pocket. "Because, I'm not sure I should—"

"I'll just be a few minutes," I said. "Then I'll be out of your way."

The man seemed hesitant, then nodded and wheeled his mop and bucket to the side, the mop handle leaning against the lockers.

He walked ahead of me and turned left before the double doors. He pulled his hand from his pocket with a large ring with at least a few dozen keys. "It's locked all the time now. Like the gym, kids aren't supposed to go in there without supervision." He walked ahead of me, picking through his ring of keys and stuck one of them into the lock on the door. "But they find a way in there somehow. I don't get paid enough to deal with them sneaking in there." He worked the key in the door.

"What's your name?" I said, standing behind him.

He looked back at me, over his shoulder. "Kevin."

"Oh," I said. "Your last name Smith?"

Kevin stopped and gave me a look. "How'd you know that?" He removed his key from the lock and pulled open the door.

"You're the one who found him," I said.

He held the door open for me and gestured for me to walk in ahead of him. "Yes, sir. That was me."

I walked ahead of him into the locker room, stepping across the black rubber mats on the floor. To the left was a room with wooden benches and blue lockers on the walls. The air was steamy. The smell of powder and overly strong deodorant, mixed with bleach, hung in the air. I said to Kevin. "There's nobody in here now, right?" I didn't want to walk in on some high school kid changing.

Kevin shook his head. "Like I said, they're not supposed to be in here. But they get in." He looked at his keys and shrugged, slipping them in his pocket. "They don't listen to me either way. Some of them have real attitudes too. Not that I was any saint when I was a kid, but..."

He stepped ahead of me and I followed him down a short hall. He walked past the bathroom stalls with the closed blue doors and sinks on the other side of the room. He stopped at a door propped open with a rubber wedge. "So what exactly are you looking for?" He nodded through the doorway. "Showers are in there."

I stepped past him.

He stood in the doorway, leaning against the side. He was looking at my business card again.

I noticed a tattoo of a snake wrapped around a cross, on his forearm.

I poked my head around the tiled wall and looked in at the showers. It was one wide-open area with six shower heads on each side. The tiles on the walls were blue. Those on the floor, white. A single covered drain sat in the middle of the floor.

I was a late bloomer and never one of those kids comfortable with the group shower. I looked down at the drain.

Kevin was now standing outside the showers, looking in at me.

"So I understand the place was flooded?" I said.

"Not the whole locker room. Just that area there. The shower area." With his black boot, he lightly kicked the six or so inches of tile, meant to keep the water inside the shower area.

"So how long've you been working here, for the school?" I said.

"Oh, I got the job a few months back, in the fall."

"What a first year on the job, huh?" I said. "Find your boss dead?"

He nodded.

I crouched down over the drain. "You from Jax?" I looked back at Kevin.

"Nah. Georgia." He pulled a toothpick from the pocket over his chest, slipped it in his mouth.

"Oh yeah?" I said. "My mother's from Georgia. Whereabouts?"

He stared back at me, pulling the toothpick from his mouth. "You don't mind, I have to get back to work." He grinned. "Gotta get those floors in the hall waxed."

I stepped out from the shower area as Kevin walked away and went back to leaning in the doorway. "So you were working during the winter break?" I said.

He nodded. "I had to come in a few times that week. There was a basketball game here the night before. I came in to clean up the mess."

"High school team?"

"Church league. They use the gym in the winter, a couple nights a week. At least they used to. School's put a stop to it for now."

I looked back toward the shower area. "Anybody else in the school that day? Or the night before?"

"Besides the kids, and whatever parents were here? I couldn't tell you. I would think the sheriff's office would have that information, no?"

I didn't respond. "So what do you know about Barry Hawkins coming in here, using the weight room?"

"What do I know?" He shrugged. "Not much. I don't know if he was supposed to be here. I mean, being the principal, I guess he did what he wanted. But honestly, I don't know much about it. Like I said, the sheriff's office might have whatever it is you're looking for."

"So who was it, knew he was here using the weight room?"

"Who knew? It was... I guess it was his wife. As far as I know, she told the sheriff's office why he was here."

I found the whole thing to be a bit odd. Why would the principal sneak into the school gym to use the weight room? And why would he use showers meant for student athletes? The guy sounded a little strange, you ask me.

"Have you ever seen him in here before?" I said. "Working out? Or using the showers?"

Kevin shook his head, running his hand over his thick mustache.

I turned from him and stepped back into the shower area.

According to the report, Mr. Hawkins had slipped on the tile and fell backward, cracking his head when he fell. Kevin Smith found him at seven oh five in the morning.

Kevin stood watching me.

I had to be careful with each step, although my Top-Siders were decent on slippery surfaces. But the tiles were slippery. "What do you use to clean these?" I said.

"What do I use to clean what? The showers?" He slipped his hand in his pants pocket and pulled his ring of keys from inside. He walked away without a word. I heard the squeak of a door opening.

Kevin walked back over, holding a large spray bottle. "This is the stuff. It's an industrial cleaner. Kills all the bacteria and whatever else leaches off these boys' dirty bodies. Ask me, I'd say it's mostly bleach."

I took the bottle, looked it over, and sprayed it on the tile below me. I crouched down and ran my hand over it. "You'd have to be careful, make sure it all gets washed away?"

Kevin nodded. "We bring in a hose, make sure we get it all off."

"Was this sprayed on the tile the night before Barry was in here, by any chance?"

Kevin stared back at me for a moment before he answered. He shook his head. "Not by me."

"Are you the only custodian?"

"We have a couple part timers. But they don't have keys. And none of them were here that week."

I looked along the tiled wall at the plastic soap and shampoo dispensers between each showerhead.

I heard a loud bang and looked at Kevin.

"What was that?"

The bang was followed by laughing and loud music.

I walked out from the shower area and followed Kevin out the door into the main area of the locker room.

Kevin walked ahead of me and stopped where a group of teenage boys were sitting in front of the lockers. "Hey, you know you're not supposed to be in here!" he yelled.

There were seven of them, had their shirts off, showing off their youthful builds packed onto their skinny frames.

"We just gotta change," one of them said. "Give us a minute."

The laughing continued, acting as if neither Kevin nor I were standing there. "We gotta get our stuff." The boys opened lockers, and one of them whispered something I couldn't quite hear. They all turned toward Kevin and started laughing.

Kevin pointed toward the door they'd somehow opened, although I wondered if he'd even locked it behind us. "You get out of this locker room," he yelled.

One of the other boys, the shortest one of the group but built up a bit with muscle, nodded our way. "What's the matter? Are you afraid one of us might die if you make the tiles too slippery again?"

The boys all laughed.

Kevin looked at me, shaking his head. "No respect."

One of the other boys called out to the shorter one. "Hey, Zack, catch." The boy threw what looked like a can of beer in the air.

The kid, Zack, caught it in the air. He cracked it open, tipped his head back, and guzzled at least half the can.

Kevin walked toward them. "You can't drink that in here." He stopped and stood in front of the door.

But the teenaged boys acted like Kevin wasn't even there, ignoring him as they got dressed into street clothes, drinking their beers. They all slammed their lockers and started toward the door.

The short kid, Zack, brushed by Kevin as he walked past him.

I grabbed the kid by the arm. "Hey!" I said. "Show some respect."

The rest of the boys kept walking and left the locker room.

Zack ripped his arm from my grasp. "Keep your hands off me, old man."

*Old man?*

He shoved me in the chest and ran out of the locker room after his friends.

I knew I was wrong for grabbing the kid by the arm. I'm not even sure why I did it.

Kevin said, "You have to be careful around here, grabbing kids like that."

"I know," I said. I was embarrassed. "You just let him knock into you like that?"

"I'd love to grab a kid like that, smash him into the wall and teach him a lesson." He shrugged. "But I can't. Especially not that one."

"Who is he?" I said.

"A spoiled brat. Shows zero respect to anyone. You should've heard the way he'd talk to Mr. Hawkins." He shook his head.

I looked toward the door, where Zack had walked out.

"Who is he?" I said.

Kevin shrugged. "Another rich kid, thinks he's better than everyone else. Transferred over from one of those private schools."

"Does he have a last name?"

Kevin looked around the locker room, nodding. "Mazer. Zack Mazer. Played football here, although I hear he never made it off the bench."

"He played for Ray Rivers?" I said.

Kevin gave me a look. "You know Ray Rivers?"

I nodded, and left it at that.

# Chapter 8

IT WAS DARK OUT on my way to Alex's house, and I had my eyes up in the rearview mirror watching a set of headlights behind me. I couldn't say for sure if I was being followed, but it certainly felt that way.

Every turn I made, the headlights seemed to follow.

I turned down Alex's street with the car a good thirty feet behind me. I pulled over, thinking whoever it was would pass if he wasn't following me. But as soon as I did, the car stopped. I watched it turn into a driveway. I assumed it was one of Alex's neighbors.

But looked back over my shoulder. The reverse lights went on and the car backed out onto the street. It drove in the opposite direction, away from me.

I spun my car around and went after it, putting the Mustang's engine to work as I sped through the neighborhood. But when I got to the turn, where I could have gone left or right, there was no car in sight.

I spun the car around and headed for Alex's.

I pulled in the driveway and parked behind her Jeep. It was dark enough out that I could see clearly into her well-lit house.

She had lights on in every room and I could easily see into all of them.

I walked up the porch and looked in the window to the left of the door at Alex, standing over the stove. Her dog, Raz, sat on the floor next to her, his eyes up, tail wagging.

I knocked on the glass and watched her turn, wipe her hands on a cloth, and tuck her hair behind her ear. She walked out from the kitchen and the door opened. "I was wondering where you were," she said. "Did you get my text?"

I pulled out my phone, looked it over and turned the screen to her. "I guess I did." I read what she'd said and smiled. "No, I haven't eaten."

She held the door open for me. "I sent that an hour ago."

"Sorry," I said, stepping in behind her.

Raz gave me his customary nose-in-the-crotch greeting but hurried after Alex going back into the kitchen.

Alex went back to the stove, and Raz sat right back in the same spot, watching her.

"Smells good," I said. I pulled up a chair at the pub-height table in front of the window on the other side of the kitchen.

She glanced back at me. "You can have some," she said, looking down at Raz, "but it's his food." She stepped from the stove to the refrigerator and pulled out two bottles of beer. She popped the cap off both bottles and placed one on the counter in front of me.

I picked up the bottle and looked it over. "Pumpkin beer?"

"Is that all right?" she said. She must have noticed the funny look on my face. "Try it. It's good."

"Pumpkin belongs in pies. Period." I studied the label, took a sip and had to figure out if I liked it or not. "I can't imagine drinking more than one," I said. I took another sip. "Doesn't anybody drink normal beer anymore?"

Alex scooped whatever was in the pot into a glass bowl, opened the freezer and took out a couple of ice cubes. She placed them in the bowl with the food and placed it on the counter. She crouched down to pet Raz. "I'm sorry, you're going to have to wait for it to cool, okay?"

"I didn't know you made his food," I said. I got up from the chair and walked to the stove, looking inside the pot. "Is that edible? I mean, by humans?"

She nodded. "It's real food. Salmon and rice, spinach, broccoli, butternut squash…"

"Oh," I said. I leaned over the pot and sniffed. "If you didn't tell me it was dog food I'd try it."

She made a face, laughing. "What's the difference?"

I shrugged. "I don't know. Now that it's in my head…"

Alex laughed and rolled her eyes. She opened the door to the fridge. "You want me to make you something to eat?"

"No," I said. Although I was hungry. "You don't have to do that."

"I know I don't have to. But you need to eat something, don't you?"

I smiled. Alex was good to me. Although sometimes she treated me like a kid.

It was always hard to put a finger on what our relationship had become. I don't think either one of us really knew, and we'd, for the most part, given up trying to figure it out.

Sometimes, like our friend Billy would say, we acted like an old married couple.

Being business partners, we did what we had to so we could avoid any kind of relationship that might mess up the business. But it wasn't easy. Not for me, anyway.

Alex had lost her husband a few years back after he went into a fire and never came out. He was a Jacksonville firefighter and the reason she moved to Jacksonville in the first place. Me? I was divorced from a fairly short marriage to my first and last wife.

Neither Alex nor I had gotten into any kind of serious or long-term relationships with anyone else after our past experiences.

"I spoke to Mike earlier," Alex said. "He said he doesn't see any way Barry Hawkins' case would be opened to further investigation."

"Really?" I said. "Even after the anonymous call the sheriff's office received?"

Alex nodded. "He said they get ones like it all the time, especially after an odd death. He said with all the amateur sleuths out there, all these true-crime podcasts popping up, everyone wants to get in on it. Everything's a murder to them."

"Really?" I said. "You think some podcaster called the sheriff's office?" I sipped my beer. "You didn't tell Mike about what Ray said about Shondra and Barry, did you?"

"No, I didn't see any reason to. We don't even know if it's true."

"Even if it's not, it would still be a motive," I said.

Alex gave a slight tilt to her head. "You sound like you think Ray killed the man."

I shook my head. "No. I'm just saying... Mike gets wind of it, whether there was an affair or not, he'll want to hear Ray's side of it."

"Because it's a motive," she said. "So I think we have to be careful with our assumptions. But right now, at least as far as Mike's concerned, Barry Hawkins' death was accidental." She turned back to the counter. "Did you find anything at the school? I thought you were going to call me, after you left."

"Sorry," I said. "I stopped off at the boat to change my clothes, get the smell of bleach off my hands."

"Bleach?" she said.

"Whatever they use on the tiles in the showers in the boys' locker room at the school. It was all over me."

Alex nodded. "I wasn't sure what you thought you'd find there anyway. You know the sheriff's office scoured the place."

"Well," I said. "I met Kevin Smith, the custodian at the school."

There was a loud sound outside, like glass had shattered. I looked outside through the window and saw taillights from the vehicle driving away.

I ran from the kitchen and out the front door, jumping over the stairs from the porch and across the grass to the driveway.

A car drove away, and I could only see the taillights through the trees. The vehicle's brake lights came on, and I saw the right one wasn't working.

Alex walked up behind me. "What happened?" she said.

I walked toward my car and saw the rear window had been smashed. "You've got to be kidding me." I walked up to it and looked in the back seat, covered in shattered glass. I opened the passenger door and lifted the latch to push the backrest forward.

There was a brick on the back seat. I picked it up and showed it to Alex.

She looked toward the street. "Did you see the car?" She walked down the driveway and stood at the end, staring in the direction the vehicle had gone.

"I couldn't make out what kind of vehicle it was, but I'd have to say it was some kind of truck or SUV. One of the brake lights was broken."

I held the brick in my hand and looked up at the house. Raz was in the window watching us.

Everything outside was dark and quiet.

"Someone followed me here," I said. "I thought maybe I was being paranoid, but—"

Alex walked up the driveway to where I stood, outside the Mustang. "Followed you from where?" she said. "The school?"

"Maybe," I said. "I ran into some kid there. What a little punk." I was embarrassed to tell her what I had done to maybe provoke the tossed brick. "I grabbed him by the arm."

"You what?" she said. "You grabbed a minor? Inside the school? You grabbed him by the arm?"

"I overreacted," I said. "Kid practically dropped his shoulder into the custodian. I wish I hadn't, but..."

Alex looked toward the street. "So you think this kid could've done it?"

"I don't know." I started toward the house. Alex followed behind me.

We went inside, and Alex pulled containers out of the refrigerator. "You'd better eat. I know how you are when you're hungry."

"I didn't grab him because I was hungry. He was a punk. Almost knocked this guy down."

"He's not an old man, is he?" she said. "He couldn't take care of himself?"

I nodded. "Sure, he could have. He's a good size himself. Like I said, I just reacted."

She sighed, shaking her head. "I'm making you something to eat." She pulled out some bread from a cabinet and went to work, facing the counter. "So what was this kid's name?"

"Zack. Zack Mazer. His parents are rich," I said.

Alex looked at me. "What's that have to do with anything?"

"I'm telling you what I was told." I picked up my beer, although I still hadn't gotten used to the pumpkin flavor. It didn't help that it had gotten warmer.

She finished whatever she'd made me and brought the plate over, placing it down in front of me. "You like avocado, right?"

I nodded and pushed the beer aside, grabbing the sandwich with both hands and taking a bite. I knew I looked like a pig but felt like I hadn't eaten in three weeks.

Alex put a stack of napkins in front of me and sat down across the table watching me.

I wiped my face. "I'd like to find where this kid lives. If there's an SUV in the driveway with a broken brake light, I'll know it was him."

"Then what?" she said, a smirk on her face. "Kick the door down?"

I grinned and took another bite of the sandwich. I washed it down with warm pumpkin beer. "I'll make him pay for it."

Alex shook her head. "If you really think it was him, you could just go to the police?"

I laughed. "I think I can take care of it myself."

"What if you show up, say he did it. And then he tells his parents you grabbed him by the arm? Then what?"

Alex got up and grabbed the bowl of dog food from the counter and put it down on the floor. "Sorry for the late dinner, Raz."

Raz dug into the bowl and devoured his food. He was as hungry as I was.

Alex stood in front of the window and looked outside. "You want me to grab the vacuum? Help clean up that glass?"

"No. But thanks. I'll stop at the car wash. You'll ruin your vacuum." I looked over at Alex, her reflection coming back at us from the window. "I meant to ask you why you keep your blinds open this late? I drove up, and could see everything you were doing."

Alex shrugged. "I never get used to it getting dark so early." She walked out of the kitchen, came back a half-minute later with her Glock by her side. She placed it down on the table.

"What's that for?" I said.

"I don't know if the kid threw that brick or if it was someone else. I'd like to at least be prepared if whoever it was comes back."

# Chapter 9

I parked across the street from Douglas Williams High, watching the students drive into the student parking lot. The cars ranged from old clunkers with faded paint and loud mufflers to brand new cars that cost more than I made in any given year. I never knew what it was like to be the rich kid with a brand new car. I had a different one every few months, usually because they wouldn't last. I'd buy them myself, with my own money. I remember the handful of kids at school who'd turn sixteen, show up the next day with a BMW or Mercedes. A birthday gift from Mommy and Daddy.

There were a number of SUVs pulling into the parking lot. But it was the black Range Rover, an older model, that caught my eye, turning into the lot on two wheels, tires squealing.

I watched it turn into a parking space. And when the driver hit the brakes, I noticed one of the lights didn't work.

I watched, waiting for the driver to step out.

The school bell rang. A herd of teenagers started to run toward the entrance. But whoever was behind the wheel of the Range Rover didn't appear to be in much of a hurry. I watched, waiting.

And when he finally stepped out, I saw it was exactly who I was expecting: the kid from the locker room. Zack Mazer.

I watched him walk toward the building, taking his sweet time. He didn't seem to be concerned with being late.

He stepped to the entrance and turned, glancing my way before opening the door and disappearing inside.

I knew there was a chance he could've recognized my car. But I wasn't overly concerned if he had. In fact, part of me wanted him to know I knew he was the one who tossed the brick through my window.

There were a couple of smaller pickup trucks sitting behind the parking lot where Zack had parked. A group of men were doing some kind of construction. I got out my binoculars to get a closer look, and realized they were repairing a brick wall that looked like it had collapsed.

I stepped out of the car and walked across the parking lot. There was a pile of newer bricks on the ground, near where the wall, with mostly broken bricks, was in need of repair.

"What happened?" I said, walking up to one of the men mixing a bucket of cement by hand.

He looked up at me. "One of these kids drove into the wall." He laughed. "Happens a few times a school year."

I had the brick that landed in my back seat in my hand and showed it to the man. "Any chance this brick is from this wall?"

The man took it from my hand. "You get it from here?" He looked it over, picked up one of the bricks on the ground and held the two next to each other. He looked at me, like he was still waiting for my answer.

"Someone threw it through my window," I said.

He raised his eyebrows. "No kidding, huh?" He nodded, put both bricks down on the ground. "It's definitely from this wall," he said.

"I figured." I nodded toward the brick I'd handed him that he'd placed on the ground. "Mind if I take that back?" I said.

He shrugged, picked it up and handed it back to me. "We're replacing them anyway."

"Thanks." I walked away, the brick in my hand, and pulled my phone from my pocket to call Alex.

She answered on the first ring. "Where are you?" she said. "I thought you were going to call me?"

"I'm calling you now," I said. "I'm at the school."

"Douglas Williams? What are you—"

"I came here hoping I'd see Zack Mazer. Sure enough, he showed up driving a Range Rover. The brake light's not working."

"You need to get out of there," she said. "You can't be hanging around a high school. It's kind of creepy."

I had just gotten into my car. "I'm leaving now."

"Are you coming back to the office?"

"Not yet," I said. "I was going to go see his parents. Let them know what a punk their kid is."

"Tell me you're not serious?" she said. "You think he's driving the only car with a broken taillight?"

I looked down at the brick on the floor of the passenger side. "I have the brick right here next to me. It's from a busted wall, here at the school." I pulled away from the curb and headed down Sam Hardwick Boulevard toward Saints Road.

"Why don't you let it go?"

"Let what go?"

"Let it go. This kid. I mean, we have more important things to do."

Alex was always the voice of reason. But it didn't mean she was always right.

"Any chance you'd be able to look up their address?" I said.

"What? No! I'm not looking for their address, Henry. You can't... Are you going to mention to them you grabbed the kid's arm? How do you think that'll go over? You don't think he's going to tell them that some strange man in the boy's locker room grabbed his arm?"

I didn't respond.

"Let it go," she said.

I turned left and stopped at the red light. "What fun is that?"

"I'm hanging up," she said.

I didn't think she was serious. But the line went dead. "Alex?" I looked at the screen and she was gone.

• • • • • • • • • •

I pulled into a 7-Eleven parking lot and parked around the side of the building. Alex was better than me at finding addresses. And being at the office, she had access to software I didn't have on my phone. But I searched on my phone anyway, hoping to find a residential address for the Mazer family.

But instead, the first result was for Mazer Accounting Services. I tapped on the website and saw a photo of the president right there on the home page. Hair slicked back, arms folded across his chest, John Mazer wore a bow tie I'd have to admit didn't quite sit with me.

I never understood why anyone would wear one, other than with a tuxedo. *To each his own*, I thought.

I clicked on the contact page and saw Mazer Accounting Services was in Deerwood. Just ten minutes away.

I pulled out of the 7-Eleven parking lot and set out on Cape Horn drive to Beach Boulevard and jumped on 295. I thought about calling Alex back, let her know what I was doing. But I didn't need to hear from her how foolish, maybe childish, she felt I was acting.

The idea behind a kid getting away with throwing a brick through my window wasn't just about me getting revenge. I wanted the parents to know what kind of kid they'd raised. Although seeing he was driving a Range Rover that likely cost thirty or forty grand, assuming it was used, said something about the parents.

At least to me, it did.

I took the exit for Town Center Parkway and followed it into Deerwood. I turned into the parking lot of the modern office building, with tinted windows making up most of the front of it.

There were a dozen cars in the parking lot, but spaces at the front. I parked next to a Mercedes and walked under the porte cochère, through the revolving doors, and into the lobby.

I stopped and looked at the sign to the right of the elevator. There were at least thirty businesses listed on it, Mazer Accounting Services being one of them.

Suite 206.

I pressed the button and waited for the elevator door to open, watching the illuminated arrow above it.

The bell dinged and the door slid open.

Inside the elevator, standing in front of me, was a man with a bow tie like the one I'd seen in the photo on his website.

John Mazer stepped off and walked past me without even acknowledging my presence. Not even a respectful nod my way.

I watched him walk toward the revolving door, carrying a brown leather briefcase.

He appeared to be in a rush.

"Are you John Mazer?" I said, before he made it to the door.

He stopped and turned to me. He nodded. "Can I help you?"

Mazer looked just like he did in his picture, the way his light-colored hair, clearly thinning, was slicked back on his head.

I couldn't help but look at his bow tie and he followed my eyes to it.

He straightened it out.

I wasn't sure I trusted a man wearing a normal tie. This guy wore a bow tie with some kind of floral design printed on it. I had my doubts about him.

John Mazer was shorter than he looked in the photo. Although I remembered the image on his website showed him from the chest up, so it was hard to tell anyway.

"You're Zack's dad, is that right?"

He looked at me with a bit of suspicion in his eyes. After a moment, he nodded. "Zack?" He nodded again. "And, who are you, exactly?"

"I'm 'exactly' Henry Walsh. And I hate to tell you this, but your son owes me a few hundred bucks."

"A few hundred dollars?" he said, as if he was too proper to use the word bucks. "For what?"

"I can give you all the details if you'd like. But your son threw a brick through my car window."

At first, he appeared surprised. Then his expression changed to one of disbelief, shaking his head. "It's very likely you're mistaken," he said. "How can you accuse my son of such a thing?"

I told him about the brick and the burnt-out brake light. And how I believe he might've followed me to Alex's house from the school. I left out the part about me grabbing his arm.

"I'm sorry," he said. "You must be mistaken. Zack would never do such a thing." He squinted his eyes. "What time did this allegedly take place?"

"A little before seven o'clock last night," I said.

"Before seven?" He shook his head. "Zack was home, having dinner. He was home from working out at the school with his friends. I'd say... I'm certain... he was home by six thirty."

I stared back at him. I wasn't surprised the father was covering up for his own kid. What father wouldn't? But I wasn't buying it. "My father used to think I was pretty innocent too," I said. "Parents never want to believe their kids would do wrong."

"If you think you're going to get Zack, or me, for that matter, to pay for some window you have no proof he broke, then—"

"He drives a black Range Rover, right? Couple years old? And, by the way, you might want to get the brake light replaced."

He stared back at me with a blank look on his face. I couldn't tell if he was stunned by my accusation, upset with his son, or simply wasn't about to believe a word I'd said.

"Listen," he said. "I don't need something like this to get blown out of proportion." He stepped toward the desk against the wall to the left of the elevator, where I would have expected a security guard to be seated.

Maybe they only worked nights.

He put his briefcase on top of the desk and worked the combination lock at the front of it. He popped open the lid and reached inside, pulling out what looked like a checkbook. He took out a pen and leaned over the desk, the checkbook open and the pen in place, ready to write. With his back to me, he said, "How much would you like?"

"Actually," I said. "What I'd like is for your son to apologize to me.  I'm not here for your money."

He turned to me. "Excuse me?"

"I said, I mean, the check is great. I thought it'd be an important lesson for him. Show him there are repercussions for his actions."

John Mazer cleared his throat. "I'm sorry, Mr..."

"Walsh," I said, my eyes on the check. "Henry Walsh."

"Mr. Walsh. I will deal with my son. It's none of your business how I handle it." He turned back to the desk. "Now, please tell me how much you would like me to make this out for. I've wasted enough time."

He didn't even want to know anything about what had happened. He wanted to write the check, make the problem go away.

"I don't know yet," I said. "I wasn't expecting you to just write me a check."

He scribbled on the check and tore it from the checkbook. He turned to me, the check in his hand. "Here," he said, handing it to me. "I'm sorry for your troubles." He opened the briefcase, put the checkbook inside and closed the lid. He turned the lock's combination and headed for the door, the briefcase in his hand.

He walked out without another word.

I looked at the check in my hand, surprised to see it was for one thousand dollars.

# Chapter 10

I DROVE STRAIGHT TO RR Sporting Goods in Beachwood hoping to talk a little more with Ray. I wondered about the Mazer kid. I wouldn't put it past him for a minute he'd pull a stunt. Maybe the kid didn't like the idea he wasn't seeing the field. Maybe Daddy had something to do with Ray being fired.

I had called Alex at the office a couple of times, but she didn't pick up. I tried her cell, and she hadn't answered that either.

I had a feeling she was annoyed enough with me she might've been ignoring my calls. It wasn't something she'd normally do, but lately she'd gotten more easily irritated with me. Or with my decision making. We'd gone through a rough patch. Not only business-wise, but personally. It seemed every time we started to get closer to each other, one of us would back away.

What we had together was hard, if not impossible, to explain. So it was just best I never tried to. Even in my own mind, trying to figure out what there was between us bordered on frustrating.

I parked on the street in front of Ray's store and stepped out of the Mustang. I looked at my screen to see if I'd somehow missed Alex. But she hadn't called.

I walked up to the building and looked in through the glass display window. Gloves and bats and spring sports equipment were on display with the white, faceless mannequins dressed in sports uniforms. One baseball, the other soccer.

But through the display, into the store, I'd expected to see Ray. Or at least some lights on in the place. But it was dark. The lights were off.

I stepped to the glass door at the entrance and pulled on the handle, but it didn't open. The door was locked. I looked at my watch. According to the sign on the other side of the glass, the store opened at nine. I knocked on the door. Nothing. Using my hands to shield the bright sun reflecting off the glass, I tried to look around inside. As far as I could see, Ray wasn't there. At least not out front.

I looked across the store toward the doorway behind the counter, then the curtain running across it. Maybe my eyes were playing tricks on me, but it appeared the curtain moved. I knocked on the door's glass one more time.

I wasn't sure if the curtain had moved but wondered if it was Ray back there, why he wouldn't let me in. That was assuming it was him.

I looked both ways along the sidewalk, noticing the building next door. There was a sign for a dry cleaners, and from what I could see, the place appeared busy. I walked toward it but turned left down the alley between the two buildings, past a couple of steel trash cans and out into a parking lot along the back of the two buildings. There were only a handful of parking spaces, one occupied by an older Nissan Maxima with a dent on the rear passenger door. There were no other cars back there.

I turned left and stopped in front of the rusted, gray steel door. It was the back entrance to RR Sporting Goods, with a handwritten sign taped to the door. It read PRIVATE ENTRANCE.

I tried the doorknob, expecting it to be locked. And although the knob didn't turn, the door pulled open as if it hadn't latched closed. I opened the door and stuck my head inside. "Ray?"

I stepped inside with the door open so I could see. But I stepped away, and it closed behind me. I stood in almost total darkness, although light slipped through the curtain running across the doorway leading to the front of the store.

"Ray? You in here?" I heard a humming noise and felt a light breeze from overhead. I looked up and, in the darkness on the ceiling, could make out a slow-moving fan. It made a ticking noise. I looked at the curtain across the doorway and wondered if the fan had made it move when I was looking in through the front door.

I felt around on the wall for a light switch, stepped back to the door and opened it to let some light in. I stepped away and jumped when the door slammed closed behind me. I used the flashlight on my phone, although it didn't work very well after a couple of drops. "Ray?" I said.

I shined the light from my phone around the space and saw a mattress on the floor beside a milk crate with magazines inside it. There was a blanket and pillow.

Shelves on the wall to my right were filled with boxes. I stepped to the doorway and opened the curtain to let light in, still looking for a light switch. I looked around the area filled with mostly boxes and random pieces of sports equipment. There was a set of golf clubs leaned up against the wall.

Other than the humming, ticking fan, the place was quiet.

There was a narrow door.

I looked down at the screen of my phone and saw I had a text from Alex:

*Call me ASAP*

I also noticed I'd missed her call, my ringer being turned off.

I reached for the knob on the narrow door, about to open it, when it swung open hard and fast and knocked me back. I tried to catch myself but stumbled over a stack of boxes, crashing to the floor.

A figure I couldn't quite see charged at me, swinging an object. I felt the pain as whatever it was struck me in the head as I tried to get to my feet.

I was hit again, using my hands to block my face. But although I stopped a direct hit, whatever it was struck just over the nose. I felt the warmth of my own blood pour down my face. It dripped into my eyes, making it harder to see than it already was.

I stumbled, trying to get to my feet. I threw a box and whatever I could grab at whoever was standing over me. I was hit, multiple times, shielding my head and face with my arms. I crawled on the floor, if only to somehow save myself from a beating, and reached for the golf bag I saw moments earlier.

My face ached and burned. I was almost blind but felt for a club, taking another hit to the back of my leg, behind my knee. But I somehow made it to my feet and came up swinging the club left and right like a baseball bat.

I heard the door open. Light filled the back of the store. But I still couldn't see. My eyes were blurred and stinging. I squeezed them hard, trying to clear them.

I opened my eyes and could see just enough to make out the objects around me. Boxes thrown, and the set of golf clubs on the floor, I was pretty sure my attacker was gone.

I stumbled for the door and made it outside. My eyes were still blurred, but I could see enough to know whoever it was had disappeared.

I touched my hand to my face, looking at the blood on my fingers. I went back inside and propped the door open with one of the boxes. I tore open three different boxes looking for some kind of cloth. I pulled out a T-shirt from one of them and held it against the front of my face, trying to stop the bleeding.

When I saw a light coming from the floor, I realized I'd dropped my phone. I reached down to pick it up and saw someone was calling. But I couldn't make out who it was. It didn't matter. I tapped the green button and put it up to my ear. "Yeah."

"Henry? Where are you?"

It was Alex.

I needed a second to gather myself, using the T-shirt to try and clear my eyes. "I'm... I'm at Ray's store." I squinted, the bright sun pouring down from the sky. "Can I call you back?" I said. I looked around and beyond the chain-link fence enclosing the parking lot. The Nissan Maxima was still there, parked in the same space behind the dry cleaners.

"Henry, listen," Alex said. "There's been some news. I just got off the phone with Mike." She paused. "Shondra Rivers is dead."

# Chapter 11

"YOU NEED TO GET to a doctor," Alex said, standing in front of me out in the street in front of Shondra Rivers' house, looking over my face. "Is it still bleeding?" She stepped to the back of her Jeep and came back with a towel. She pressed it against my face and took the bloody T-shirt from my hand, putting it inside a plastic bag she tossed in the back of her Jeep. She nodded toward the rescue vehicle. "Don't you think you should at least have one of the paramedics take a look at it."

"It's fine," I said, taking the towel from Alex but keeping it pressed against my face. Although my face actually hurt when I spoke. The upper part of my head felt like it had been cracked open.

There were four Jacksonville Sheriff's vehicles parked in the street. One rescue vehicle was in the driveway, backed up toward the door. Another one had parked out on the street with a fire engine parked behind it, in front of a neighbor's house. The coroner's van was parked closest to the door.

The maroon Crown Victoria with faded paint was parked half in the driveway, two wheels on the lawn.

The car belonged to Detective Mike Stone.

Mike walked out from the front door and stuck a cigarette in his mouth as soon as he hit the steps. He stopped in the walkway, cupping his hand over the top to give it a light, walking across the grass toward me and Alex standing outside my car, parked near the road.

His eyes were fixed on mine as he approached. His eyebrows furrowed, his eyes squinted, he came closer and studied my face. The cigarette hung from his mouth. "What the hell happened to you?"

I didn't answer.

Mike looked at Alex. "What happened to his face?"

I said, "Fender bender, on my way here."

Mike gave me a look, like he wasn't buying it.

Alex looked past him toward the Rivers' house. "So, what's the story?"

Mike looked over his shoulder.

A man and woman from the coroner's office wheeled out Shondra's covered body. "She was stabbed in the chest. The cleaning lady found her in bed."

I pulled the towel from my face. "In bed?" I said.

Mike took a drag from his cigarette, shifting his stance. "Cleaning lady found her." He turned, his head following the body being wheeled toward the coroner's vehicle. He pulled his pants up from the belt, smoke rising up in front of his face. He took the cigarette from his mouth and gave Alex a nod. "I called because I know you've been dealing with the husband. And we haven't been able to locate him, so I'm wondering which one of you wants to tell me where I'll find him?"

I shook my head and shrugged. "I have no idea."

"We tried calling him at his store," he said. "But nobody answers the phone."

I kept it to myself that I had just come from Ray's store. I gave Alex a quick glance, hoping Alex would do the same.

One of the paramedics walked up behind Mike, staring at me. He pointed with his thumb over his shoulder. "I was standing over there, couldn't help but notice your face." He leaned in close enough I could smell the coffee on his breath. "You want me to bandage that up for you?"

I shook my head. "It's nothing."

The man slipped a pair of rubber gloves on his hands and reached his hand out to touch it. "I'm not sure it's nothing," he said, looking at the bloody towel in my hand. "That's quite a bit of blood."

"Why don't you go ahead and throw him in the back of that rescue, take him to the ER?" Mike said. He looked at me suspiciously, then walked away past the other officers and in through the front door.

Alex followed behind me and the paramedic, toward the rescue vehicle in the driveway.

The paramedic, an older gentleman with short white hair, stepped up and into the back of the truck. He came out with a large blue leather bag. "What's your name?"

"Henry."

He stepped down and crouched in front of me, looking in my eyes with a penlight, studying my wound. "Well, it's possible you could use stitches." He stared at my wound. "So what happened?"

"Fender bender, on the ride here," I said. "Just put a Band-Aid on it," I said. "I'm sure I'll be all set."

"There's a chance you'll end up with a scar if you don't get this stitched up. I'm sure you don't want that, right?"

I shrugged. "I have plenty. I'm told it adds character." I grinned but felt the pain in my face when I did. I also had pain in the back of my head and down behind my knee. "Do you have an ice pack by any chance?"

The paramedic nodded, working on the wound over my nose. He removed a wet cloth from a plastic pouch and wiped down my face. Then he took a long cotton-tipped stick from a paper sleeve and dipped it into a brown bottle, then touched the end of it to my wound.

It burned like he'd poured battery acid on my face. "Hurts more than the wound," I said.

"Sorry," he said. "It's a pretty good one you got here. A lot of swelling." He nodded at Alex. "Up inside, see that refrigerator on the right? The ice packs are in there. Take as many as you need." He continued working on my wound.

"Were you inside the house?" I said.

The paramedic stopped what he was doing and nodded. He looked away for a moment, toward the coroner's vehicle backing out of the driveway. "Did you know her?"

"You could say that," I said.

I left it at that.

Alex stepped down from the back of the vehicle with an ice pack in each hand. She squeezed one to get it working and handed it to me, ice-cold to the touch.

I placed the ice pack on the back of my head.

The man crumpled papers from the bandage packaging in his hand and removed his rubber gloves, balling them up in one hand. "You should be good," he said, looking around me at the back of my head. "You bang the back of your head too?" he said.

I nodded, looking away.

He stood up and said, "Then I'd suggest you swing by the ER, get yourself checked out."

"Maybe he's right," Alex said, looking down at me.

"I'll be fine." I took the ice pack off the back of my head and pressed it against my forehead. I turned as the paramedic climbed up into the back of the vehicle. "I understand she was stabbed?" I said.

He looked around, climbing down from the vehicle. He slammed the doors closed on the back of the vehicle. "I'm not sure I'm comfortable discussing what I saw in there with you or anyone else, outside of the sheriff's office."

"I understand," I said. But persisted. "Was the cleaning lady still here when you arrived?"

He was clearly hesitant to answer a single question. But I gave him an easy one. Interrogation 101. "She was out front, in the driveway." He looked around again. "I think she's gone. She didn't speak English." He nodded toward Mike, walking out from the building. "You'd be better off asking the detective these questions."

I looked at Mike and turned back to the paramedic. "Yeah, sure."

Alex walked after Mike as he headed over to his car.

I said to the paramedic, "Did you happen to notice anything else when you were in there?" I'd hoped I could get whatever I could out of him, knowing there was little chance Mike would give us much of anything. At least not at first. The paramedic had a surprised look on his face. "Are you a cop?"

"I'm a private investigator. And Mrs. Rivers... I was actually doing work for her husband."

"Oh," he said. "That explains the questions." He pulled open the driver-side door to the truck, reached for the grab bar, and pulled himself up inside. He held his hands on the steering wheel and looked straight ahead. After a brief pause, he looked down at me, standing outside the vehicle. He looked back and forth, keeping his voice low. "She'd only been stabbed once. In the chest. I'm not a detective, but it didn't appear there was much of a struggle. She was on her back, in her bed. If you ask me, I'd say she was asleep when it happened."

I pictured Shondra's face, and the last time we talked to her in the parking lot where she worked. "Was the knife still in her?" I said.

He shook his head. "Not when I got in there. No weapon was found. Not that I know of."

"But you're sure her death was caused by a stabbing?"

"I mean, I saw nothing to indicate otherwise. Puncture wound over the heart."

# Chapter 12

It was late in the evening, and I still hadn't spoken to Ray. He hadn't answered any of my calls. And I'd tried him a dozen times. Alex hadn't spoken to Mike since the morning when we saw him, and we had no indication anyone from the sheriff's office had found Ray to, at the very least, tell him his wife had been killed.

That was, of course, assuming he didn't already know.

It would be naïve of me, or even foolish, to believe Ray Rivers wouldn't be a suspect in his wife's death.

But in the early stages of the police investigation, there appeared to be little proof. Other than a body. No weapon had been found, at least as far as I'd known.

I took a ride by Ray's house. I didn't think he'd be there, although I did expect to see officers and detectives from the sheriff's office.

Yellow tape surrounded the property.

I was surprised to see the one vehicle in the driveway belonged to Ray. It was his Suburban.

I turned in and parked the Mustang behind it and walked up to the front door.

Ray was standing on the other side, watching me.

He had tears in his eyes. "Henry?" he said, pushing open the screen door. "What are you doing here?"

I shrugged. "Looking for you," I said. I reached out and shook his hand, told him I was sorry for his loss. I looked around the front of the house and toward the street before I stepped inside. "Where are the cops?"

"They just left."

"And they said you could stay here?"

He shook his head. "I left when they did. Told them I wouldn't be back. But I..." He wiped a tear from his cheek. "I had to come back."

I looked him in the eye. "This is a crime scene, Ray. They're not going to want you in here."

"It's my house," Ray said. He started down the hall and into the kitchen.

I closed the door and stood in the foyer, in front of the stairs. I watched Ray, his wide body just about filling the width of the hall. His head looked to almost hit the top of the doorway as he stepped into the kitchen.

Was I watching a man who killed his wife?

At that point, I had to give Ray the benefit of doubt.

Most of the lights were off, other than a lamp in the room to my left and lights in the kitchen. The sound of sports, coming from a TV in the other room, made it seem for a moment there hadn't been a murder in the house. I looked up toward the top of the stairs and the open hallway. It was dark up there, lights off.

I walked down the hall toward the back of the house.

Ray was standing at an island with a bottle of liquor in front of him.

"When did you find out?" I said.

"This afternoon. I was at my store, couple officers from the sheriff's office came by." He had a glass in his hand, whatever inside it clear, with a couple of ice cubes. The label on the bottle said Grey Goose Vodka. Ray took a sip from his glass. "I'll be honest, when I first saw them, I was sure it had something to do with Barry." He wiped a tear from his cheek and leaned in close, looking at my face.

"What happened?"

I touched the bandage above my nose, between my eyes. I looked at him and couldn't help but wonder if he had some idea about it. "I'll tell you all about it in a moment."

His mouth started to open, like he wanted to say something. But he remained quiet. His eyes were behind me.

I looked over my shoulder into the adjoining room to see a TV up on the wall over the fireplace, tuned to a college basketball game on ESPN.

Ray had the remote in front of him, pointed it toward the screen and lowered the volume. "Duke and UNC," he said. "Big game." He threw back what was left in his glass and picked up the bottle. He topped off the glass but didn't pick it up. Shaking his head, he looked down. "I just can't believe she's..." He started to cry but wiped the back of his big hand across his eyes. "I'm sorry."

"Nothing for you to be sorry about," I said.

"After the detective came to the shop, I closed up, of course. Came right here. He followed me, asked me a few questions but said there'd be more. He asked me about you."

"Detective Stone?" I said.

Ray nodded. "Yeah. Stone."

"What'd he say?"

Ray shrugged his big shoulders. "They don't know much, it seems. Asked me if she had any enemies. Asked about her family, most who live across the country. Friends…"

"But did he say anything else? About you?" I said. "I assumed they wanted to know where you were?"

Ray sipped his drink. "He kind of put me on the defensive," he said. His tongue sounded a bit tangled from the booze. With the half-empty bottle of vodka and the cap with the torn label still attached to it, I'd assumed he'd had more than a few drinks.

"He looked surprised when I told him I hadn't been living here," he said. "Then, of course, he wanted to know more about our relationship. Why I'd moved out. But I asked the detective to cut me some slack. I'd just found out my wife was dead. And here's this cop, peppering me with questions."

"Stone can be a little aggressive," I said. "But he's a good detective."

Ray had his eyes down toward his glass and held on to it in front of him. "I asked him to give me a break, and promised I'd go down to the station in the morning."

I thought for a moment. "Did he ask you where you were?"

"Yes. And where I'd been staying. I was kind of embarrassed, telling him I'd been sleeping in the back of my store."

"And what about this morning?" I said. "You tell him you were at the store?"

Ray nodded with a touch of hesitation, turning his head, his eyes going away from me.

"Ray?" I said.

He turned back to me.

"That's not true," I said. More a statement than a question.

Ray cocked his head back. "What's not true?"

I looked him in the eye and pointed at the bandage above my nose. "You want to know where I got this?"

Ray stared back at me, waiting.

"It happened at your store."

A confused look took over his face. "Huh? At my store? What... I don't understand. How could—"

"I was there in the morning. Right before I got the call about Shondra."

"You got a call about Shondra? You knew about it this morning?"

"My partner, Alex, got word. Apparently, he didn't mention it to you, but Detective Stone knows we'd been talking to you. He's a friend. Well, not exactly a friend of mine. Of Alex's. They've known each other for quite a while. He called Alex because he was trying to find you. And if you told him you were at your store, when I know you weren't..."

"Henry, no. Listen, I—"

"You start lying to the cops now, you know how it's going to look?"

Ray closed his eyes and hung his head. "I panicked, all right? I just... I don't know why I lied." He raised his eyes to mine. "But I was there for most of the day. I opened early, had to take off for a couple of hours." He narrowed his eyes, his gaze on the bandage covering my wound. "Can you tell me what happened? How you got hurt at my store?"

"How about, first, you tell me why you weren't there? Because, the truth is, if I were the person in charge of investigating what happened to Shondra, I'd not only be suspicious of a man who not only said he was somewhere he wasn't, but wondering about his frame of mind, considering he believed his wife was possibly having an affair."

The expression on Ray's face tightened. "Are you trying to say I killed my wife?"

"I'm simply telling you how things look," I said.

Ray stared back at me with a look that said he was worried. And maybe a little mad. He took a deep breath and exhaled, shaking his head.

I looked over the bottle of vodka. It wasn't my kind of drink. In fact, it reminded me more of something you'd use on a wound than put in your body. But I couldn't let Ray stand there, finish the whole bottle by himself.

"You mind, I get a glass?" I said, looking around the kitchen. "Unless you have something else? Whiskey?"

Ray shook his head and held up the bottle of vodka. "This was Shondra's. She never even opened it. Not much else in the house though." He grabbed a glass from the cabinet and placed it down in front of me. "You want ice?"

"A couple of cubes would be good," I said.

Ray opened the freezer door and put the ice in the glass. He stepped to the island and filled the glass from the bottle, slid the glass across toward me. "I'm sorry I lied. I told you, I was... I know how this can look. It's always the husband, isn't it?" He picked up his glass and shot it back. "I'll tell Detective Stone the truth, when I go over there in the morning."

"You might want to maybe sober up soon, get a good night's rest. Get your story straight." I sipped my drink and looked at him over the glass. "You're not sleeping here, are you?"

Ray shrugged. "I don't know."

"The cops told you not to be here." I looked at the clock on the stove. I thought maybe neither of us should hang around much longer. It was, after all, a crime scene. "You have an alibi?"

"An alibi? You mean, this morning?"

"Last night and this morning. They don't know what time this happened yet."

He nodded. "This morning, I was running errands."

"Is there someone you saw? Someone you talked to?"

Ray shrugged. "The woman at the post office, I guess?"

"She'll know you? If she needs to vouch for your whereabouts?"

"I-I don't know. Maybe."

"Maybe?" I said. "Maybe won't be good enough, Ray."

He looked over at the TV. "You're talking like I'm guilty."

"All I'm doing... I'm just advising you to get your story straight. Before you go in and start answering questions. I know how this works, Ray. You slip up, throw any more lies Stone's way, he's going to come after you."

Ray filled his glass halfway with another shot but didn't respond to what I'd said.

"And I'm not just talking about telling them you lied about being at the store, when you weren't. You need to come clean about your belief Shondra and Barry had an affair," I said.

"What?" His eyes were wide open. "Why? I didn't kill her. And I don't know if they were having an affair or not. What good would that even do? Besides put me at the top of the list as a suspect?"

"Because once they start to dig, if they determine there was, by chance, an affair... and then someone finds out you knew about it—"

"How would they?" he said, shaking his head. "Nobody knows but you."

I wasn't sure he understood what I was trying to say. "Ray, I'm not going to be able to lie for you."

"Why would you have to lie? Just keep your mouth shut," he said, appearing a bit agitated. His voice and his movements were getting sloppy. "Not telling someone something they don't need to know and lying are two different things."

I shook my head. "You're wrong. And you need to understand that."

Ray ran both hands over his face and held them there for a moment. Tears came down his face, and he wiped them with the back of his hand.

# Chapter 13

IT WAS TEN THIRTY in the morning, and Alex hadn't gotten much out of Mike after Ray had gone to the station, as promised, for questioning.  And Ray hadn't answered my phone calls either.

I turned down North Catherine Street toward the side lot where Mike normally parked his Crown Vic outside JSO headquarters.

It was parked where it always was, in the last spot on the other side of the chain-link fence between the lot and the sidewalk. As soon as I pulled up to the curb, we spotted Mike standing just outside the building having a smoke.

Alex rolled down her window on the passenger side. "Mike!"

He looked around like he was unsure where the voice was coming from. But then he looked our way, taking his time before walking toward us, the cigarette hanging from his mouth.

He stepped to the edge of the curb and walked to the rear of my Mustang, looking at the missing window. "I could write up a ticket for that, you know."

"For what?" I said. "No rear window?" I looked at Alex, rolling my eyes.

Mike stepped over to Alex's window, crouched down and looked in. "You hear about your friend?" he said.

"Ray?" I nodded. "He was here already?"

Mike took a drag from his cigarette  and took a step back from the car. "He's lucky we let him leave."

I had to lean down toward the passenger side, my head almost on Alex's shoulder so I could see Mike's face outside the car. "Why's that?"

Mike shrugged, shaking his head. "Well, he lied about being at the store in the morning. Although, so far it looks like his wife'd been dead through the night. Killed sometime between, say, midnight and five a.m. Initial reports. Said he sleeps in the back of his store, which I found kind of hard to believe. Sad, really. Guy played in the NFL, doesn't have the money to go to a hotel?"

I didn't respond, Alex turning toward me with a quick glance.

"Anything else?" I said, hoping Ray had mentioned he believed Shondra and Barry Hawkins were having an affair. But I wasn't at the point where I was going to tell Mike anything I wasn't supposed to. Not yet, anyway.

"Something doesn't smell right with the man," Mike said. "I can't put my finger on it. He was very—"

"The man has to be in shock," Alex said.

Mike frowned. "Are you going to start defending the guy? Neither one of you know a thing about him, and now, here you are—"

"We're not defending anyone," I said. "But I know how you guys operate. I think it's a little too convenient to point your finger at the victim's husband as a real suspect this early in your investigation."

Mike laughed. "Oh, is that what you think?" He dropped his cigarette on the ground. "I'll make a mental note. Should I check with you once I have any other suspects? In case you want to presume they're innocent?"

"Isn't that how the law works?" I said. "Innocent until—"

"Oh, just shut your mouth, Walsh. Will you?" Mike threw up his hands and started to walk away. "Like I need to answer any of your questions." He stopped, mid-step. He pointed with his finger to his chest. "The way you two act... like I have to tell you anything? You think I work for you or something?"

"Well, technically," I said. "We do pay your salary."

Mike stepped closer to the car, looked in the window at me, past Alex. He narrowed his eyes, a snarl on his face. "Give me a break with that foolish garbage," he said. He looked toward the back of the Mustang. "You can't even afford to fix a broken window. You expect me to believe you actually pay taxes?" He slapped Alex on her arm, hanging out the window. "Like I told you the other day, you ever decide to get back into legitimate law enforcement where you don't have to keep working with this clown, I got someone who wants to talk."

I looked at Alex, but she stayed facing Mike. She had, no doubt, hoped I didn't hear what Mike had said to her. Or hoped I wouldn't ask what he meant. So I let it slide. At least for the time being. I looked out the window at Mike. "Can you at least tell us what else Ray told you?"

He shook his head. "No, I can't. And I'm not sure there's anything you don't already know. There were no real revelations, other than they were separated. Clearly not a happy couple." He looked me in the eye. "But if I find out you're holding anything back that gets in the way…"

I had a pretty good feeling Ray hadn't said a word to Mike about his belief Shondra'd had an affair with a man who, coincidentally, was also now deceased. Although it hadn't been believed Barry had been murdered.

Shondra had been.

I stepped out from the driver's side and stood with the door open. I leaned on the roof and looked across it at Mike. "So you don't have anything," I said. "Certainly nothing to even consider him a real suspect. Am I right?"

Mike reached inside his blue Jacksonville Sheriff's Office jacket, pulled out a pack of cigarettes. "What I don't get," he said, "is what makes you think I have to discuss any of this case with you?" He stuck a cigarette in his mouth and held it between his teeth, a cocky grin on his face.

Alex stepped out from the car and stood on the other side of it, on the sidewalk, next to Mike. She looked at him and said, "What Henry's asking is if Ray told you anything that would maybe raise a red flag. We're not trying to cross you or anything, Mike. So I'm not sure why you're getting so upset. We just want to know."

Mike cupped his hand over his cigarette and gave it a light. He looked from me to Alex, his scrunched eyebrows low over his squinted eyes. "Why do I get the feeling there's something one of you isn't telling me?"

I didn't answer.

Alex leaned against the door, facing Mike. "Did he mention anything about…" She gave me a quick glance over her shoulder. It was like she'd changed her mind about telling Mike what we knew. But it was too late.

Mike took a step closer to her. He looked over at me, across the roof. "One of you had better tell me what's going on," he said. "Withholding evidence, or any information, from an active investigation is—"

"We're not withholding anything," Alex said. She stepped in front of Mike. "It's just that... Ray had promised Henry he'd share something with you, you might find important. In fact, it is important. It doesn't sound like he did?"

"Jesus," Mike said. "Will one of you spit it out? Before I have to bring you both inside?" Mike took a drag from his cigarette. "The truth is, the man closed up like a clam. I mean, he didn't refuse to answer questions. But once he realized where this could be heading, he asked if he needed to get a lawyer. I told him he wasn't being charged or even suspected of anything at that point, hoping he'd willingly clear up a few things. Of course, I didn't deny obtaining legal counsel was a good idea." He looked from me to Alex. "So who's going to talk?"

Alex looked at Mike. "He didn't tell you he thought his wife was having an affair?"

Mike's eyebrows shot up on his head. "Shondra Rivers was having an affair? And Ray Rivers knew this?" He shook his head. "He didn't say a word." He stuck the cigarette in his mouth. "Any chance you know with who?"

I wasn't going to let Alex be the only one to do what we'd hoped Ray was going to do on his own. "Barry Hawkins," I said.

Mike again seemed surprised. As much as I'd expected. "The dead principal? From Douglas Williams High?" He looked from me to Alex. "Is it true?"

Alex shrugged. "We don't know. Ray doesn't even know. It was just speculation on his part. And Shondra denied it."

"We asked her," I said. "She said Ray was a jealous man. She said he was paranoid."

Mike cocked his head back. "You talked to the victim? Before she died?"

"Well, Detective," I said. "I assure you she didn't tell us after she was dead."

Mike gave me a look like he wanted to jump across the roof at me. "You know what I'm saying... you goddamn smart-ass." He looked at Alex. "Why didn't you tell me any of this before?"

Alex shrugged. "Like I said, Ray promised Henry he'd tell you. We thought he'd keep his word. For his own sake."

# Chapter 14

Ray was behind the counter, the phone up to his ear. He looked up at me when I walked into his store, gave me a nod, and continued talking, his voice low.

He hung up a few moments later.

"Sorry about that," he said, writing something down on a pad in front of him.

"How come you haven't answered my calls?" I said.

"Oh, uh, my cell phone..." He looked down toward the floor as he stepped around from behind the counter. "I was upset. I actually..." He looked up at me, a crooked grin on his face. "I smashed it."

"You smashed your cell phone?" I was surprised. But I guess I understood.

"You know, I lost my head."

I nodded. "You can't check your voicemails?" I nodded toward the phone, a landline, on the counter. "I left you a couple."

"Oh, yeah. Uh, you know, it's been crazy all morning. I went and talked to Detective Stone. And, I got in here late and everything, so..."

"You talk to a lawyer?"

Ray pointed with his thumb over his shoulder, toward the counter. "That's who I was calling."

"You have one you know?"

Ray shook his head. "No. I left a couple messages. I hope to hear back soon."

I was hesitant to tell him why I was there and wondered how he was going to react. "I spoke with Detective Stone," I said. "And have something you need to know. About what you and I talked about last night."

Ray stared back at me. "I hate to admit it," he said. "What we talked about... I drank quite a bit. It's all a bit foggy."

I looked out toward the street. "Where's your Suburban? You didn't drive here last night, did you? You said you were going to call a cab."

Ray nodded, leaning back with his hands behind him, against the counter. "I did call a cab. But I fell asleep waiting for it. Slept on the couch, at the house. Drove here this morning, changed before I went to talk to the detective."

"Your car's in back?"

He nodded.

I might've purposely been taking my time, before I got to the real reason I showed up at his store. Finally, I said, "Why didn't you tell them about Shondra and Barry? You promised me you would."

Ray shook his head. "It would have been worse if I told him," he said. "There was... it made no sense to put myself in position to, I mean, you already know how it'll make me look, they find out I—"

"You can't keep something like this from them," I said.

"I told you, I'm not even sure they were having an affair. Maybe Shondra was right. Maybe I am just a jealous, paranoid man."

"That's the part, Ray, doesn't look good."

"Huh?"

"I told you last night, you can't withhold information. I can't either."

Ray took a deep breath and exhaled. He nodded, like he understood. But the man was a bit thickheaded. "Listen, Henry. I appreciate you coming by, trying to be helpful and all." He looked out toward the street. "Right now, I don't need a private investigator. I need a good lawyer, clean up this mess before it gets out of hand. That's my priority. You understand what I'm saying?"

I nodded. "Of course I do. I get that. But I wish you'd take my advice, and—"

"What I'm saying, is, I don't need your advice right now." He forced a grin. "I appreciate it though. I do."

Part of me wanted to laugh. It was like Ray was firing me even though he'd never actually hired me. Right then I had to question what I was even doing. Why was I trying to help a man who clearly was going to do what he felt he needed to do?

"That's fine," I said. "But you need to understand." I paused. "I had to tell him," I said.

Ray stared back at me, folding his arms across his chest. "What?"

"I told the truth, Ray. I'm sorry. It's what I do."

"The truth? You told who the truth? What the hell are you trying to tell me?" He straightened up from the counter and took a step toward me. He inhaled, making his chest expand, holding his breath.

I swallowed hard, my throat bone dry, like it was going to crack. "Mike Stone knows. I told him you suspected Shondra and Barry Hawkins were having an affair."

Ray gave a tilt to his head; his eyes squinted hard. He unfolded his arms and started toward me, his eyes locked on to mine. "You told him?"

My body tensed up, seeing in Ray's eyes that he was ready to snap. "I had to. It's—"

His voice grew louder. "I told you something in confidence. Just like when you went to Shondra, without asking me first. I told you to keep your mouth shut!"

I took a few steps back from him as he stepped toward me. "Take it easy, Ray. Let me explain."

He continued toward me, shaking his head. "You threw me under the bus, Henry. Just like everyone else. I trusted you, man. And now, you know what you've done? They're going to come after me. And it'll be your fault!"

I looked around for something to protect myself, having a good feeling I was going to need to. I put my hands up. "Ray, I'm going to ask you to calm down. Listen to me for a minute."

He took another step in my direction, then charged forward. He came at me, moving fast for a man his size. I turned to get away, but he took a wild swing and hit me hard in the back of the head. He punched so hard, it felt like I'd been kicked by a mule.

I stumbled forward, in the direction away from him, but quickly got my footing. I turned, my hands up, ready for another wild swing to come my way. Ray threw another punch but I ducked under it, came up with a right hook. I hit him right in the gut. But it was like my fist had struck a slab of meat.

The look on Ray's face, I'm not sure he felt it. He took another swing but I got my hands up again and blocked it. But the force of his punch sent me into the clothing rack. Clothes came down with the hangers as I tried to catch myself from falling to the floor.

"Ray, stop!" I yelled, trying to get up.

He jumped forward, stood over me, and lifted me off the floor by my arm. But with my free hand, I threw another punch, a wild one, and caught him in the jaw.

He barely budged. He dragged me by the arm, twisting it like he was going to rip it from the socket. My body dangled beneath him as I tried not to move so my arm wouldn't dislocate more than it felt like it already had.

I got in another punch, this time hitting him on the side of his head.

He let go of me this time, fell back into the display of socks and knocked it over as he hit the floor. He pushed himself up slowly, staring back at me, breathing heavily through his nose like a bull.

I backed off, looking down at him. "Ray, that's enough!"

He touched his mouth with his hand and looked at the blood on his fingers. He was up on his feet and, without a word, charged after me once again, driving his shoulder straight into my chest. He sent me backward across the floor, my feet moving under me but with such force I couldn't stop the momentum.

We crashed into the door. It swung open and the plate glass shattered, coming down on top of us as we fell outside and both landed on the sidewalk.

I felt a sharp pain in my leg and looked down. A piece of glass was sticking out from below my knee.

An older couple was walking past the front of the store as it happened, both startled by the crash and two large men hitting the pavement, glass all around.

The woman screamed.

Ray rolled off of me and looked at the couple, shaking his head. He stood over me, looking me in the eye. "I'm... sorry. Henry, I'm..." He turned from me without another word and ran back into the store.

The old couple helped me off the sidewalk without saying much. They both seemed to be in complete shock from what they'd witnessed.

"Watch out for the glass," I said. I looked down at the blood pouring down my leg and into my shoe. I reached down and gave the piece of glass a good yank and dropped it on the sidewalk.

"Ray!" I yelled, looking into the store. I limped with my first step, feeling plenty of pain.

The old woman had her phone out, tapped the screen and held it up to her ear. "Yes, I'm in front of RR Sporting Goods. Yes, that's right, in Beachwood. We need the police." She looked down at my leg. "And maybe a rescue."

I called out for Ray and walked back into the store. But as soon as I stepped over the threshold, I heard the scream of an engine. I walked back outside to tires squealing, a black Chevy Suburban turning around from the back of the building, almost up on two wheels as it cut the corner, hit the curb, and bounced into the street. Ray was behind the wheel and continued at a high speed, fishtailing as he cut off oncoming traffic and took off. He disappeared around the corner at the end of the block.

· · · • · • · • · · ·

I excused myself from the officer standing next to me outside Ray's store, walked past the sheriff's office vehicles and crossed the street to where Alex had parked.

She stepped down and toward me, looking me up and down as we met in the middle of the street. "Are you okay?" she said, glancing down at my bandaged leg.

I nodded.

"Can't you go a day without getting hurt? Or beat up?"

I cracked a smile, although more than the pain in my leg, I was bothered by seeing Ray lose his temper the way he had.

Although I'm not sure I could blame him.

"He really just took off?" Alex said as we stepped up onto the curb in front of the store.

"He apologized to me, after we'd gone through the glass."

She studied at the metal frame of the door at the entrance and looked down at the glass somebody had swept into a pile against the building's brick exterior.

The faded maroon Crown Vic pulled up and double-parked, blocking half the street. Mike stepped out, walked toward me with meaning. He stopped on the sidewalk, looked me up and down, shaking his head. "What's wrong with you?" He continued into the store, stopped inside the door, and looked around before walking back outside. "What'd you do?" he said.

"Told him we told you about the affair."

"Why didn't you let me handle it?" he said. "You don't think I was going to perhaps mention to him, he'd left out a minor detail in our discussion this morning?"

My phone rang and I looked at the cracked screen. It had already been fairly beat up but had only gotten worse when a three-hundred-pound man landed on top of me, knocking it out of my hand.

With the cracks and the glare from the sun, I couldn't see who it was. I stepped from Mike and Alex and under a shadow from the other end of the building. I answered, "Henry Walsh."

"Henry? It's Dad."

"Dad? Oh... hey. I, uh... Is it all right if I call you back in a few minutes? I'm kind of in the middle of—"

"Mom's in the hospital," he said, without giving me a chance to cut him off. "She took a pretty bad fall at the house."

Everything around me seemed to come to a halt, my mind focusing strictly on my father's voice.

I walked away from the building, past the dry cleaners, and stopped when I was away far enough from everyone else. "Is she all right?"

The line was quiet.

"They... the doctor... he wants her to rest. She fractured her foot, and cut her hand." He paused. "She hit her head pretty hard."

"Oh, Dad," I said. "But she'll be all right?" I said. "What exactly... How'd it happen?"

Again, the line was quiet. My father was pretty tough, but their move to the Gulf Coast—for no reason other than to enjoy the back nine, as Dad liked to call it, with a change of scenery away from Fernandina Beach—hadn't gone as planned.

But nothing ever does.

"Can I talk to her?"

Another moment of quiet. "She's resting," he said. "They're going to keep her overnight at the hospital. So maybe if you call me later." He paused. "I want you to be prepared, Henry. She... she may not know who you are."

Ray throwing me through that door didn't bring me half as much pain as hearing my father say my own mother might now know who I am. It had been a few years since she'd been diagnosed with Alzheimer's. The progression seemed to be slow, as they said it might be. But it didn't mean it stopped.

And I'd feared the day she wouldn't remember me.

"She's having trouble remembering much of anything right now. She doesn't even know she fell. The doctor said it may be temporary... from the trauma. Of course, with Mom's Alzheimer's..."

"Should I come down?" I said.

"I was hoping you'd ask," he said. "It would be great to see you. I know you're busy. But if you had time, I could buy your ticket if you—"

"What? No, please. You don't have to buy my ticket. Things are all right," I said. "I'd probably drive, anyway."

My father was always trying to help me. Even as a grown man, he'd slip me a twenty-dollar bill whenever he saw me. He knew what it meant to run your own business, and how the trade-off of never having a boss was having some days, or months, where cash could be a little tight.

I looked down the sidewalk toward Alex and Mike as they both walked into Ray's store. I started walking toward them. "Let me figure some things out. I'll call you back a little later."

I hung up and walked into the store behind Mike and Alex.

Alex turned to me. "Everything all right?"

"Yeah. Good." I tried to fake a smile. But I could tell by the way Alex looked at me she knew I wasn't telling her the truth.

Mike stood behind the counter, the phone up to his ear. He opened the curtain over the doorway and looked in the back. The lights were on this time. He hung up his phone and tucked it on his belt, turning to me and Alex. "Ray Rivers was in an accident. Drove off the road about five miles from here."

"Is he all right?" I said.

Mike shook his head. "Not sure. He's not dead. But crashed into a tree in front of the CVS, off Town Center Parkway."

# Chapter 15

I'D GOTTEN WORD SOMETIME in the afternoon that Ray had sustained minor injuries from the crash, although he had refused a trip to the hospital.

After dropping my car off at a repair shop to get the window fixed before my trip down to Naples, Alex and I headed back to the office. I sat on the couch under the window, having a tough time trying to focus. I couldn't quite figure out how a simple case we were never officially hired to be involved in quickly blew up in my face.

Alex had been quiet since we'd gotten back to the office, spending most of the time at her desk, her eyes on her laptop. Neither of us had much to say, and there was something in the air between us I didn't feel very comfortable with.

She looked up from her desk, staring at me.

"Everything all right?" I said, looking back at her.

She took a moment before she spoke. "Do you want to go *alone* to Naples?"

"Alone?"

She nodded. "I didn't know if maybe you wanted some company on the ride."

The truth was, I didn't mind the ride alone. I often preferred it. The quiet. Some music. Long drives were something I didn't do enough. "It's not exactly a vacation," I said. Although it wasn't that I didn't want her to go.

She laughed. "I just, you know, with your mom and everything. I didn't know if there was something I could do to help out somehow?"

I thought about it. And for some reason tried to play it cool, like I didn't want her around. "I thought maybe someone should keep an eye on the office. Especially if something happens with Ray."

She shook her head. "Ray's not our client. He never was. And you heard Mike. He was pretty clear he'd appreciate it if we'd back off."

"Of course he wants us to stay out of it," I said. "He says it every time we're involved in a case. It's like he's afraid we'll find something before he does."

Alex rolled her eyes. "Even if Ray was a paying client, what he did to you is reason enough to let it go." She stood up from her desk and walked toward me. "Go see your parents. Take care of your mom. And your dad. They need you."

I swallowed hard and nodded. I had to think for a minute, turning with my arm up on the back of the couch. I looked out toward the river. "You know, if I was in Ray's shoes, I might've done the same thing."

Alex looked down at the bandage on my leg. "He could have killed you."

I leaned forward, my elbows rested on my knees. "All I'm saying is the man trusted me to keep quiet. And I opened my mouth when I shouldn't have."

Alex gave me a look. "Technically," she said, "you weren't the one who told Mike. But the fact is, we had to do what was right. So stop feeling guilty about it. Ray should've been straight with Mike from the beginning."

She was right. Ray hadn't been straight with Mike when he should have been. Believing your wife was having an affair is a fairly obvious motive.

"You think Mike's going to go after him?" I said.

Alex brushed a strand of hair back from her face and shrugged. "I think the fact they were separated, Ray was living in the back of his store, and he believed she was cheating on him."

"But, no evidence."

"Yet," she said.

I turned again and stared out at the river. "I think I'm going to take my boat out when I get back," I said. "I don't remember the last time I was out on the water."

"I never understood why you never take it out."

"I guess because I bought it as a place to sleep," I said.

Alex walked back to her desk and looked at her laptop.

We were both quiet for a couple of moments.

"So, do you want to come to Naples?"

Alex looked up.

I stood from the couch and looked at my watch. "I'm probably going to leave as soon as the car's ready."

"Tonight?" she said, looking surprised.

"Yeah, why not?"

She stood from her desk. "I... I'd have to get packed and—"

"I'm probably only staying for a couple of nights. It's tight in the condo."

"You sure there'd be room for another body?"

I nodded. "You can bring Raz. I'm sure you don't want to leave him behind. Not while he's still healing."

"Really?" she said. "I don't think your parents would want him around. Especially, your mom coming home from the hospital and... Can you at least check with them first?"

"I already did."

She gave me a funny look. "You did? But, so you..."

I shrugged. "I was going to ask if you wanted to come."

She smiled, nodding, and didn't say much else.

. . . . . . . . . . .

Alex grabbed the remote and turned on the TV we had up on the wall. I wasn't paying much attention to it until she told me to look.

A live broadcast on News4Jax was on the TV with Mike Stone and a captain with the Jacksonville Sheriff's Office standing next to him.

I got up from my desk and stood with my arms folded in front of me, watching the two surrounded by reporters in front of Ray and Shondra Rivers' house.

Alex raised the volume as we listened to the captain announce the cause of death of Shondra Rivers was officially homicide. They asked for the community's help finding the killer and to call if anybody had any information.

Not a word about Ray.

"Are there any suspects at this time?" one of the reporters asked.

The captain, who had done the talking up to that point, turned to Mike.

Mike stepped forward. "The investigation has just begun. We will release more information when it becomes available."

. . • . • . • . • . .

Alex's bag was out on the porch at her house, with Raz sitting next to it on the top step. His tail wagged as I walked toward him.

He knew we were all going on a trip.

Alex stuck her head out the front door. "Come on in. I'm almost done."

"I'll wait out here with Raz," I said. I walked up the stairs, sat next to Raz, and rubbed the top of his head, thinking.

I was worried about my parents. Worried about what it was going to be like seeing them again. It had been a few months. Things had changed since they'd moved. My father had become my mom's caretaker, after for most of his life having it be the other way around.

Raz shifted his body, resting his chin on my thigh, his eyes up on mine.

And I hated the idea I'd be showing up kind of a mess. I'd removed the bandage above my nose, but the wound and black and blue wasn't something I could hide. I had a slight limp, at least when I thought about the pain in my leg. Not to mention the bandage on my lower leg—the other one—where the glass had stuck me.

And it seemed like it all could have been avoided.

Alex came out the door and pulled it closed, locked it, double-checked the locks and yanked on the knob. She picked up her bag and nodded toward my car. "You sure that thing's going to make it all the way down there?"

"All the way?" I said. "It'll get us close." I grinned

Alex laughed.

"Besides, it'll run better with the new window. They cleaned the inside too."

She walked alongside me, Raz between us. "What's a new window got to do with how your car runs?"

"Seriously? You've never noticed a car runs better when it's clean? Or when you get some kind of cosmetic repair?"

She stopped and looked at me like I had three heads. "No. Never."

I grabbed her bag from her shoulder and walked ahead of her. I slid the key in the lock on the trunk and opened the lid, then placed her bag inside, next to mine.

She walked over to her Jeep and checked the roof and doors. "I wish I had a garage," she said.

"Are you worried about leaving it?" I said. "You want to drop it off at the office? Billy will keep an eye on it."

"I hope nobody drives by, decides to toss another brick."

"I don't think he'll do it again," I said.

Alex looked at me. "Nobody's admitted to anything," she said, then turned back to the house. "Oh, you know what? I almost forgot Raz's things!" She ran toward the house and up the steps, unlocking the door and going back inside.

She was back out a moment later, carrying a canvas bag with shoulder straps. "That would have been bad," she said, shaking her head. "I don't know where my mind is lately." She reached in the bag and pulled out Raz's leash and clipped it on his collar, then opened the passenger door and pushed the back of the seat forward.

Raz climbed inside and lay down on the seat.

"He looks better," I said, watching him from outside the driver's side, the door open.

We both got inside the car.

"He's doing a lot better." She turned in the seat, reached over and rubbed his head. "Right, Raz?" She pulled her seat belt on.

"You have everything?" I said.

Alex nodded. "Are you sure your parents will be okay with us bringing Raz?"

I smiled, turning the key in the ignition. The engine roared. "They'll be happy to see us. All three of us." I backed out from the driveway and felt a lump in my throat.

I was afraid my mother wouldn't know who any of us were.

· · · · ● · ● · · · ·

We'd been on the road for a couple of hours. Alex had called Mike but he never answered. The message she left asked him to call her back.

"I thought we weren't going to worry about Ray," I said.

She nodded. "We're not. But I thought I'd tell him we'll be out of town. Who knows."

I said, "Why didn't you just say that on the message?"

I kept my eyes on the road but I could feel her staring at me.

"Just because we're not working on the case doesn't mean I want Mike to think we've disappeared."

"Oh," I said. But I wondered if that was the real answer.

The truth was, some of the hostility between me and Mike stemmed from Alex being in the middle of us. Mike and I both had a relationship with her outside of work. And although I wanted to think me and Alex were different. I wasn't sure that was true.

It was dark out, and I noticed the glow on Alex's face when we passed under the lights over the highway.

She shifted in the passenger seat, turning to face the other way like she was going to take a nap.

Her phone buzzed in the center console and she picked it up, looking at the bright screen. "It's a text from Mike. He wants to know if we've heard from Ray."

I shrugged, shaking my head. "Why would we have heard from him?"

She tapped with her thumbs, replying back.

Her phone buzzed again. "He said they can't find him."

I was trying to look at her phone and swerved a little over the line on the highway.

"Pay attention to the road!" she said.

I picked up my phone, although I hadn't looked at it since we'd hit the road.

"Didn't I just say to pay attention to the road?" She grabbed the phone from my hand and looked at the screen. She looked up at me. "It's Ray," she said, turning my phone. "A text."

I reached for it but Alex pulled it back, out of my reach. She looked at the screen and read his text:

*I'm sorry about what happened. I understand what you had to do. I hope you forgive me. The cops are looking for me.*

"When did he send it?" I said.

"An hour ago."

I reached and grabbed the phone from her, tapped on Ray's number and put the phone up to my ear. I tried to keep my eyes on the road.

It rang six times, then went to voicemail.

"Ray," I said. "It's Henry. Sorry, I missed your text. Call me back. I'm on the road."

"If there's a chance he's running from the police, and now he's calling you while he's on the run..." She shook her head. "I know you can't help yourself. But we can't get caught in the middle of this."

"How do you know he's running?" I said. "I'm sure he doesn't know what to do." I looked at my phone. "Why wouldn't he answer?"

Alex's phone rang. "It's Mike," she said. She answered and put it up to her ear. "Mike?" She listened. "Yeah, I saw it. What's going on?" She was quiet again.

"Can't you put it on speaker?" I said.

She looked at me and said to Mike, "You mind if I put you on speaker?" She tapped the screen and put the phone, screen up, on her lap. "Mike?"

"Yeah. Listen, Rivers has disappeared. We need to talk to him. He's not doing himself any favors hiding from us."

"How do you know he's hiding?" I said.

Mike didn't answer.

"Maybe he's waiting to talk to a lawyer," I said. "You told him to get a lawyer."

"Do you have something on him, Mike?" Alex said. "Or is this because of what we told you?"

He paused before he answered: "I can't go into anything right now. But like I said, he's not doing himself any favors hiding from us. And we just got another call on the anonymous tip line, saying Ray Rivers is the killer."

"You thought it was a hoax the first time they called," I said. "Now, you believe it?"

"We didn't have a murder victim at the time," Mike said. "Barry Hawkins wasn't murdered. Shondra Rivers was."

Alex and I both looked at each other. We both knew there was nothing else we could do.

"So do me a favor," Mike said. "You hear from him, you'd better let me know."

Alex and I stayed quiet. Neither of us said a word about the text we received from him.

"You there?" Mike said. "I don't like the silence."

"We've told you all we know," I said. "I get the feeling you're jumping to a conclusion."

Mike laughed into the phone. "Besides being a little naïve, Walsh, you know what your problem is? You trust the wrong people."

Alex shook her head, giving me a look like she wanted me to let it go.

Other than the roaring engine and the rumbling tires on the road beneath us, it all got very quiet.

Alex lifted the phone. "Mike? Mike?" She looked at the screen. "He hung up."

# Chapter 16

I turned down Beach Resort Drive and into the parking lot at my parents' condo. My father was sitting on a lawn chair outside his door, waiting for us.

He stood, and I could see the excitement on his face.

"Hey, Dad," I said, stepping out of the car. I was, of course, happy to see him. But also a little anxious knowing all he'd been dealing with.

He was strong, but everyone has a breaking point.

We hugged and held on for a moment longer than normal. I cleared my throat, fighting back tears as I stepped back from him.

"I hope we didn't keep you up," I said.

Before he could reply, Raz jumped out from the back seat, tail wagging as he galloped toward my father.

He bent down, rubbing Raz's face with both hands. "Hey, boy. Nice to meet you."

"This is Raz," I said.

Dad stood up as Alex came around from the trunk of the car with her bag. "Hi, Alex."

She stepped toward him and they hugged. "I hope you're okay with Henry bringing some extra baggage," she said.

Dad laughed. "You're always welcome." He looked down at Raz. "You, too, Raz."

"How's Mom?" I said, anxious to hear.

Dad sighed, nodding. His eyes went to the ground before he raised them up to mine. "She's doing okay. She'll be home in the morning. They wanted to run some more tests."

"How'd she fall?" I said.

"The bathroom. I wish... I should have been keeping a better eye on her. The floor was wet." He reached for Alex's bag, taking it off her shoulder without asking.

"You look good," I said. And I meant it. He was nearing eighty. Although thinner than the last time I saw him. But you could still see it in his arms and shoulders. He was still strong. "Are you still going to the gym?"

"I try. But it's hard leaving Mom home alone. Sometimes her friend'll come over and stay with her; gives me time to get out, do some things." He opened the door and waited for Alex to go in ahead of him.

I stepped past him after Alex, and Dad, his voice low, said, "Are you going to tell me what happened?"

I stopped and looked at him like I didn't know what he meant. But his eyes were on the wound above my nose. I shook my head. "No." I grinned and continued into his house.

The smell of home hit me right away. Even though it was a different place, and it had been a few years since they'd moved to Naples, it reminded me of my home on Fernandina Beach, where I was raised.

The place, of course, was smaller than the house. And although they brought most of the same furniture, it was new and modern with light-colored walls and hardwood flooring. The TV was to the right, and across from it, on the other wall, was the floral couch and matching recliner they'd had for at least twenty years. The only thing that was new was the rug laid over the hardwoods. I looked toward the adjoining kitchen, separated by a long counter with stools facing the space.

Even the kitchen table was from our old house.

He pointed with his thumb toward the open doorway to the left. "I don't know if"—he cleared his throat—"you two can figure out the sleeping arrangements. We have the spare bedroom." He nodded toward the sofa. "That's a pullout."

I'd slept on it before. And the fact it was two decades old didn't make the so-called mattress the most comfortable night's sleep.

Dad shrugged, stepping toward the front door to make sure it was locked. "I'll mind my own business." He'd never asked about me and Alex, outside of our working relationship. And I was sure he didn't want to know the situation.

I'd done my best to make it clear Alex and I were business partners and friends. And there was nothing more to it. Although bringing her with me to Naples may have told a different story.

He looked out through the open blinds toward the parking lot, then twisted them closed. "So the Mustang's running all right?"

"It made it here," I said. "I've put some money into it. More than I wanted to. But it runs well. It still needs a paint job.

And the A/C should probably be replaced before the summer. Luckily it hasn't been that warm up there."

"No?" he said. "Been warm here. I actually miss the cooler nights."

I nodded toward the bedroom with the door open, off the living room. "Alex, you and Raz can take the bedroom. I'll sleep out here, on the pullout."

"You sure?" she said. "I can sleep on the—"

"The bedroom is yours." I gave her a look and picked up her bag from the floor. I brought it into the bedroom and placed it next to the bed. Alex walked in behind me.

Dad yelled from the kitchen, "You've got your own bathroom in there too." I walked out from the bedroom, and he looked at his watch. "I know it's kind of late, but if you want a beer or a drink, I stocked up. Before you got here."

I didn't tell him how long we were staying. I wasn't sure. But I had a feeling he was expecting it to be more than a night or two.

"Don't let us keep you up," I said. "But I'd love a drink."

He shook his head, waving me off. "I don't go to bed as early as I used to." He pulled glasses down from a cabinet. "You want a glass of Jack?"

"Are you having anything?" I said.

He nodded. "Hopefully, it'll help me sleep."

I walked into the kitchen and sat down on one of the stools at the counter, looking around the room. There were photos on the wall. I stood up and walked over one of my sister. "So, Mom... Have things been getting worse? Her memory?"

Dad had his back to me but looked back over his shoulder. Good days and bad," he said. But it was like he didn't want to get into it. "Does Alex want Jack? Or something else?"

"She'll have a beer," I said.

He nodded. "Oh, that's right." He reached for the refrigerator door and pulled out a bottle of Yuengling. He held it up and looked at the label. "Does she like this?"

I sat back down at the counter. "She's not picky."

Dad cracked the cap off the top and placed the bottle down next to me. He put two ice cubes in each glass and poured a heavy shot of Jack over the top.

Alex came out, already changed into a hooded sweatshirt with running shorts and her hair up. I caught myself staring at her but looked away before she noticed, although my father noticed my gaze and seemed to chuckle as he put the glass in front of me.

"That's yours," he said to Alex, nodding toward the bottle of beer. "You want a glass?"

She picked it up and shook her head as she took a sip. "This is good, thanks."

Dad raised his glass. "Here's to Mom's health," he said. He walked to the sliding glass door on the other side of the kitchen, stood with his back to us, not saying a word.

I glanced at Alex and said to Dad, "She's going to be all right. She's stronger than both of us put together."

He turned from the window, nodding. He wiped at the corner of his eye with the back of his knuckle. "I know." He took a deep breath and exhaled. "She'll be happy to see you."

But I could see it in his face; the moment he said it, he was worried it might not be the case.

We both knew there was a chance Mom might not know who I was.

"So," he said. "How's business?" He pulled up a chair at the round, dark-wood kitchen table. "Have a seat, tell me something exciting."

Alex and I moved from the counter and sat down at the table across from him.

I sipped my drink and looked out the window. It was pitch black outside. Although they didn't have a direct view of the water, it was a stone's throw away. Which was all they ever wanted. We didn't live on the water growing up on Fernandina Beach but close enough at the time. It was a great place to be raised, but my parents had good reasons for wanting to move away and try the opposite coast.

"Well," I said. "It's been kind of slow. We almost had a client who is now a suspect in his wife's murder."

Alex gave me a look like she'd hoped I hadn't brought it up.

But I knew Dad could use something else to talk about, to distract him. He enjoyed hearing about my work.

"What's that mean, almost had a client," he said. "Is he guilty?"

I shrugged, shaking my head as I sipped my drink. "We don't know. But he came to us before his wife was killed." I grinned. "I know that sounds a little strange."

"So what was the case? Unrelated?" he said.

I leaned forward on the table, holding my glass with both hands. "Did you hear anything about the principal who died at Douglas Williams High School?"

Dad shook his head. "I haven't been paying much attention to things up in Jax. I don't even watch the news much anymore."

I continued, "Well, funny, but he slipped in the shower at the school. But didn't survive."

"Quite a coincidence," he said. "So that was the investigation? The principal?"

I shook my head. "You remember Ray Rivers?"

"Rivers?" He nodded, his eyebrows raised. "Hell of a football player. Even when he was a young kid. He played at your school until his parents moved him to, uh..."

"Douglas Williams," I said. "That's the school where Barry Hawkins—the principal—died in the shower."

Dad looked confused. "What was the principal doing in the shower at the school?"

I tried to explain and told him as much as I could about all that had happened, although as I spoke I realized what few answers I had.

"And now Ray has disappeared?" Dad said. "Sounds guilty to me, don't you think?" He pointed toward the wound on my forehead. "Does that have anything to do with it?"

"This?" I shook my head. "I don't know."

He leaned back, folding his arms at his chest. I could see in his eyes he was thinking through everything I'd told him.

Dad never wanted to be in law enforcement, but his brother was, up in Pennsylvania. Dad went in an entirely different direction. He loved baseball, and coached for most of his life. But "work" was running a watch-and-clock repair business he owned in downtown Fernandina Beach.

"So, are there any other suspects?" he said, leaning forward with his hands on the table.

Alex smiled and put the bottle up to her mouth. She'd been around Dad enough to see how interested he got in our work and wouldn't stop asking questions until he'd had enough to satisfy him.

"Like I said, Ray was almost a client. At this point, we're not involved in the investigation."

"So, is that it? For excitement?" Dad said.

I was hesitant to go into it, but I knew my father'd get a kick out of the brick going through my back window. Of course, I left out the part about me grabbing the kid's arm. I pulled the check from my wallet and showed it to him.

"The father wrote you a check? Didn't even care if his kid did it or not? Or make him apologize?" He shook his head. "You wonder why these kids are so screwed up today."

Alex cut in. "Well, we can't say with one hundred percent certainty the kid's the one who did it."

"But the father wrote a check anyway?" Dad leaned back and folded his arms. "Just like those parents, out in Hollywood, paid  someone to take the SATs for their kids. Some of them even made up fake pictures, made it look like their kids were on a team... sports the kids never even played before. All to get them into some fancy college." Dad held his glass between both hands. "I understand wanting to take care of your kids, but you have to know where to draw the line."

"I agree," I said, hoping to leave it at that.

Dad got up from the table and nodded toward me. "Then you have the parents get involved in sports at the school because they think it's going to make a difference for their kid. Even if he stinks."

"From what I heard, this Mazer kid wasn't a very good ballplayer."

"He played football?"

I nodded. "Ray was his coach. And, just like you said, the parents seemed to be involved. His mother's the treasurer for the booster club."

"Treasurer?" He laughed. "That's who usually has their hand in the pot."

"What's that supposed to mean?" I said.

"I remember when you were in school. You may not have known, because they kept it quiet, but a couple, I don't even remember their names, they were involved in the booster club. Turns out they stole a couple grand from the school."

"From the booster club?" I said.

Dad nodded. "Was someone we all thought had money, too. But they were taking money from the kid's sports to pay their damn mortgage." He grabbed the Jack Daniels from the counter and topped off my glass. He'd hardly touched his drink. He said to Alex, "Would you like another beer?" But before she answered, he had the bottle out of the fridge, opened, and in front of her. He sat back down and picked up his glass. "I'm not telling you anything you don't already know, but just because someone appears wealthy, you never know what's behind the curtain. The wealthy people I've known, half are up to their eyeballs in debt. Can't make the house payments, drive around in the fancy cars, do what they can to keep up whatever appearance they're after."

Alex and I both laughed.

She gave me a look, like she'd finally figured out where my attitude toward rich people came from.

Dad stood up again from the chair. "I'm going to bed," he said. "Would like to be at the hospital at eight."

I looked at the clock on the wall, the same one Mom had hand-painted when I was a kid. It was after eleven. "Good night," I said. "We'll be ready to go in the morning."

Dad looked around the kitchen and toward the room with the TV. "Where's Raz?" He laughed. "There he is, sleeping on the couch. He walked past me and put his hand on my shoulder. "Good to have you here, Henry." He nodded at Alex with a grin. "Make yourselves at home."

# Chapter 17

Mom was seated in a chair in the corner of her room, fully dressed with her bag next to her at her feet—a medical boot on her left one—her eyes up on the TV. She had a bruise on her head, worse than mine, and a cast on her arm.

The machines next to the empty bed beeped. A nurse came over the speaker on the wall, calling for "Dr. Carter."

Dad walked ahead of me and Alex toward Mom. "Good morning, Marie."

She looked from the TV. "Shhh," she said. "I'm watching something."

"Marie?" Dad said.

She turned again, nodding. "George?" She finally cracked a smile. "I was wondering when you'd be home."

"We're not home, Marie."

"Is everything all right?" she said, a concerned look on her face.

She still hadn't acknowledged I was there.

"Everything will be fine," Dad said. He glanced at me and said to her, "Did you see who's here?"

I smiled and walked toward her. "Hi, Mom," I leaned over and gave her a hug and a kiss on the cheek.

She looked up at me without saying a word. She looked at Dad, over at Alex, then back to me. A smile broke on her face. "Henry? What are you doing here?" She reached up for my hand and I helped her to her feet. She wrapped her arms around me and squeezed hard, like she did when I was a kid.

I looked at Dad standing next to us. He had tears in his eyes. He put his hand on my shoulder and walked past me. "Let me go get the nurse, see if we can get her out of this place."

Mom watched Dad as he started to step out into the hall. "Where's he going?"

I held her hand. "He'll be right back." I turned, reaching out for Alex. "You remember Alex, don't you?"

I hoped she did.

She looked at her but I could see in her eyes it didn't seem to register. She slowly shook her head. "She's your wife?"

"No, she's my... Alex is my partner." I wasn't sure, in that instance, exactly how to answer.

My mother let go of my hand and looked down toward her lap. She raised her eyes to Alex. "I'm sorry I don't remember you. I have something..." She pointed to her head. "My brain." She shrugged. "Oh, I don't even remember what it's called."

Alex gave her a thin smile and leaned down, giving my mother a hug without saying much else. She didn't have to.

My mother kept her eyes on Alex, like she was studying her, looking her up and down. "You're very beautiful," she said, turning toward me. "You're lucky, Henry." She looked back at Alex, narrowing her eyes. She tapped her chin with her finger, then smiled. "Alex?" With a nod, she said, "You have a dog, don't you?"

Alex's smile grew. "Yes, Raz."

"We brought him," I said. "I remember how much you liked him when you came home a few months ago."

"Home?" she said. "From where?"

"From here. In Naples."

She looked at me, shaking her head. "I live in Fernandina Beach." She rolled her eyes with a slight laugh. "Naples? Why would I live in Naples?"

Dad walked in behind a nurse pushing a wheelchair.

"Are you ready to get out of here, Mrs. Walsh?" the woman said. She pushed the wheelchair closer to Mom and helped her move to it from the chair she was sitting in.

Mom looked past the nurse at Dad. "Did you hear what Henry said? He thinks we're in Naples."

· · · · ● · ● · · · ·

Mom was resting in her bed, and Dad took a nap on the recliner in front of the TV. He had a book on his lap and I grabbed it, placed it on the side table next to him. Raz was on the floor next to him, his eyes open but he looked bushed. Like my parents, Raz was getting up there in age.

Alex and I decided to take a walk to the beach and enjoy it while we could.

I stopped in the parking lot before we got to the walkway to the beach, and I tried to stretch out the kinks I had in my back.

"What's wrong?" Alex said.

"My back. That pull-out sofa's been around for a long time. It makes my bed on the boat feel like it's from a five-star hotel."

Alex got behind me and tried to help me with my pain, running her hands up and down my back. "You should get a massage." She stepped next to me and started walking again. "I saw a place around the corner. It'd be good for you. Relieve some stress."

"I've never had a massage," I said.

"Really?"

I nodded but didn't go into why.

We continued our walk, neither saying much. I took in the beach smell in the air, giving me a sense of calm I hadn't felt in quite a while. I hadn't done much thinking about Ray Rivers, trying to force myself to let it go and spend my energy on my parents and my potentially short visit.

We stopped as soon as we could see the water.

"It's beautiful," Alex said. "I understand why your parents moved here." She turned to me. "But it can't be easy for them, being here all alone."

I nodded, my eyes scanning the water.

"But what are you going to do?" she said. "Drive down here every time something happens?"

"What are you saying, I should move to Naples to take care of them?" We walked across the sand toward the water. I stopped. "Although, not a bad idea."

She grabbed my arm and pulled me along. "I don't know if that's what I'm saying. But you're going to need to figure it out. It's important. We're at that point in life…" She let go of my arm and ran ahead of me.

It hurt my leg to try and do the same, but I started into a slight jog anyway.

Alex was acting strange, the way she was talking. I could tell she was getting at something but wouldn't come out and say what it was.

She slowed down and looked back at me, smiling as her feet touched the water. She brushed her hair back from her face.

"What are you trying to say?" I said. "Is something wrong?"

She looked out toward the water. "I think we need to both think about making a change."

"Change?" I said. "In what way? Move to Naples?"

She cracked a slight smile, looking down toward the sand. She raised her eyes and said, "The business has almost no income. If I hadn't somehow put some money aside over the past couple of years, I'd be in big trouble. I'm broke, Henry. This business venture... it hasn't been as fruitful as I'd hoped."

"We need to get a client," I said.

She looked at me and nodded. "You think?" She laughed, but it seemed to be filled with frustration more than anything. "We can't keep doing this. I know you don't care about the money. But from a business perspective, we can't continue doing things the way we have been."

She continued walking and I followed her along the water. The warm sun beat down on us from above.

"Does this have anything to do with what Mike said to you? Something about getting back into law enforcement? I didn't want to ask. And I could tell you didn't want me to hear about it the way I did, but..."

She kept her eyes straight ahead, walking with her feet in the water. It was like she didn't hear what I'd said. But I knew she had.

"Are you thinking about going back?" I said. "Back into law enforcement?"

She stopped and looked into my eyes. "It came up out of the blue. Mike knows someone up in Virginia, looking for a detective. I'm not even sure it's an option. But I can't lie to you. I've been thinking about it."

The only reason Alex ever left law enforcement in the first place was because she was injured as an officer up in Virginia, where she's from. At the time, she was investigating a burglary. Her hand slipped through a basement window, severing her nerves badly enough she wasn't even able to hold a gun.

But after a few years, the feeling in her hand came back to normal. As far as I knew, she'd never thought about going back to law enforcement.

But, apparently, she had.

I didn't hear her phone ring, but Alex pulled it from the pocket of her shorts. She looked at the screen and put it up to her ear. "Mike?" I watched as her eyes widened as she listened, nodding. But she wasn't saying a word.

"What is it?" I said, knowing by the look on her face Mike had delivered some big news.

She stared back at me, still nodding her head as Mike carried the conversation on the other end of the phone. "But how can you..." She nodded. "In custody? Already?" She nodded again, listening to the call. "Okay, yes. I get it, Mike. I didn't think you'd move this—" She closed her eyes, pushing her hair back on her head. "All right. Yes. Okay. Thanks for the call, I guess."

She ended the call and stared at the phone for a moment before raising her eyes to mine.

"Is it Ray?" I said.

She paused, then nodded. "They took him into custody. They're charging him with murder."

# Chapter 18

Alex sat with Mom outside on the deck behind my parents' condo. I stayed inside and helped Dad make sandwiches.

Mom seemed to be doing all right. It was nice to spend the day with her. Although she couldn't remember falling, and didn't know why she had a cast on her arm, she seemed to at least know who we all were.

Dad turned to me from the counter with two plates in his hands. "You all right?" he said. He put the plates down and leaned on the counter with one hand, the other on his hip. "You're being awfully quiet."

I nodded, trying to force a smile. "Yeah, no, everything's great." I grabbed the other two plates with the sandwiches and nodded, heading toward the back door to the deck.

"Henry?" he said. "You know you can talk to me."

I stopped before I got to the door and looked back at him. "Let me bring these out. I'm sure Mom and Alex are hungry."

Alex got up from the table and slid open the screen door, taking the two plates from my hands.

"The one on the left is Mom's tuna sandwich," I said. "The other one's for you. It's all vegetables from Dad's garden."

She looked me in the eye and smiled, turning toward the table. She placed the dish in front of Mom and helped push her chair closer to the table. She opened up a napkin and placed it on Mom's lap.

I stepped back into the kitchen.

Dad was still standing there, watching me. I knew he was waiting for me to talk. And he wasn't going to give up.

He knew something was up.

"I didn't want to talk about it," I said. "But I might as well tell you. They've arrested Ray Rivers for his wife's murder."

Dad looked a little surprised, but not entirely.

"I guess I'd be foolish to think it wasn't going to happen," I said. "Especially, the detective on the case seemed to've had his mind set from the beginning." I thought for a moment, glancing out toward Alex and Mom. "The truth is, I feel somewhat responsible."

Dad removed his Boston Red Sox cap and scratched his head. He'd been a Red Sox fan since he was a little kid. "Why would you feel responsible?" he said.

I shrugged. "Well, Ray turned to me to help him. And I think, I guess, I might've let him down. I don't know if Alex and I did the right thing, telling her friend Mike that—"

"He's the detective?"

I nodded. I'd forgotten he'd heard enough of my cases over the years to know Mike Stone was often a fixture in most of them.

"So what do they have on him?" Dad said.

"I don't know yet. We still need to get the details."

"Get the details? Why? You told me he wasn't your client, didn't you? I know you always want to be the one to find the answers. You were like that when you were a kid. But in this case, from what you've told me, I don't see why you want to make it your concern anymore. Sometimes you just have to walk away."

I stood staring at the plates on the counter in front of me. I picked both up and stepped toward the door. "Let's go eat."

Dad walked out behind me. "I hope you're not going to take off to go back because of this," he said.

Mom had taken a bite of her sandwich and looked up at me. "You're leaving?"

I shook my head and gave Alex a look out of the corner of my eye. "No. Not now."

The four of us sat and ate our lunch, quiet for the most part, although I did what I could to keep the small talk going to keep Mom engaged.

· · · ● · ● · · · ·

It was getting dark out and we were all clearly tired. Dad was in the bedroom helping Mom get ready for bed. Alex and I crashed, sitting on the couch together. I had the remote in my hand, clicking through the channels. I tossed the remote to Alex. "Nine hundred channels, there's never anything on." I got up and walked through the kitchen and looked out past the deck into my parents' yard. Each unit had its own space fenced in. It was enough room for a little privacy and a small garden.

Dad had squeezed as many vegetables as he could into a fairly tight space he enclosed with chicken wire.

I sipped my Jack, finished it down to the ice cubes and wasn't sure I needed any more. Over the past five years, I'd only lived on a boat, other than the year I spent living in an apartment out at Neptune Beach. I always found myself feeling trapped being stuck indoors. And the boat, for the most part, was just a place to keep my bed while, for the most part, being outside.

I didn't see the way most people lived as healthy, surrounded by walls without fresh air or sunshine, going from the office to the car to the grocery store and back indoors once home.

I was sure we weren't meant to spend so much of life indoors.

I turned from the door and looked at Alex, watching me. She had stepped to the counter and leaned on her elbows, standing on the living room side. She held a bottle of beer in both hands. "What's going on with you?" she said. "You seem restless." She grinned. "More than usual."

I thought for a moment before answering. "Well, it's a weird time. With Mom, of course. I hate seeing her go through this. It's hard on Dad too. And with what you said, about the business... about this opportunity you have." Facing the door, I said, "And I can't help feeling... I keep thinking, Ray's behind bars, and I—"

"I heard what you were saying to your dad earlier." She stepped toward me and rested her hand on my back. "We don't know what they have on him. They didn't arrest him; they can't arrest him, just because he thinks his wife had an affair."

I looked out through the screen, listening to the waves crashing in the distance. It was a peaceful sound.

"There's nothing we can do right now," she said. She hadn't taken her hand from my back.

I looked her in the eye and we held each other's gaze.

Alex leaned into me and we kissed.

We weren't even drunk, and for the first time we did something I'd pictured in my mind but never let happen, other than one time neither of us remembered very well.

I felt like a kid in high school, kissing a girl in my parents' kitchen, the thrill and nerves thrown together. I hoped Dad wouldn't come around the corner.

I slid open the screen door. Alex and I stepped outside.

We kissed again, and I didn't want it to stop. But I pulled back from her, brushed a strand of hair from her face and looked her in the eyes. "What are we doing?"

She didn't answer, our eyes locked.

My phone buzzed in my pocket. And for some reason, I don't exactly know why, I pulled it out and looked at the screen. It was Billy.

"Hey," I said, answering.

"Am I bothering you?"

I looked at Alex as she walked away, toward the other end of the deck. She stood at the top of the steps with her back to me.

"What's up?" I said.

Billy must've noticed in my voice, my brain was scrambled. "Everything all right?"

"With me? Yeah, good. Everything's..."

Alex walked past me, slid open the screen door and walked inside.

Billy said a couple of things but I wasn't even listening, watching Alex through the screen as she sat down at the table in the kitchen. My brain was calling me an idiot. I still wasn't sure what made me answer the phone. "Can I call you back?" I said.

"Actually, I was just calling because someone was here looking for you."

"At the restaurant?"

"Yes. A lawyer. He left his business card. He said he was hoping you'd call him right away."

I took a quick look at my screen and saw I'd missed a couple of calls with private numbers. There were no messages. "A lawyer, huh?" I said.

"He knows you from high school."

"High school? What's his name?"

Billy took a couple of seconds to answer. "Uh, his name's Wendell Richards."

"Wendell Richards?" I remembered him from high school. Or maybe even before high school.

"A big kid?" I said, thinking back to the last time I saw him.

"Well, he's not exactly a kid, Billy said. "And if, when you say *big*... I guess, you could probably say he's on the heavy side, if that's what you mean?"

"Yeah, I guess so. I know I'm not supposed to say this, but you could say he was the fat kid in class. You know, back when you only had a couple of overweight kids?"

Billy laughed. "I know what you mean. But he's a grown man. An attorney. I'm sure he'd love to hear you remembered him as the fat kid."

"I didn't mean anything by it." I looked through the screen door again and Alex was no longer in the kitchen. "He didn't say what he wanted?"

"I didn't ask."

I slid open the screen door and walked inside, reaching for the junk drawer where I'd hoped to find a pen and piece of paper to take down Wendell's number. I found a pen; there were at least fifty of them, but no paper. I pulled out my wallet for one of my business cards. "Go ahead," I said. I leaned on the counter with the phone pressed between my shoulder and ear. I wrote Wendell Richards on the back of my card, and took down the phone number from Billy.

I looked at the clock on the stove. "How long ago was he in there?" I said.

"He left a few minutes ago."

I left the card with Wendell's number on the counter. "Thanks for the message," I said. "Did you hear the news about Ray Rivers?"

"I did. You believe it?"

I thought for a moment. "I don't know if I have a reason not to."

"See you when you get back," he said, and hung up.

I left my phone on the counter and walked into the other room. "Sorry about that."

She shook her head. "Don't be. I'm sorry. We never should have—"

Dad walked out of his bedroom and into the kitchen. He was wearing pajamas, something he didn't do when I was younger. It used to be boxers and a T-shirt or shorts. I guess you wear them as a kid, then wait until you're an old man to start putting them on again.

He got himself a glass of water, took a pill from a pill box by the phone, and walked back toward his bedroom. "I'm hitting the hay," he said. "See you in the morning." He closed the bedroom door behind him.

"What did Billy want?" Alex said, getting up from the couch and coming toward me. I had a feeling she was going to act as if nothing had just happened between us.

I held up the card with Wendell's number on it. "This lawyer showed up looking for me, at Billy's Place."

"Did he say what he wanted?"

I shook my head, walked back into the kitchen and dialed the number. "No, but I'm not going to wait to find out." I leaned back against the counter, the phone up to my ear.

Alex sat down at the table watching me.

The phone rang and was answered on the second ring.

"Wendell Richards."

"Wendell? It's Henry Walsh."

"Henry! Hey, it's been a long time, hasn't it? Thank you so much for calling me back right away. I wasn't sure I was going to hear from you."

"Why's that?"

"I didn't know if you'd already assumed what it's about. And, well, my new client is the one who's asked me to talk to you before anyone else. But he said you may not be willing to help. I understand there was, well... a slight conflict between the two of you."

I didn't have to think more than a handful of seconds to realize who he was referring to. "Ray Rivers?" I said.

Alex stared back at me.

I could hear voices in the background, but I had a feeling it was a television. "Hang on a moment, okay?" Wendell said. And the sound in the background was gone.

"I'd heard you were a private investigator," he said. "In fact, I'd almost called you a handful of times before. I'm always on the lookout for a good private investigator. There are some real beauties out there... wouldn't be able to find the last chip in the bag, if you know what I'm saying."

I'd never heard that one before and wasn't sure it even made sense.

"You didn't answer me," I said. "Is your client Ray Rivers?"

"Oh yes. Sorry. I was just... I'm defending Ray. I don't know what kind of details you have about the case the sheriff's office has against him. But I'm going to need some help. And Ray seems to think you're the man for the job. If you'd be willing to help."

Wendell's accent was a little more Southern from what I'd remembered. It was almost like he'd come up with a little more twang to it than you'd expect.

"You don't think he did it?" I said.

Wendell let out a slight laugh. "I don't ask if my client committed a crime," he said. "My only question is whether or not the prosecution can prove it."

I thought about his stance, which I assumed was the job of any good defense attorney. I tried to look at things the same way, but it wasn't as cut and dried in my business. Working for someone I knew was guilty would never be an option.

Wendell said, "So are you willing to meet me, so we can talk?"

"I'm not sure I know much more about the case than you do," I said.

"I'm not asking you to come in so I can pick your brain."

"So, what exactly are you asking?" I said.

"I'd like to hire you."

"*You* want to hire me? Or Ray?"

"Well, I mean, the check'll have my name on it, if that's what you're asking?"

I could see the look in Alex's eyes, anxious to hear what was going on with the call. I looked toward the closed door to my parents' bedroom.

I knew helping Ray would mean I'd have to leave Naples.

"I'm out of town right now."

"I'd hate to break up your vacation, Henry. But I'd be lying if I told you we had plenty of time."

I stepped to the screen door and looked outside. "The earliest I can meet is tomorrow afternoon."

"Can we say two o'clock?" Wendell said.

I looked at my watch. "Where's your office?"

"Fernandina Beach. Right downtown. Not far from where your daddy used to have his watch repair business."

# Chapter 19

WE HAD A LONG goodbye and left my parents' place early in the morning, promising I'd be back as soon as possible. Mom cried when I left, Dad wearing sunglasses to hide whatever was going on underneath.

I looked over my shoulder at Raz, sacked out in the back seat.

My mind was going in a million directions, thoughts jumping from Mom to Ray Rivers to Shondra and Barry Hawkins, the kid smashing my car window... to me and Alex. I couldn't imagine doing the work without Alex, if she did decide to leave, get back into law enforcement.

I thought about Naples, if I could ever live there... maybe start another business.

But they were all just thoughts fighting each other in my head. Too many at one time swirling around in my little brain. I glanced over at Alex facing the passenger window. She hadn't said a word for the first hour and a half of the ride.

I made a quick stop for coffee, bought Alex a tea, and jumped right back on the road. The silence continued, until I finally asked her if she thought it would make sense for us to take the case.

She shifted in her seat and looked at me, one leg up under the other. "I think there's something about Ray I don't like. He clearly has a nasty side." She shrugged, her paper cup of tea resting on her thigh. "If we put everything else aside... simply look at what he did to you." She looked straight, toward the windshield. "We'd always agreed if either of us weren't comfortable with a client, we'd walk away."

I thought for a moment. "Does it make a difference if he wouldn't be our direct client?" I said. "I mean, we'd be working for Wendell Richards."

"I'm not sure I care who signs the check," she said. "Not if we're trying to help a man who could potentially be guilty."

"What ever happened to *innocent until proven guilty*?"

Alex rolled her eyes. "You know what I'm saying. You asked me what I thought. And I'm telling you. I... nothing has ever felt right about any of this, going back to when he first called you."

"The story's changed," I said. "At the time, his wife was still alive."

She looked to her right, out the window. "I don't understand. I don't know why you've been so caught up helping this man. You said yourself you hardly knew him as a kid. It's not like you—"

"Weren't you just crying about our lack of work?" I said.

"I wouldn't call it crying," she said, staring at me sideways. "You don't have to be like that."

I let out a sigh, nodding. "I'm sorry. I didn't mean to. I'm just saying, from a business perspective, it's a legitimate investigation. And we'll get paid for it. Isn't that what you want?" I looked over my shoulder at Raz. "It could be enough to pay off that credit card you put Raz's surgery on. And you never know if Wendell has something else for us, down the road."

"So, you're saying now you're interested in taking a case, just for the money?"

I stared ahead, taking the ramp for Polk Parkway toward Orlando. I hesitated, opening my mouth but holding back from what I wanted to say. I removed my sunglasses. "I'm interested in getting our business back on track so you won't leave."

· · · • · · • · · · ·

Billy had offered to watch Raz, so we dropped him off at our office and jumped right back on the road for Fernandina Beach.

I parked the Mustang on Centre Street in front of the brick office building with the blue awnings over the glass doors, two blocks from the building where my father's watch-and-clock repair shop used to be.

We went inside and down the long, quiet hall. The building was old and had a damp, mildew odor inside, like most buildings near the water. We continued past a dozen doors, most closed, and stopped when I saw the gold plaque on the wall that said Attorney Wendell Richards, Esq. Suite 113.

The gray-haired woman behind the desk gave us a smile. "Good afternoon," she said.

The waiting area in the office had two leather padded armchairs against the wall and a coffee table with magazines neatly fanned out on top of it. There was a painting of a beach—I wasn't sure which one—hung on the wall over the chairs.

"We're here to see Wendell," I said.

But before she could answer, a man taller and wider than I remembered, wearing white suit pants and a powder-blue shirt with red suspenders and a matching tie, stepped through the doorway to the woman's right.

I remembered back, even when he was younger, he wore suspenders. But back then he looked like Spanky from the *Little Rascals*. His appearance seemed to be well-planned. The white suit, you'd see the Southern attorneys wearing on TV, topped off with a matching hat.

Wendell approached me. "It's been a long time," he said. He shook my hand with a firm grip, although a bit damp. He held his grip longer than I preferred.

"It has been," I said. "You don't look any different." I didn't mean it to be an insult or compliment. Just a fact.

Wendell laughed and rubbed his big stomach with both hands. "Oh, I'd say I put on another fifty pounds since high school, but I do appreciate you saying that." His eyes went right to Alex, stepping past me to shake her hand. "You must be Alex." He waved for us to follow him and headed through the doorway, down a short hall, and through a set of double doors.

We stepped into a large space with a desk on the far side, two chairs in front of it. To the right was a window overlooking the parking lot, a couch and coffee table in front of it. Two matching wingback chairs were on the other side of the coffee table, right and left of the couch at an angle. The room was large enough with different areas sectioned off: the desk, the seating area, and to the left was a table with six chairs around it.

Wendell turned once we were inside and pushed the doors closed. He walked around to his desk and gestured for us to sit in the two chairs across from him.

The three of us sat down, and Wendell slipped on a pair of reading glasses, opening a manila folder in front of him. He studied whatever was on the top page and handed it to me. "This is the latest report," he said.

I reached out and skimmed over it.

He said, "I understand you're both friendly with the detective on Ray's case?"

I nodded. "Well, I'd say Alex and Mike are friends." I held up the police report and handed it back to Wendell. "I've already seen this one," I said.

Wendell took the paper back. "Oh, sorry." He slipped it in the folder and handed me another sheet of paper. "They found the knife at his store."

I looked at Alex, her facial expression showing she was ready to walk out of there.

"That's not all," he said. "There was an earring, belonged to Ray. Found it in the bedroom."

"What kind of earring?" Alex said.

"One belonged to Ray. He's already admitted to the sheriff's office he hadn't left it there when he first moved out. Said he wore it often."

"I assume this was before he had legal representation?" I said.

Wendell nodded. "I think he was trying to be honest with them, considering he hadn't been completely upfront at the beginning." Wendell shifted in his seat. "So, as you can see..."

"What's the defense?" I said. "Somebody tried to set him up?"

Wendell looked down at his desk, straightening out the papers in the folder. He raised his eyes. "A neighbor told police he was outside the house, around eleven o'clock."

Alex gave me a look, and again, I thought for a moment she was going to get up and walk out.

"He was at the house?" I said. "Before she was killed?" I closed my eyes and ran both hands over my face.

"He did admit he was there. He never tried to hide that fact. But he never spoke to her. He never went in the house," Wendell said.

None of this looked good. "There's a weapon and an item placing him at the scene," I said. "What do you really expect us to do?"

He looked from me to Alex, then back to me with a crooked grin on his face. "Find the real killer."

I leaned forward, my elbows on my knees, not sure what to say. Alex looked to have already checked out of the conversation. I looked at Wendell, and he had that same crooked grin on his face. "The pay is twenty thousand dollars."

Not a bad number.

"It's a generous amount of money if we can wrap it up fast. But I'm not sure that's possible. It ends up taking us six months..."

Wendell leaned forward on the desk. "Well, here's the thing." He adjusted the knot on his tie. "It's likely this could go to trial in two weeks. I'll give you ten up front. The remaining ten once you wrap it up."

"Guaranteed? I said.

Wendell nodded. "Of course. Your time is money. I realize that. This is a big case."

I leaned back in the chair and looked at Alex staring back at me.

I knew as much as she'd love the money, a case that's doomed to fail was something we both preferred to walk away from.

I looked across the desk at Wendell. "Where's Ray right now?"

He looked at his watch. "He'll be released sometime in the morning. They're a little backed up at the courts this week. Once they set bail, we should be able to get him out of there, first thing."

"Any chance we can talk to him?" I said. "Before we give you our answer?"

Before Wendell answered, Alex grabbed my arm. "Can we talk, in private, for a couple minutes?"

We both turned to Wendell as he stood up from his desk, nodding.

"I'll tell you what," he said. "I'll step out for a few minutes, give you some privacy." He walked past us and out of the office. "I'll come back in a couple of minutes, or give Margaret a shout when you're ready. She knows where I'll be." He walked out and pulled the double doors closed behind him.

I stood up from the chair and walked to the seating area with the couch in front of the window. I looked out into the parking lot at a dark blue Mercedes with LAW-ER1 on the registration plate. I assumed it was Wendell's and hoped he knew how to spell lawyer. I said to Alex. "I know you don't want to do this," I said. "So if you want to walk away..."

She sat still, staring back at me without answering. I got the feeling she wasn't sold either way.

"We have to ask ourselves if Ray deserves a fair shot," I said.

"They found the weapon," she said. "And it's not the only evidence."

"You think it's a coincidence someone was in that store when I was there?" I said.

"I thought about that," she said. "I wish you'd told Mike about what had happened to you, at the time."

"Either way. It's possible I walked in on someone planting that knife."

# Chapter 20

ALTHOUGH I'D NEVER BEEN known to take a case just for money, the decision became easier when Wendell promised another ten thousand on top of the initial proposed fee for our services. And by the time we were back at the office, Alex and I had both fully committed to helping prove Ray's innocence.

Whether we believed he was innocent was another story.

It didn't mean we had an answer or were foolish enough to believe we were even close to having another suspect. Just making the decision to take the case was a start.

We knew we were under the gun. And with less than two weeks until trial, time wasn't on our side. We had a short list of people we wanted to talk to, if for no other reason than to get a hook in the water.

The truth was, we had no suspects at all.

And like pulling a name from a hat, we started with Mindy Hawkins.

We pulled up in front of Mindy's house. A Volvo station wagon was parked behind her Lexus, a FOR SALE sign in the rear window. Funny, it was the same model we had when I was a kid, the Volvo 240 station wagon. We had a yellow one.

The one parked in the driveway was blue, though the paint was faded. It had a University of South Carolina sticker on the bumper.

I wasn't in the market for another car but couldn't help but wonder about the asking price. I liked the old vintage cars.

We parked out on the street and walked up the driveway. I looked inside both cars as we walked past, toward the front door. I rang the doorbell, and after at least a minute, the door finally opened. It was Mindy's sister, the one we'd met the first time we stopped by to talk to Mindy.

"Oh, uh, we were hoping to talk to Mindy? If she's home?"

She looked me over, then Alex, shaking her head. "You were here the other day, weren't you? The private investigators?"

I nodded. "I'm Henry." I gave a nod to Alex. "This is Alex."

Alex said, "You're Kim? Did I get that right?"

The sister nodded. "Is there something I can help you with?"

"We'd like to talk to Mindy," I said.

Kim held a stare on me for a moment, slowly shaking her head. She looked back into the house. "I'm sorry. It's just not a good time for her. She's lying down."

"Oh," I said. "Is she sick?"

"She's resting. It's been a long few weeks for her. I'm not sure what you want to talk to her about, but between Barry's death and another friend of hers who recently died…"

"Are you referring to Shondra Rivers, by any chance?" I said.

Kim nodded. "Yes. It was quite a shock to Mindy. So, if you don't mind, I'll tell her you stopped by." She started to close the door.

But I stepped forward and put my hand up to stop her from closing it. "If she's feeling all right, I mean, if she's not ill, I'd still like to talk to her. It's important."

She looked at my hand on the door. "What are you doing?"

"Please," I said. "We won't take long."

"Weren't you already here? And she told you she'd call you when she was ready to talk? I heard her tell you that."

I sighed, turning back to Alex, unsure of how forceful I wanted, or needed, to be.

Alex said, "If you could please let her answer for herself, and ask her if she'd speak with us? We'd really appreciate it."

Kim looked over her shoulder into the house then turned back, shaking her head. "I'm sorry." She pushed my hand from the door and closed it. The locks clicked on the other side.

"Well, that was a little odd," I said. We both stepped from the door and walked along the driveway toward the street. I pulled open the Mustang's driver-side door and looked across the roof at Alex. "Talk about making it look like you have something to hide."

Alex shrugged, shaking her head. "Make it that obvious, it's usually not the case."

We both stepped inside the car.

Alex turned to me from the passenger seat. "It could just be that she's protecting her sister. She has been through quite a bit. And if she was, perhaps, friendly with Shondra..."

"But was she?" I said. "It's likely Mike talked to her about the alleged affair between her husband and Shondra. If that's the case, I could see how overwhelming it'd all be."

Alex nodded. "Maybe it sank in a little more, if that's the case. Even if she didn't believe it the first time."

I looked up at the house and pulled out my phone. "What if I call her? Maybe she'll answer, instead of having to deal with her personal gatekeeper."

"I was actually surprised you walked away like that. It's not like you to give up so easily," Alex said.

"What was I supposed to do? Push her out of the way? Kick open the door?"

Alex grinned. "You had a look on your face. I thought you were going to."

I started to drive away but hit the brakes when I saw the front door open and Mindy Hawkins step out onto the top step.

"Guess she's feeling better?" I said. I backed the car up to the same spot I'd just pulled away from.

Alex and I got out again and walked up the driveway.

Mindy met us halfway, the three of us standing to the side of the Volvo.

"I thought your sister said you weren't able to talk," I said. "I'm sorry for disturbing you. I know it's been a difficult few weeks."

"That's putting it mildly," she said, looking down toward the pavement.

She looked different from the first time we met her, but I couldn't quite put my finger on what it was. She looked tired, her eyes sunken in. She wore no makeup.

Mindy brushed a strand of hair from her face. "My sister treats me like I'm the little sister. But don't take it personally. She did the same thing to the cops when they were here. But I had to let him in."

I looked toward the house and saw the curtain move on the picture window. "Your sister's not careful, it'll come across one of you has something to hide," I said. "Not a good look when the sheriff's office comes around."

Mindy nodded, shrugging her shoulders. "I know. I told her the same thing."

"Would it be all right if we sat down somewhere?" I said, hoping we'd be invited inside.

Mindy pointed toward the left side of the house. "We can sit in the back." She looked up at the blue sky, although the big tree in the middle of the yard created a lot of shade over a good portion of the driveway. "The sun's bright out back, and I could use some vitamin D. I haven't left the house much these past few weeks." She walked ahead of us and onto a walkway toward the back.

We followed her through the gate to a black iron fence enclosing a modest-sized backyard. You could see the neighbors' homes on all three sides of the yard, but trees and shrubs created enough of a border to block most of the view.

We sat at a table on a stone patio twenty feet or so from the house, almost in the center of the yard. It was surrounded by flowering shrubs and flowers.

Alex looked toward the house. "Does your sister live around here?"

Mindy shook her head. "She'd been living down in Miami. But she's been staying here."

"For how long?" I said.

"Since before Christmas."

"That's a long time for a guest," I said. "Does she work?"

Mindy looked at me from across the table. "Is this why you're here?" she said. "To ask about my sister?"

I shook my head. "Before we go any further, you should know we're working with the attorney representing Ray Rivers."

Mindy lowered her eyes to her hands folded in front of her. "I didn't want to believe there was anything between Barry and Shondra." She raised her eyes. "I'm still not sure I believe it. But from what the detective who was here told me, it's the apparent motive."

"There's no evidence to say your husband and Shondra were having an affair," I said. "But if Ray believed it to be the case..."

"I've heard the evidence is pretty strong." She looked across the yard, toward a small pond with the fountain. Quiet for a moment, she looked back at me. "I can't help but wonder if Ray had something to do with Barry's death. I... I know it was an accident. The police, the detective who was here, didn't seem to believe there was any evidence yet to say otherwise. I can't help but think if Ray killed Shondra because he believed she had an affair."

"Like I said, we're working with Ray's attorney. It's our job to prove Ray is innocent."

Mindy raised both eyebrows, her eyes opened wide. "It sounds to me the sheriff's office has the evidence they need. I'm not sure what you expect to find."

"There are a lot of missing pieces," I said. "Fingerprints are lacking, for one. And the truth is, I'm siding with the belief the weapon was planted."

The French doors on the back of the house opened and Mindy's sister stepped outside. "Mindy? Is everything all right?"

Mindy looked up at her, nodding. "Everything is fine. We're just talking."

Kim walked over to the table, resting her hand on her shoulder. "I think you should come inside. The detective told you not to talk to anybody else."

"He did?" I said.

Mindy looked up at Kim and shook her head. "I'm fine. Please, Kim. Go back inside. I'll be in shortly."

Kim stood still, not moving.

"Please," Mindy said. "Go inside."

Kim let out a sigh and walked back toward the house and inside without another word.

I looked at the windows and couldn't see her once she went inside. But I had a feeling she was watching us.

"I'm sorry about that," Mindy said.

"It's all right," I said. "It's nice to have someone looking out for you." I shifted in my chair, leaning forward on the table. "Just a couple of things I'd like to ask about, and we'll leave you alone. Can you tell me about Barry working out at the school? That was not allowed, as far as I know. And why would he take a shower there instead of coming home?"

Mindy looked away, her eyes out toward the back of the yard. "I thought you wanted to talk about Shondra?"

"If you could just answer the question."

She looked at Alex when she answered. "He told me the night before, when he went to bed earlier than normal, said he was leaving early to go use the equipment at the school. That's all he said. When I woke up, he was gone."

"And what time did you wake up?"

She shrugged. "I... I'm not sure. Maybe eight o'clock, or—"

"And did you communicate with him at any point?"

Mindy looked straight into my eyes. "Why are you asking me these questions? I guess I'm confused. I realize you believe there could've been an affair between Barry and Shondra, but..."

"We're just trying to piece some things together," Alex said.

"I'm having a hard time understanding why he would go to the school to work out," I said. "It was during the winter break, when the school was closed. And then he was gone for four or five hours? And you didn't communicate with him at any point while he was gone?"

She shook her head, looking down at her hands on the table. "Barry seemed to be under a lot of pressure. He didn't like going to the local gym. He'd always run into a parent or someone involved in the school. You don't get a lot of privacy as a school principal."

"And the only option was to go use the school gym?" I said.

Mindy shrugged. "I don't see why you find it so strange."

I thought for a moment, looking around the yard. "Do you still have his phone?" I said.

She shook her head; her eyes squinted as she stared back at me. "I'm sorry," she said, her voice cracking. "I don't want you or anyone else digging into Barry's life any longer." She stood up from her chair. "Can't you just let the man rest in peace?"

The French door swung open and Kim rushed outside. She put her arm around Mindy's shoulder and turned with her toward the house. She looked over her shoulder, shooting daggers with her eyes toward me and Alex. "If you don't leave right now, I'm calling the police. And if you show up here again, that's exactly what I'm going to do."

Kim walked away, her arms around Mindy. They both walked into the house, and the door slammed closed behind them.

# Chapter 21

"WHY ARE YOU GOING this way?" Alex said. "I thought we were going to the school admin building to talk?"

"Quick detour," I said. "I want to drive by Ray's store."

"For what?"

I gave her a quick glance. "Talk to the owner of the business next door."

"The dry cleaners?"

I nodded. "Never got a chance to, but would be worth asking if he's seen anything suspicious around. Especially when I was attacked back there."

We stayed on Route 1 for three miles and turned off onto Beachwood Boulevard. I looked at my phone, wondering why Wendell Richards hadn't yet called to follow up about Ray's release.

I turned right and thought I'd find a parking space at the front of Ray's store. But even though the CLOSED sign hung on the entrance, the spaces along the curb in front of the store were all taken. One car was a black Mercedes sedan, another a white BMW SUV, and then two Teslas. I drove slowly, looking inside the store.

I was surprised to see there were people inside.

"Who's that?" Alex said.

I turned around in the middle of the street and parked on the other side, across from the store. "I have no idea."

We got out and crossed the street. I looked toward the dry cleaners, but the place appeared dark, at least from what I could tell from outside. The sign on that store also said CLOSED.

We stepped up onto the sidewalk and looked into Ray's store through the large square window, to the right of the door, past the mannequins. Three men in suits were inside. Another man faced them, appeared to be doing the talking—much younger, with jeans and cowboy boots and a black T-shirt.

I pulled on the front door to the shop, but it was locked. The men looked toward us as I knocked on the glass someone had obviously replaced. "Can I come in?" I said, knocking loud. The glass was clean, all the stickers and signs taped to it before now gone. The only sign was the one that said CLOSED.

The younger man of the group, the one in the jeans and T-shirt, walked toward me. He crossed his arms in front of his body, like an umpire calling a runner safe on base. He shook his head, his voice muffled as he said, "Not open," from behind the glass. He turned to walk away, but I knocked again and yanked on the locked door's handle.

The young man walked toward me again, running his hand over a dark, slicked-back head of hair. He put his face close to the glass. "Go away!" he said. "The store is closed!" He stared out at me, his eyes narrowed, shifting his eyes past me toward Alex. He gave her a nod, looking her up and down.

I yanked on the door and pounded on the metal edge around the glass. I pointed at the lock, a set of keys dangling on the other side. "Unlock this door. What are you doing in there?"

The three men looked a bit terrified, looking at each other, saying something I couldn't hear. The young man guided them toward the doorway behind the counter. He pushed the curtain aside and led them into the back. He walked through and came toward the entrance.

He turned the key in the door. The bolt clanked and he pushed it open, just enough to poke his head outside. "What the hell is your problem, buddy? Didn't you hear me? The store is closed. You'd better get lost, before I call the cops."

He tried to pull the door closed, but I stuck my foot out to stop it. "What are you doing in Ray's store?" I said.

The young man had a smug look on his face. "I don't know if you watch the news, buddy. But Ray's not coming back."

He kicked my foot out of the way and tried to pull the door closed. But I grabbed the handle with both hands and held it from the other side.

"What the..." He also used both hands and tried to pull it closed. "I'm calling the sheriff's office!" he said, his voice strained as we both pulled on opposite handles.

The men in suits looked out from the doorway behind the counter, watching us. They looked alarmed and confused, looking at each other, speaking a language I didn't understand.

I got the door open enough to get my foot back between the door and the jamb. "Tell me what you're doing?" I said. "Who are you?"

"I'm the owner," he said through his strained voice.

I shook my head. "Ray Rivers owns this place."

"I own the building," he said. "Mr. Rivers is going to the pokey. As far as I'm concerned, he's out of business." He reached his hand out and tried to push my hands out of the way. "There's a sporting goods store about a mile away, you need something, you crazy son of a—"

I shoved my body inside and got the door open.

The young man backed away, pulled his phone from his pocket. "I'm calling the cops." He tapped the screen and put the phone up to his ear.

"Wait," I said. "I don't care if you own this building or not. Ray's not been convicted. You don't just take away a man's livelihood." I looked him over. "What are you, twelve?"

The young man still had the phone up to his ear. "Yes, I'd like to report an, uh... an assault. A breaking and entering. At RR Sporting Goods."

I looked back at Alex, standing outside but holding the door open behind me. "I guess this must be Chance Greenberg," I said. "The guy who wouldn't replace the security cameras." I turned back to the young man. "Hang up the damn phone. We'll leave when you tell me what you're doing."

He seemed hesitant, looking from me to Alex, the phone still up to his ear. Finally, he said into the phone, "No, it's nothing. I'm sorry. I'll call back if I need you." He tapped the screen but kept the phone in his hand.

I looked toward the men at the back. "Who are they?"

Chance gave me a look. "None of your damn business."

"Are you trying to sell Ray's store?" I said. "You ever hear: innocent until proven guilty?"

Chance laughed. "You ever hear, I own the joint. I can do what I want?" He pulled at his shirt, straightening himself out, then turned to the men in the doorway toward the back of the store. Chance instructed them, "Go check out the back. I'll be with you in a moment."

I said to the men, "Don't listen to this kid. It's not for sale."

The men still had confused and nervous looks on their faces. They walked into the back room.

Chance lifted the phone, put his finger on the screen. "I'll give you ten seconds to walk out of here. Or I'm calling them back."

"Henry," Alex said. She gave me a nod for me to follow her outside. I hesitated but finally went out the door after her.

Chance hurried over to try and lock the door, but before he could, I shoved at it from the outside, pushing it closed hard and slamming it into his face. He stumbled back, dropping his phone, grabbing his face with both hands.

He yelled something through the glass, but Alex and I were already crossing the street.

"Was that really necessary?" Alex said, the usual reprimand for my sometimes juvenile behavior. "What is it with you, knocking around kids lately?"

I stepped to the driver-side door and ducked inside. "He's not a kid," I said.

I drove straight ahead but did a quick U-turn in the street, parking in front of the dry cleaners next door. "I wonder if he owns both buildings."

Alex looked out her window at the building. "This place looks like it's out of business."

I opened my door and stepped out, looking inside the building. But there wasn't anything at all inside. It was a big, open space without the counters or equipment that was there just a couple of days before. "There were a dozen people in here. There was a counter, a cash register. It's all gone. This place looks like it's out of business."

Alex stepped out on the other side and stood on the sidewalk. "How could it be?"

She looked toward Ray's store. "Maybe this kid's selling the building?"

I reached inside and turned off the engine, walked around the front of the car and between the two buildings into the back parking lot. I turned left and pulled on the back door of RR Sporting Goods. Although it was left open last time I was there, when I'd been attacked, this time it was locked.

I looked down at the ground. And in the grass growing up through the asphalt, behind a trash can I didn't remember seeing, was a long, black piece of metal. I picked it up and showed it to Alex. "I wonder if this is what I was hit with?"

She took it from my hand. "What is it?"

"It looks like a baluster. From a fence."

"It looks like the one around Mindy Hawkins' house, doesn't it?" Alex said.

I shook my head. "Her fence was real iron. This is aluminum."

She took it from my hand and looked at my face, her eyes toward the wound that had already started to heal. "You really think this is what someone hit you with?"

I took it from her, shaking my head. "No. I'm just guessing. Maybe it was already here, or inside. Maybe Ray'll know something about it."

I put my ear against the thick steel door to see if I could hear the men inside. But it was quiet. "How can this guy kick Ray out of here already?" I nodded toward the back of what was formerly the dry-cleaner's building. "And what's up with this guy? Suddenly out of business?"

"And how could this kid be here so soon, already showing off the place to prospective buyers?"

I looked around at the empty parking lot and walked between the two buildings toward my car. "These young real estate investors, they're all about the money. They're not in it to help the little guy. Not like they were in a past generation. I'd say ruthless is a good way to describe them. It's not like the old days, someone could pay a fair rent, open a store or a restaurant. Today it's more important these investors get every penny they can, couldn't care less about the neighborhood or the community and all the history they'll bulldoze into nonexistence for another buck."

Alex gave me a look. "I didn't know you were so bothered by commercial real estate."

I laughed. "My father was smart enough to buy the building where he had his shop. But the man who bought it from him, when Dad retired, raised the rent on the other tenants. Doubled it. All five businesses closed. And that man didn't care. Like I said. Ruthless. Dad always felt guilty about it, wished he'd never sold the building."

"But they wouldn't have been able to retire if he hadn't sold it."

We stepped out onto the sidewalk. The cars that had been parked in front of Ray's shop were all gone. I watched a white Tesla pull away from the curb fifty feet away, Chance Greenberg behind the wheel, looking our way as he drove by.

# Chapter 22

We walked down the hall on the second floor at the Duval County school administration building and turned at the door with the sign outside that said Financial Services.

Linda Green stood with her back to us over a copy machine. The machine clanked and swooshed with each sheet it spit out into a pile.

"Excuse me," I said.

Linda turned, tapped a button, and the copier stopped. The office was quiet. "May I help you?"

"I hope so," I said. "We spoke to you the other day, came in here looking for Shondra Rivers?"

She swallowed, closing her eyes for a moment. "You must not have heard, but Shondra—"

"We're well aware of what happened to her," I said.

Linda exhaled, like she'd been holding a breath. "Right, sorry. I've just... it's been a bit of a shock to us all." She looked at both of us, then seemed to force a smile. "Is there something I can do for you?"

"Do you have a few minutes to talk?" I said.

"Does it have to do with Shondra?"

I nodded and handed her my card. She looked it over. "You're a private investigator?"

I repeated my question. "Can we talk?"

Linda looked hurried, picking up the stack of papers from the copy machine, placing them down on a small metal table next to it. She straightened the pile before looking back at me. "I have to get to a meeting in a few minutes." She looked up at the clock on the wall over the door behind us.

Another woman walked out from around the corner behind Linda, smiling at me and Alex. "I'm heading out for lunch, Linda. See you in half an hour." She left the office without another word.

I said to Linda, "We won't take a lot of your time."

She looked around, appearing hesitant. There was no doubt she was nervous, but I wasn't sure if that's just how she was. She picked up the stacks of paper from the table and carried them, pressed against her chest. She walked away from us and started through a doorway to the left. "Follow me. My office is down this way."

We walked after her through the doorway, down a short hall, and into a modest-sized office. It smelled like food. Maybe it was mustard, but I couldn't quite identify the smell. On my left was a small wooden desk with a brown lunch bag opened on top of it. A half-eaten sandwich sat on top of wax paper. Next to it was a can of diet soda with a straw sticking out of it.

"Are you trying to eat your lunch?" Alex said.

She shook her head, walked to her desk and stuffed the sandwich inside the bag. She rolled over the top of the bag and tossed it in the trash can next to her desk. She pointed at the small round table with four chairs a few feet away, on the other wall opposite her desk. "Please, have a seat."

Alex and I both pulled up a chair and sat down, our backs to the door.

Linda cleared the mess of papers on the table and placed them on top of a short bookcase up against the wall a few feet from where we sat.

"So, you're a private investigator?" she said, her eyes on me but shifting from me to Alex.

"We both are," I said. I pointed my thumb toward Alex, seated to my right. "This is Alex Jepson."

Alex took out one of her business cards and pushed it across the table toward Linda.

"Are you in some way associated with the sheriff's office?" she said. "I ask because a detective stopped by this morning, asking questions about Shondra." She picked at a fingernail, her eyes on her hands. "He wanted to know about her relationship with Ray, and if I happened to know anything about it. But I didn't know much about it, other than he'd moved out of the house."

"She didn't talk about it?"

Linda shrugged, shaking her head. "I wouldn't say we were ever close enough to get into something like that." She looked at her watch. "I'm sorry, but I'm going to have to get to that meeting in a few minutes. The superintendent gets very upset if anybody's late." She grinned, a fine line between her dry, pink lips.

Linda seemed like a nice enough woman. It was hard to tell if she was in her thirties or fifties. She looked young, but there was also something old about the way she acted. It might've been the way she dressed in her long, flowered skirt and the dark, buttoned sweater over her white blouse. Or how she kept her dark, slightly grayed hair in a bun. You might think she looked like a school librarian. Or what you'd imagine one to look like.

"You never got the feeling she was in trouble for any reason?" I said. "Any kind of issues with anyone from the office?"

She had her hands folded on the table, her eyes down for a moment as she shook her head. "Shondra got along with most everyone, as far as I know." She shifted in her chair. "He seemed like a nice enough man."

"Ray?" I said. "I want to remind you he hasn't been to trial," Alex said.

"Oh, but it sounded like, talking to the detective, he had no doubt it was him."

I leaned forward on the table. "If the detective was one hundred percent sure Ray did it and had everything he needed, you think he'd be coming here asking questions?"

She nodded, like she understood my point.

"Innocent until proven guilty," she said, a slight smile on her face.

"Would you mind telling me what's behind Shondra moving to another department?"

"I don't know what significance that would have."

I thought it was an odd response. I said, "Does that mean you're not going to tell me what happened?"

Linda swallowed, like she was trying to hide it. "I... well, I guess what happened is, uh, Shondra wasn't performing up to expectations. So, at the time, we agreed it would be best if she was moved to another department. They had an open position in Human Resources, and she had some experience in that department."

"Was this, by any chance, your decision?" Alex said.

She picked at her fingernail again, her eyes on her hands. "Sometimes we have to make tough decisions. I liked Shondra. As a person. But we're a very large school department, covering the entire county. One hundred ninety-six schools. When someone makes a mistake, it can cause very significant problems."

"So she made one mistake?" Alex said. "And was removed from her position?"

Linda was still, looking at Alex for a moment like she was trying to think it through before she spoke.

"I can't get into every detail with you. I mean, there were numerous errors. Some clerical, and, well..."

"Had she made these mistakes before?" I said.

"I've only been director of the department for eight months. But"—she nodded—"it's been... I started to notice her making more mistakes, around the time she and Ray started having trouble."

I stared into Linda's eyes, but she looked away. "I thought you'd said she didn't talk about it with you?" I said.

"Oh, well, it's not that she didn't talk about it. I guess, well, we all knew what was going on."

"You mean, everyone in this office?" I looked toward the door.

"Oh, well, it's just me and Jodi here now. She's the one who left for lunch."

"So it was just the three of you?" Alex said.

Linda nodded. "For the most part, yes."

"For the most part?" I said.

"We hire temps once in a while. But they're usually only here for a few hours. I hardly ever remember their names."

Linda looked up at the clock on the wall behind her. "I'm sorry, but I have to go now." She stood from her chair and pushed it back under the table. She picked up the papers she'd brought in from the copy machine and carried them with her into the hall.

Alex and I followed her out, down the hall and back to the front area with the copy machine and the waiting area. I stopped at the open doorway and turned to face her. "We may be in touch again," I said. "But thank you for your time."

She gave a nod. "Maybe it's better if you call me first." She walked around the corner and down the hall toward her office. She came back with her business card and handed it to me. "This is my direct line, here at the office. I'd appreciate it if you'd call first, in case I'm not available next time."

· · · · ● · · ● · · ·

Alex's phone rang, and she looked up at me from her desk. "It's Mike." She appeared hesitant to answer it, but she had no choice. He had already called twice and she didn't take his calls. She cleared her throat. "Mike? How's it going?"

It had been almost two days since she'd spoken to him, and the way word traveled, I was certain he had to have known we were hired to help in Ray's defense.

"I saw you called," she said. "But you didn't leave a message, so I just assumed..." Alex stopped, listening to Mike on the other end. She looked over at me and rolled her eyes, nodding until she finally had a chance to get a word in. "I was going to tell you, Mike. But..." She was quiet again. He wasn't going to let her talk.

I watched as she got up from her desk and walked toward the window. She stood with her back to me, the phone against her ear. "Mike, I'm sorry. I really am. But if that's the way it has to be, then—" She shook her head. "Yes, we know there's incriminating evidence. But finding a weapon, no fingerprints..." She listened again.

I couldn't tell if Mike was yelling or just acting like a whiny child. Which, to me, he had a habit of doing.

"Why are you so upset?" she said, turning from the window, shaking her head.

I had my feet up on my desk, my eyes on Alex. I raised my voice enough, hoping Mike might hear me through the phone. "He's upset because he's afraid we'll make him look bad."

Alex shot me a look, shaking her head at me. She wasn't interested in me stirring the pot, although sometimes it was my favorite thing to do. "We're not going to get in your way," she said. She stepped away from the window and started pacing back and forth in front of the couch. She pushed her hair back and left her hand there, on her head. She looked at me, nodding. "Yeah, he's right here." She held the phone with her arm outstretched, toward me. "He wants to talk to you."

"Me?" I said. I reached up for the phone. "Hey, Mike. Long time no..."

"What's wrong with you, Walsh?" he said. "Between you and Alex... I don't get it. You're the one who came to me, told me the guy was lying, and now you're—"

"I never said he was lying. And neither did Alex. So don't try and put words in our mouths. Holding information back and lying are two different things."

Mike laughed. "You're a beauty, Walsh. The guy throws you through a glass door, could've killed you, and then you go running back to him. For what? Just so you can make a few bucks?"

"Give me a break," I said. "First of all, what happened between me and Ray is not an issue. I learned a long time ago not to take things too personally. You should give it a try. And, secondly, you know the last thing that drives me? Money. So don't make such a foolish statement."

Mike didn't respond.

Alex was back at her desk with her laptop, her eyes on the screen.

I said to Mike, "And you're acting like this is the first time it'll be our job to prove you wrong. Why're you making such a big deal about it now?"

"You've never partnered with Wendell Richards," he said. "I don't know what you know about him. But the man's a snake. He doesn't care about justice. And he'll bend the truth any way he has to just to put another notch in his belt."

The truth was, I didn't know much about Wendell Richards. At least after high school. And even then I barely remembered him. I hadn't even known he became an attorney. It wasn't like he was some big-time lawyer where I'd see his name all around town.

Although, apparently, it wasn't the first time Mike had to deal with him.

"I don't know what to tell you," I said. "We've been hired to find the truth."

"I already know the truth," he said. "Ray Rivers killed his wife."

I laughed. "See, that's the problem, Mike. You've already made up your mind. You're fixated on proving you're right, bringing a man who could be innocent down in the process. Does it ever cross your mind you could be wrong?"

He huffed into the phone. "All I'm telling you is to stay out of my way. You cause any issues with my investigation, I'm going to come down on you. You understand?"

"Now you're threatening me? You think you can stop me." I looked over at Alex walking to her desk. I said to Mike, "You think you can stop us from doing our job?"

Mike started to say something else, but I tapped the screen and ended the call. I walked over and put the phone down on Alex's desk.

"You hung up on him?" she said, looking at her phone.

I nodded. "I don't know how you deal with him as much as you do." I walked to the couch and sat down, leaning forward on the edge of the cushion.

"We can't work against him," she said. "Getting him any more upset than he already is, isn't the best approach."

"Are you saying I'm supposed to let him threaten me? Push us around?" I shook my head. "You know it's not my only motivation, but I'm just being honest when I say proving him wrong would be pretty satisfying."

"A bit petty, don't you think?" she said.

I shrugged. "Maybe."

# Chapter 23

Alex and I followed Wendell Richards into his office, my heart racing in my chest, with a touch of anxiety running through me. Ray was already there, sitting on the couch with his back to the door, his right arm up on the cushion, looking toward the window.

It was the first time Ray and I had seen each other since we not only crashed through the door at RR Sporting Goods, but also since he'd been arrested for his wife's murder.

Ray turned to us as we walked in toward him. His eyes went right to mine.

Wendell pulled the double doors closed. "I'm guessing I don't need to make any introductions?"

Ray pushed his big body from the couch and came toward me. He didn't look good; there was a bruise on his head similar to mine I assumed he got from his car accident. He also looked like he hadn't slept much, if at all, the bags under his eyes looked like deflated mini footballs. He stepped in front of me and reached out his hand. "I hope you forgive me, for the way I acted," he said, using both hands to shake my hand. "Thank you for accepting to help me, Henry." He shifted his eyes to Alex. "Thanks to both of you."

"Well, I don't think we need to rehash all of that," Wendell said, stepping around his desk. He stood behind holding on to his oversized leather office chair. "Ray knows the mistakes he's made. But the four of us together are going to find a way to get him out of his predicament. Let's see to it justice falls on his side."

Ray sat back down on the couch.

Wendell nodded toward the two wingback chairs right and left of the coffee table in front of Ray. "You and Alex, make yourselves comfortable." Alex and I sat, and he wheeled his oversized leather chair out from behind his desk. He stopped on the opposite side of the coffee table, across from Ray. He seated himself and looked at me, then Alex, on either side of him. "Can I get either of you a drink before we get started?"

We both shook our heads.

Wendell had a pad in his hand and leaned back with one leg crossed over his knee. "So," he said, again looking from me to Alex, "any progress to report?"

"Progress?" I said. "We've just started. I can't call much of the preliminary steps *progress*. Not at this early stage."

"Well, as you know, time is not on our side."

I nodded. "I'm well aware of that." I wasn't sure if Wendell was just trying to set the tone and ensure we all knew he was basically in charge, or if he was putting on a show in front of Ray. If there was one thing I didn't like, it was an unreasonable, pushy client. But I held my judgment.

I went ahead and told them about our conversation with Mindy Hawkins and our brief sit-down with Linda Green at the school administration building.

Ray was surprised to learn Shondra had been removed from her position at the school department.

"Why wouldn't she have told you what happened?" I said.

Ray shrugged. "I guess it happened after I'd moved out. It's not like we were having a lot of conversations after that point. But as far as I know, she was good at her job. In fact, she'd been looking forward to a promotion. But they brought someone in from the outside."

"Linda Green?" Wendell said.

Ray and I both nodded.

"Linda Green is the one who got the position Shondra'd been hoping for."

"Shondra was expecting to get that promotion?" Alex said.

"You bet," Ray said. "She was as upset as I'd ever seen her. But that all happened around the time she started acting funny with me. Being distant. So it wasn't like we got into any discussion about it. In fact, I can't tell you the last time we had much of a discussion about anything."

Wendell said, "So you had already split up when they moved her into another position?"

"Uh-huh."

The four of us sat quiet for a handful of seconds.

Wendell took notes on his pad resting on his thigh.

"Now, Mindy Hawkins, who at first I'd asked if she'd ever suspected Barry was unfaithful, looked at me like I had two heads. But this time, the police actually brought it up with her. So this time she didn't deny it. But she also doesn't want her husband's name dragged through the mud. I think she'd prefer to brush it aside."

"I understand that," Ray said. "At this point, you could say I'm in the same boat. I just want to prove my innocence. Proving whether or not Shondra had an affair doesn't do me much good."

I leaned forward in my chair. "Well, we need to look at the big picture, Ray." I looked at Wendell, watching me but staying quiet. I shifted my glance back to Ray. "So, as much as you may not want to talk about it, I was hoping you could tell me when you first suspected something was going on between them."

Ray took a moment before he answered, finally nodding as he moved his eyes around the room. "Shondra was going out a lot. She never used to. Was pretty much a homebody. I guess maybe she just wanted to get away from me, which didn't sink in at the time. Usually she wouldn't even tell me where she was going. So, one night I followed her and she ended up at Wilmington's Restaurant. You know where it is? Downtown?"

I nodded.

"Well, I pulled in, watched her park and go inside. She was alone, but I didn't follow her in. I went out and had a couple of drinks, had to think if I was wrong for following her."

"She is your wife," Wendell said.

Ray gave Wendell a short grin, nodding. "When I drove back again an hour later, her car was gone, and I saw Barry leaving the parking lot. Someone else was in his car but I couldn't see if it was her or not."

"You don't think it could've been a coincidence they were at the same restaurant?" Alex said.

"Especially if you didn't actually see her with Barry," I said.

"Well, I went home. And when she finally showed up, must've been midnight, I asked her who she was with at the restaurant. She went crazy, screaming at me for following her. Said I didn't trust her, that I was paranoid and jealous."

I leaned back in the chair and thought about when I'd asked her about having an affair. She used those exact words: paranoid and jealous. So I, at least, felt Ray was telling us a true story.

I said, "What about Barry? You never said anything to him?"

Ray shook his head. "This all happened after I was fired. So, no. Barry and I hadn't talked at all. I wanted to. I still hadn't gotten an answer why I was fired, never mind if he was messing around with my wife." Ray looked toward the floor.

Wendell paused, then gave me a nod. "You said you had some questions you wanted to ask Ray?"

"Well, of course, I'd like to know about the night before Shondra..." I said to Ray. "Can you tell me what happened at the house that night? I understand you were there?"

"My house? I just... I wanted to talk to Shondra."

"At eleven o'clock at night?" I said.

Ray ran both hands over his face. "I know how bad it looks. But it's the truth. I had a couple of drinks at Stegman's Pub. I called her. And when she didn't answer, I went over to the house."

Looking at Wendell, I said, "The sheriff's office has his call to her phone on record, correct?"

He nodded. "Yes, sir. All of them. Ray made a handful of calls to her cell and home phone. All on record."

"But no messages?" Alex said.

Wendell and Ray both nodded.

"What did you tell them—the police—about making all those calls?" I said.

"Just that I was worried about her," Ray said.

"Then, you drove over there?"

"I did. But she didn't answer the door. I knocked, rang the doorbell, nothing."

"And you didn't have a key because she changed the locks?" I said.

Ray nodded. "She changed them back, maybe a month ago."

Alex said to Wendell. "Is she allowed to do that? Seeing it's his house? Assuming his name's on the deed?"

Wendell shrugged. "Better off Ray didn't have the key. There was no forced entry. So it's likely she let the person in."

"Isn't there another way to get in?" I said. "Or did she change the garage door openers too?"

Ray shook his head. "She didn't change those. But I gave her back the remote I had in my truck."

"Was that remote located somewhere in the house?" I said, looking from Ray to Wendell.

Wendell said, "I don't believe so." He turned to Ray. "Didn't the police ask you if you had the remote?"

"Yeah. And I told them the same thing I just told you."

Alex and I both exchanged a glance. It was another piece of evidence I could see going against Ray. Especially if it hadn't been located.

I sat quiet for a couple of moments, thinking through some different scenarios. None of which were helpful to Ray. "So, let's discuss the weapon found at your store."

Ray sighed, staring back at me. "I didn't do it, Henry. I swear."

I nodded. "Well, what I'm thinking about is that scene in the back of your store. I told you, I was attacked. Someone was back there. And the chance that someone planted the weapon is, well, I think it could certainly be something."

"Does the sheriff's office know what happened back there?" Ray said.

"No. Not yet. I don't want to go to them with that alone. It's not enough at this stage." I said to Ray. "Have you seen the knife?"

Ray closed his eyes, nodding. When he opened them they looked to be filled with tears. "It's a knife from our kitchen. A set we got when we were first married."

I made a mental note, whoever killed her had clearly been in the kitchen prior to her murder. Whether or not she knew someone was in there... I had to guess not. Otherwise, she wouldn't have been lying in bed.

"What about the earring?" I said. "You're sure it wasn't at the house, since before you moved out of there?"

Ray shifted on the couch, like he was trying to get comfortable. "It was with my things, at the store."

"You hadn't been wearing it?"

Ray shrugged. "I wear it all the time."

"Did you have it that evening? When you were knocking on the door, calling her?"

"No. It was at the shop with my things."

I said to Alex. "So assuming whoever I ran into in the back was planting the knife... there's a good chance they'd already been there. Took the earring, left it at the scene."

"You're saying it was premeditated?" Alex said.

"If someone planted the earring?" I nodded. "Had to've been."

Ray pointed to the earring in his ear. "This is the other one I wear more lately. Had it on when I met you at Billy's Place. It's one Shondra gave me, for our fifth anniversary."

I studied the diamond stud. Twice the size of the rock I gave my ex-wife when we got engaged.

"And you're certain that earring is the same one you left at the store?" Wendell said.

Ray nodded.

I sat quiet for a couple of moments, not sure we needed to send the conversation in a different direction. But I wondered about Ray's landlord.

"Alex and I were at your store. And we ran into your landlord."

"Chance?" Ray said, a surprised look on his face.

"Yes. He was inside with a group of men in suits."

"He was inside my store? What was he doing?"

"He knows you've been arrested," I said. I didn't want to get Ray upset, but he needed to know where things stood. "He said the store was being permanently closed."

Ray's mouth hung open, staring back at me. "What? How can he..." He closed his eyes and covered his face with both hands.

Wendell had his eyes on me, doing a lot of listening, which was rare for most attorneys I'd come across. "Tell me again who this Chance fella is?"

Ray lifted his face from his hands. "Chance Greenberg. He owns the building where I have my store."

"He can't really close down Ray's store, can he?" Alex said, turning to Wendell. She was making the assumption he'd know something about real estate law.

"I can't say what he can or can't do without seeing the lease," Wendell said.

"He can't take my store from me!" Ray said, the frustration clear in his voice. "It's all I've got."

Wendell used both hands to gesture for Ray to relax. "I'll send him a letter, make sure he understands how something like this would work." He turned to me and said, "Let's not get distracted with Ray's business." He got up from his chair and rubbed his big stomach, hooking his thumbs inside his red-and-blue-striped suspenders. With a nod my way, he said, "Anything else you need from either me or Ray, before you get going?"

"I'm not sure I'd consider this a distraction," I said. "Anybody could be a suspect at this stage."

Wendell looked at me, nodded like he agreed, and put on what looked like a forced grin. "All right. I'll leave it up to you to decide what's important or not. That's why I hired you." He rolled his chair back over to his desk. "But keep in mind, every minute counts."

Although I had wanted to talk to Ray, I wanted to remind Wendell we were barely a full twenty-four hours into our investigation.

· · · · ● · ● · · ·

Wendell led us out through the double doors and into the lobby. The desk where the old woman had sat the first time we were there was empty. "Where's your receptionist?" I said, turning to Wendell.

"Oh, she's only here a few hours a week."

I guessed Wendell couldn't have been too busy, running the office by himself. Likely answering the phones himself too. I had yet to see any other attorney in the place, guessing it was just him. Solo.

Ray stuck his head out from Wendell's office. "Thank you, Henry." He shook my hand.

Alex and I continued down the hall to exit the building, but I stopped, turning back to Ray and Wendell still standing in the doorway. "Ray, did I tell you about Zack Mazer?"

Ray stared back at me. "*Zack?*"

"You know him, right?"

"Yeah, he's on the football team at the school."

I walked back toward Ray as Wendell watched me with a curious look on his face.

I told them how it all happened with Zack, starting with the locker room, even the part about me grabbing the kid's arm. "Then the father wrote me a thousand-dollar check."

Wendell pointed with his thumb over his shoulder and into his office. "Listen, I've got work to do. Does any of this have to do with Ray's case?"

I looked at Wendell but didn't answer. I said to Ray, "You ever have any run-ins with the kid?"

Ray took a moment before he answered. "He was always a bit of trouble. He wasn't a player coaches would consider coachable. Showed no respect to me or anyone else on my staff at any time. Kid would skip practice, miss the bus, then wonder why he wasn't playing. The thing was, he wasn't good enough to have the attitude he did."

"But you know the father?" I said.

"Zack came here from a private school. I'm not even sure what happened or why he transferred to the public school. But I remember how the parents wanted to be involved in sports right away. The mother jumped right on board with the booster club, took over as treasurer. And the father, well, like a lot of parents, he thought his kid was better than he was. He actually showed up at my door one night."

Wendell seemed to stop paying attention until that point. "He showed up at your door? For what?"

Ray shrugged. "He wanted his kid to play."

"Wait," I said, glancing at Alex, her eyebrows raised looking back at me. "What happened?"

"Told Shondra he wanted to talk to me about his son. I don't know if he'd been drinking, or what. But she was pretty upset, the way he was acting."

"You weren't there?" Alex said.

"No, I wasn't. But according to Shondra, he didn't believe her. He demanded she get me. The guy wouldn't let up. She told me she threatened to call the sheriff's office, and that's when he finally left."

"You have any other problems with him?" I said.

"It was late in the season. It's not that out of the ordinary, a father wants to talk to the coach. I try to let 'em know it'll do more harm than good. But they can't help it. Guy like John Mazer, with his deep pockets, thinks money'll make up for having a kid who's a so-so athlete."

"You think he had anything to do with you being fired?" I said.

Ray looked at me and shrugged. "It crossed my mind."

# Chapter 24

I WAS ALONE AT the bar at Billy's Place, waiting for Alex to come down from the office. She had spent the ride back from Fernandina Beach on her phone doing research and wanted to run up to the office and dig deeper on her computer.

I needed a drink.

Billy came over with my glass and two cubes of ice and poured a good shot of Jack over the top of it without asking. He knew enough to know when he didn't have to. "What's the latest?" he said.

I picked up the glass and held it up in front of me. "The latest is I have some weak leads."

Billy looked surprised. "Weak leads?"

I looked around as the working crowd came in through the door, one after another, and headed straight for the bar. The dining room looked to be filling up, and within the few minutes I'd been there, most of the seats at the bar had been taken.

I said, "I was hoping it wasn't this busy."

Billy stepped to the beer tab, filled a couple of pints. "Well, someone's gotta pay my bills." He smiled as he turned and carried two beers to someone at the far end of the bar.

I hadn't talked to Billy as much as I normally did. He was a good friend. The smart one. Sometimes, in a funny way, talking to him was like talking to my dad. There was always a good mix of logic, common sense, and careful consideration.

Characteristics missing in most people.

I felt someone come up behind me and turned to see Alex standing there, looking around the bar area. "You all right?" I said. I put my hand on the stool I'd been saving next to me.

"Why's it so crowded?" she said.

I shrugged. "I have no idea. But did you find what you were looking for up there?"

She sat down. "I think there's too many people around to discuss it."

I looked at her, curious and interested, wondering what it was she'd found. But she was right. It wasn't the time or place to openly discuss a murder investigation.

The ride back from Wendell Richards' office wasn't much different from the ride back from Naples. There was something in the air around Alex and me. We both knew what it was, and in the car together, it was apparent neither of us wanted to approach it. Although we had plenty else on our minds other than our kiss down in Naples.

Sometimes drinking will push you in a direction you prefer not to go. But sometimes it's not bad. I had wondered which one of us would bring it up. But neither did.

Billy gave Alex a nod from the other end of the bar, leaned into the cooler, and pulled out a bottle of Corona. He held it up for her and she gave him a thumbs-up. He walked toward us with the bottle, wiping his brow with the back of his forearm.

Alex nodded. "Busy tonight, huh?"

"You're not kidding," Billy said. "I'm getting too old for nights like this."

The volume of the voices around the bar was beyond my comfort zone and why I normally avoided coming to the bar—any bar—during the busiest of times.

"Where's Chloe?" I said.

Billy wiped his hands with the towel he kept draped over his shoulder. "She and Jake took the night off together. So here I am, busier than expected, and I don't have my head chef or my only other bartender."

Alex lifted her beer, holding it up in front of her mouth. "Why don't you hire someone else?"

"Nobody wants to work anymore," he said. "And when I do hire someone, they don't last. Or they steal." He put two menus in front of us. "If you two want to order food, better do it soon. The kid in back's not the fastest." He looked out into the dining room. "Gets any busier..." He pushed out a smile. "I should be happy, right? All this business?" He laughed and walked away, through the swinging door into the kitchen.

I opened the menu.

Alex sipped her beer. "Maybe we should go upstairs after we finish these." She looked around and leaned closer to me. Her voice quiet, but loud enough so I could hear her, she said, "Just confirmed John Mazer has a criminal record. Was arrested for embezzlement about eight years ago as the CFO for a paper plant in Georgia."

"No kidding," I said. "Did he do time?"

She nodded. "Six months. Fined an undisclosed amount."

I closed the menu. "How long's he had the accounting business here in Jax?"

"Moved to Florida six years ago, started his firm. Looks like it's just him." She had her phone up on the bar and turned it to me. "Here's a picture of his wife, Catherine."

I looked at the glamor shots of Catherine Mazer. She was a good-looking, middle-aged woman. In the photo, she wore a sleek red dress and high heels.

Alex turned the phone back and looked at the screen. "This was a photo of her at a fundraising event up in Georgia." She tapped the phone and turned it my way once again. "This is their house. She shares plenty of photos of the inside: the new eighty-inch TV they bought, new furniture..."

"Big house for three people," I said. "You know where the house is?"

She nodded. "It's about a mile away from the high school." She swiped her finger across the screen. "Here's one of their recent vacations in Aruba. She's one of those people, not afraid to share every little detail of her life with anyone who's got nothing better to do." She tapped and swiped and turned the screen so I could see it. "Here's what she had for dinner last night. She posts just about everything she does, including every meal. Other vacations. They travel quite a bit, according to her Instagram."

"I'm not sure I understand that," I said. "I never liked looking at someone else's vacation photos *before* the internet. Now, it's all you see. Who cares? And who cares what you made for dinner?" I faced forward, holding my glass up in front of me with my elbows on the bar. "Good for you, you know how to cook." I laughed, threw back what was in my glass, and slid it toward the far edge of the bar in front of me.

"Are you all right?" Alex said. "You seem a little, uh, on edge?"

I could feel her staring at me, but I kept my eyes straight ahead. "I guess I am," I said. "Nothing feels right about this case." I nodded at her phone. "I appreciate you digging into John Mazer. But there's likely nothing there. Nothing where Shondra used to work, nothing with Mindy Hawkins."

Alex faced me. "You said it yourself. We're just getting started."

"And we're already running out of time." I tried to get Billy's attention, turning to Alex. "You know, Ray seems like a decent guy. But there's something, something I... I'm not sure I believe a lot of what comes out of his mouth."

Alex kept her eyes on me for a moment. "This is what we've been hired to do. This is what we agreed to. Something else has to add up." She picked up her beer. "Aren't you the one who had to talk me into taking this case? And made me promise I was all in? Now, what... you're having doubts already?"

I said, "I don't know if I'd call them doubts. But let's just say I'm concerned this isn't going to turn out well."

She leaned forward, her arms folded in front of her on the bar. "You always worry when we have a tough case. And every single time, you start to doubt your own abilities. But we always pull it off."

"What if, this time, the odds are against us?" I held up my empty glass for Billy and finally caught his eye. "I'm going to get one more."

Alex sipped her beer, still facing me. Her eyes were still on me.

I looked around as more people came in from outside. "Look at this place. It's a gold mine. I should've opened a restaurant."

Alex laughed. "What? Where did that come from? You don't even like to cook, do you?"

I continued staring straight ahead, watching Billy at the other end laughing with his customers, a couple of regulars I recognized. "Look at all the fun he's having."

Alex rolled her eyes, straightening out in her seat.

We both sat still. Quiet, looking straight ahead.

I looked at her. "Who said I didn't like to cook?"

Alex shrugged, giving me a funny look. "I don't think I've ever seen you cook anything."

"Where am I supposed to cook? The galley? There's barely enough room to make a sandwich."

Alex had a pleasant look on her face. "Are you telling me you're a good cook? After all these years?"

"Just because I've never put a meal on Instagram doesn't mean I don't know how to cook."

She laughed.

"I'm serious. When I had a kitchen... a real house. I used to cook."

Billy walked over, dropped two ice cubes in my glass and poured me a good shot of Jack.

"I wish I had time to chat," he said. "You want to order anything?"

I looked at Alex, and we both shook our heads. "We've got work to do," I said. "I think we're going to head out after this drink."

Billy nodded. "All right. I know how much you like crowds. I hear you. But stop back later, if you want, before you go home."

I nodded, and Billy walked away, disappearing into the kitchen.

Alex put her hand on my arm. "So when are you going to cook for me?"

I couldn't quite put my finger on what was going on. Did she want me to cook her a meal? Maybe even post a photo of it on Instagram?

"Where am I going to cook? The galley isn't going to cut it."

"What about at my house?" she said, looking quite pleased she seemed to have persuaded me to do something.

I looked her in the eye. "You really want me to?"

"Why not?" she said, holding her bottle up under her lip. "It's a date."

. . . ● . ● . . . .

I stood at the window looking out from our office toward the darkness hanging over the parking lot and the St. Johns River behind it. Most of the crowd downstairs at Billy's Place had left. I let Alex drive the Mustang home, and I was deciding if I'd spend the night on the couch, or walk home to the marina.

There was a knock at the door from the back stairs from the kitchen below. Billy walked in, looking around my office. "Where's Alex?"

"She went home. She didn't want to leave Raz alone."

Billy looked at his watch. "I just came up to say good night. I saw the light on."

"Already?" I said.

"I'm beat. Long night," he said, shaking his head. "I can't keep doing this, working behind the bar like that. It's a kid's game. I should be thinking about retirement, heading down to South Beach."

"South Beach, huh?" I said. "You ever think about living on the other side?"

"The other side of *what*? Florida?"

I nodded. "Over there on the Paradise Coast, where my parents are."

"Naples?" He shrugged. "I guess it never crossed my mind. I don't know, aren't there a lot of old, rich people around there now?"

"Can't you say that about most of Florida?" I said.

Billy shrugged. "I don't know. But why'd you ask me about Naples?"

"I guess I've been thinking about it."

"Moving to Naples?" He rubbed the back of his neck. "Because of your parents?"

I nodded but had trouble getting the words out for a moment. I had a lot on my mind and needed sleep. I hadn't even called my parents since I'd been back and felt guilty about it.

"Someone's going to have to take care of them," I said. "And, well, that someone's probably going to be me."

"Your dad's doing all right, isn't he?"

I looked out through the window, into the darkness hanging over the river. "It's hard on him."

Other than the air from the A/C blowing through the vents, my office was quiet.

"Are you heading home soon?" Billy said, reaching for the door.

I looked at the couch. It was new, and comfortable, but I wasn't sure I needed another night on a couch. "I'll probably walk home."

"You want a ride?"

"Nah. I could use a walk. It's a nice night."

"You sure?" he said, pulling open the door.

I gave him a nod. "Thanks. I'll be all right."

"Okay. See you later." Billy walked out and closed the door behind him.

............

It was almost one in the morning when I left the office, walking along Trout River Drive. The night was quiet, and I felt more awake than I had just a few hours before.

There was a chill in the air. But I didn't mind. I'd worn my jeans, although short sleeves weren't made for what felt like cooler weather coming through.

I could see the wooden sign at the entrance for the Trout River Marina on the right, still a good distance from where I was. Headlights came up from somewhere behind me and I glanced over my shoulder. A car seemed to be coming toward me, but it was back at least a hundred yards. And it was moving slowly.

I continued my walk and didn't think much about the headlights, although they continued getting brighter the closer the car got to me. I didn't look back. But I knew something wasn't right.

I picked up my pace and thought about turning into the parking lot to the building on the right, the entrance before the marina. But a ten-foot high chain-link fence separated the building's parking lot from the parking lot at Trout River Marina. I couldn't see myself making the climb.

And I was also curious about the car driving behind me.

Looking over my shoulder again, the car seemed closer. I could see my breath in the glow of the headlights, the car starting to pick up speed. I tried to get as far off the road as I could, but the area to the side was damp and muddy from a hard rain earlier in the day.

I looked back one more time, but the car was so close I had to stop and use my arms to block the bright lights. The engine roared, like the driver was giving me a warning. And by the time I realized what was about to happen, it was too late.

The car sped up and came directly at me. I tried to dive out of the way, but the car's right front quarter clipped me, taking out my legs and sending me head over heels into the fence before the marina's entrance.

I swear my body felt like the blade of a fan, spinning in the air. I tried to catch my fall but the first thing to hit was my head, clunking off the steel fence post.

I was awake. At least at first. I was on my back, staring at the dark night sky. I tried to get a look at the car, but nothing moved. I couldn't feel my hands or feet. My ears were ringing so loud, I thought my head was going to explode.

I closed my eyes, hoping it was a bad dream. Was I paralyzed? Was I dead? The ringing and everything around me quieted. But my eyes wouldn't open.

# Chapter 25

AN OLD MAN I didn't recognize crouched over me, his hand on my shoulder, shaking me. "Buddy, you all right? Hey, Buddy."

I sprang up from the cold, damp ground squinting my eyes from the sun coming up over the horizon. I looked at him staring back at me, turning my eyes toward the road and back to the sign for the Trout River Marina. For a moment, I couldn't remember how I'd gotten there or why I was there.

"You want me to help you up?" the man said, holding out his hand.

I grabbed his hand and pushed myself up from the ground. I was slightly light-headed, grabbing on to the chain-link fence to steady myself. I squeezed my eyes tight, hoping the pain in my head would go away.

The exhaust from his old pickup truck made me feel worse than I already did. The sputtering sound from his muffler hurt my ears. "You see anything?" I said.

The man shook his head. "If you're wondering if I know what happened to you, I haven't got a clue. I thought maybe you'd had too much to drink."

I rubbed the top of my head and felt a lump right near there. "I think... I think I was hit by a car."

He looked me over. "You sure? You were hit by a car? If that's the case, I'd say you're lucky to be alive."

I looked to my right down the road in the direction of Billy's Place and my office. To my left was the entrance to the marina. I nodded, pushing my hair back from my face. "Someone tried to run me down."

"You want me to call the sheriff's office for you?"

I looked at my watch. The glass face was cracked. It was a watch I'd had for twenty years, one my father had given me. "Would you mind giving me a ride to my boat? In the marina?"

The man nodded, reaching for my arm as if to make sure I didn't fall over. "Yeah, sure. Of course." He nodded toward his truck, and I stepped up into the passenger side. The dashboard was covered in papers and a clipboard and at least a dozen pens and pencils spread all over. There were a couple of empty beer cans on the floor.

He drove ahead and turned into the parking lot, went around the main building and slowed as we approached the docks.

I pointed toward my boat. "Right over there. The small one with the blue trim."

He drove ahead and turned to me, stopping a few spaces down from where my boat was docked. "You sure you're all right?"

I nodded, feeling the old bruise on my head. I had so many bruises at that point I wasn't sure which was old and which was new. "I appreciate the ride over," I said. "I guess I could've walked."

The old man shrugged, giving me a nod. "Not a problem."

I stepped out, and he slowly pulled away without another word. I reached into my pocket for a cell phone I'd bought the day before. And the screen was already cracked.

The marina was fairly quiet, without much action other than a couple of joggers and some fishermen readying their boats. I climbed up onto my boat and went down into the cabin. I didn't feel like I'd slept, although I must have been out cold for a good four or five hours.

I made some coffee and got myself cleaned up before heading back outside with my lawn chair. I sat out on the dock, trying to gather my thoughts about exactly what had happened. I sipped my coffee and called Alex.

She answered on the second ring.

"You awake?" I said.

"I just got back from a run," she said.

"You're running again?" I said and had a feeling why she might have been trying to get in better shape than she already was.

"Are you at the office?" she said.

"No. At my boat."

"Oh, good. I felt guilty taking your car, leaving you at the office."

"Well, funny thing is, I walked home and someone tried to kill me."

"Kill you? Kill you how? At Billy's?"

I shook my head, my eyes on an older Lexus pulling into the marina. I stood up from the chair and watched it drive across the lot. I had a feeling I knew who it was. "Hit and run. I was hit by a car."

"Are you hurt?"

"Hurt? I don't know. No more than normal. I think I'm okay. I was out cold for a few hours, otherwise..."

"Jesus, Henry. You're at your boat now?"

I didn't answer, my eyes on the Lexus driving slowly around the parking lot. "Hey, let me call you back."

"Wait, what? Do you need a doctor?"

"No. I'm good. Let me call you back." I hung up and started between the parked cars toward the vehicle. With the windows on the car tinted, it was hard to see the driver. My head was aching and still a bit foggy, and I needed something to eat.

I started to run after the car as it continued driving, as if at a crawl, then turned between a row of cars and headed in the other direction.

I hadn't realized what I'd hurt until I tried to cut around a parked car. My knee just about gave out and I stumbled, catching myself on the trunk of another stationary vehicle before I hit the ground. I looked up, and Mindy Hawkins was right there in front of me, staring out through her windshield.

I limped to the driver's side of her car as she rolled down the window. "What are you doing here?" I said.

She looked out at me from inside the car, sunglasses on her eyes, and the smell of sweet perfume coming from inside. She was calm. "I was surprised to hear you lived on a boat."

"So you drove out here to find out for yourself?"

She shook her head, looking past me. "Can we talk?"

I pointed toward an empty parking space a few spots down from my boat. "Why don't you park right there."

She'd put up her window before I finished and drove ahead, turned into the parking space, and killed the engine. She stepped out of her car and started toward me.

"How'd you know I lived here?" I said.

She shrugged. "I don't know. I guess I just heard."

"Oh," I said, although it wasn't something I had publicized. Not many people knew I lived there. And my small handful of friends knew enough to keep it quiet. "So, are you going to tell me why you showed up this early in the morning, out of the blue?"

"I wanted to talk to you. After the way we left it at my house..."

"It wasn't a problem," I said. "I understand you don't want your husband brought into this mess." I walked ahead of her and turned, taking her hand as she stepped onto the dock. "But the problem is, I'm not sure it's possible to untangle his name from it. It's likely there's some connection between what happened to him and what happened to Shondra."

Mindy acted as if she wasn't listening, walking along next to me. "You're limping," she said, looking down at my leg. With shorts on, she could see I had a bandage around where I'd been cut and the new purple bruise I had on the outside of my knee from where the car had hit me.

I looked back at Mindy's car and tried to get a look at the front right quarter. It wasn't that I thought Mindy Hawkins would have a reason to hit me with her car. But I found it odd she showed up at the marina, out of the blue, early the next morning after I was hit.

She wore a long black leather jacket over tight-fitting blue jeans. She was older, probably somewhere in her fifties. And attractive. She looked different than she had the last time I saw her and not what I expected, now that I was seeing her outside of her house. With the jacket and jeans and her black combat boots, the look she had might've been described as tough—a rock-and-roll look.

"Is it too cool to sit outside?" I said. I pointed with my thumb over my shoulder. "Or we can go inside." I smiled. "It's tight down in the cabin, but if you'd—"

"I like the fresh air," she said, turning her eyes toward my green-webbed lawn chair. "I had those same chairs," she said. "Mine weren't green though."

I reached up onto my boat and pulled down another one, with yellow webbing. "They were my parents' chairs, probably as old as I am," I said. I opened up the yellow one for Mindy and placed it down with the other one. "Would you like a coffee?" I said, picking my mug up from the dock.

"No, thank you." She sat down, and I sat in the other chair, not quite facing each other, but at a slight angle toward the river.

Mindy pulled out a pack of Newport Light cigarettes. I didn't picture her as a smoker. "You mind?" she said. She stuck one in her mouth.

I shook my head. "Go ahead." I sipped my coffee and looked at her over the rim. There was something odd going on with her. Maybe she'd hit a late midlife crisis. Although I wasn't really sure that was something women even went through. I didn't know her enough to make any judgment, but from the photos I saw of her online and the way her nerdy husband looked, watching her smoke her cigarette made it clear she was someone I had mistaken for someone else.

"So," I said, "Are you ready to tell me why you'd show up out of the blue at the marina where I live, this early in the morning? Should I be suspicious?" I smiled as if making light of it. But I wasn't.

She took a drag from her cigarette, nodding. "I wanted to apologize for the way I acted the other day."

"Oh," I said. "I'm not sure you did anything wrong."

"I was upset. I had hoped Barry's name wouldn't be dragged into this mess, and what happened to Shondra."

"I understand. But the thing is, I'm afraid there's some kind of connection between what happened to Shondra and what happened to your husband."

Mindy was giving me a look, her chin down as she drew from her cigarette, staring back at me with her lazy look, her eyes coming through the smoke in front of her face. She reached over and put her free hand on my thigh. "What do I need to do for you to keep Barry out of this?" She ran her hand inside my leg and I stood from the chair.

"I'm in the middle of an investigation," I said. "I'm sorry, but it's just not possible to ignore the fact he either had an affair with Shondra Rivers, or was involved in something else between the two."

She looked up at me, her cigarette up in front of her face. "Barry didn't even like Shondra," she said. "I mean, as a person. They didn't get along very well."

I wasn't exactly clear if she was trying to come up with a reason to believe her husband wasn't a cheater, or if there was something he had told her, to perhaps throw her off. I'd dealt with enough cheating husbands in my career to see them weave any lies they could to hide their infidelity.

I remembered a woman hired me when she was suspicious of her husband's claim he hated the woman's sister. He didn't even want the woman's sister around for holidays or kids' birthday parties. Turns out, the husband and the sister were in the middle of a three-year affair they'd been hiding from my client. At least until I showed up.

"Is that the only reason you came here?" I said.

She turned away from me, her cheeks drawn in as she took another drag from her cigarette. "I know you have a job to do, to help defend Raymond. But perhaps he's not as innocent as you're hoping."

I stared back at her. "Are you saying there's something I should know?"

She shifted her eyes out toward the river. "The more I thought about it... even Barry was concerned at one point about Raymond's temper."

I was slightly confused. "Can you be a little more specific?" I said. "I know Ray's temper can, I'd say, get him in trouble. But what exactly are you referring to? Is that why Ray was fired? Did something happen between your husband and Barry we don't know about?"

She stood from her chair. "Just some things Barry said. I'm not going to be the one to point the finger, make it any harder on Raymond. Because, well, I don't know if he killed his wife. But I'm telling you, the more I've thought about it, I'd hate to see someone get away with murder."

I looked out toward the parking lot. "So, just so I'm clear. First you came here to ask me not to bring Barry into this investigation more than I have to. But now you're telling me you believe Ray is guilty of murdering his wife? Without an ounce of evidence other than a feeling you have?"

She dropped her cigarette on the dock, crushing it with her boot. "I'm sorry," she said, walking toward the parking lot. "Perhaps you were the wrong person to talk to," she said. "I had hoped you'd be more understanding."

I reached for her and held her arm as she started past me. "Listen. I will do whatever I can to keep your husband from being dragged into this any more than he has to be. But I can't make any promises. And I'd appreciate it if you'd keep your opinion about Ray to yourself for now. Unless you have something more concrete to offer."

Mindy glared into my eyes, pulling her arm from my grasp.

I watched her walk across the lot until she stepped into her Lexus and left the marina.

# Chapter 26

ALEX PULLED INTO THE marina driving the Mustang and parked in the same space Mindy Hawkins had pulled out of a half hour earlier.

She stepped out from the car wearing sunglasses and a faded T-shirt from the Jacksonville Sharks baseball team.

I watched her and waited until she stepped onto the dock.

"You just missed Mindy Hawkins."

She pulled off her sunglasses. "What did she want?"

"She showed up out of the blue," I said. "I'm not even sure how she knew I lived here. But I was surprised to see her here. Although I got the feeling she was more surprised to see me standing in front of her car when she pulled into the lot."

"You don't think she was expecting to see you?"

"I don't know."

Alex looked me over, up and down. "Before you tell me what she wanted, can you promise me you're all right?"

I nodded. "Just another night in Jax," I said, smiling. I took a step and felt a twinge in my knee, getting a footing before I stumbled.

"You don't look all right," Alex said.

"It's fine." I turned the chair toward her and nodded toward it. "Sit down. I'll tell you what she said."

Alex had a take-out cup in her hand, a tea-bag string hanging over the side. "I have something important to tell you," she said. "But you go first."

"Well, she claims she was here hoping I wouldn't bring her husband into the investigation. But like I told her, there's no way I can make that promise. It's too late for that."

"That's why she was here?" Alex looked at her watch. "A little after seven in the morning, she shows up looking for you to tell you something she'd already told you?" She rolled her eyes.

"You don't buy it?" I said.

Alex sipped her tea. "I don't know. But was there anything else?"

I told Alex how Mindy thought maybe Ray really was the killer.

She said, "Why would she all of a sudden tell you that now?"

"I asked her the same exact thing. However, I advised her not to go to the cops, tell them the same thing."

"Why would you do that? If someone has a reason to believe—"

"I don't think she has much of a reason at all. It would be hearsay. She said Barry told her he was afraid of Ray's temper. She never said she saw it herself. In fact, remember the first time we talked to her? It was pretty clear she liked Ray. Didn't have a bad thing to say about him. And suddenly she's singing a different tune."

Alex had her sunglasses over her eyes and lifted them onto her head. "Can I tell you what I found last night?"

"Last night?" I nodded.

"I did some more digging when I got home. Turns out Linda Green and John Mazer have some history together. They used to work together at the same paper plant, up in Georgia."

"The place where he got nailed for embezzlement?"

Alex nodded. "Linda was second-in-command of the accounting department."

"He was the CFO, right? Was she involved?"

"It doesn't appear she was. According to the records, John and a salesman, working for one of their vendors, were the only two involved. At least, according to records. Apparently, Mazer padded invoices, putting more money in the salesman's pocket. Mazer got a cut of the extra money."

I stood up from the chair and leaned against my boat. "So what's this actually mean? Is it just a coincidence they both end up down here in Jax? We need to find out more about their relationship at the company. And what it is today."

"It might be nothing," Alex said. "But I found it interesting they know each other."

"I find it interesting this woman is in charge of the entire Duval County school system."

Alex stood up from her chair. "But like I said, she wasn't involved in the crime." She looked out toward the river. "But what if she was somehow involved?"

"I wish Mindy was still here when you showed up. I'd love to ask her about John Mazer. I wonder what she can tell us about him."

Alex said, "What if we go see her now?"

I looked at my watch and rubbed the back of my neck, feeling tight from being hit.

Alex grabbed me by the shoulders and turned me around so she could look me over. "Are you sure you're all right?"

I nodded. "I'd be better if I at least saw what kind of car it was that hit me."

"You didn't notice anyone at the bar? It had to've been someone who knew you were walking home. I can't imagine it was just random."

"You saw how busy it was. Who knows. Whoever it was could've been sitting there watching us. Or watching me from outside, waiting for me to leave the office."

Alex said, "You don't really suspect Mindy Hawkins would do something like this, do you?"

I shrugged. "I have no idea."

"What if she was driving by, looking to to see if you were dead?"

I shook my head. "My gut says it wasn't her. But whoever it was, I'm not even sure the intention was to kill me, or just try and give me a little scare."

"Someone doesn't drive a car into another human being to scare them," Alex said.

We started toward the Mustang, and Alex reached into her pocket, pulling out the keys to the Mustang. She tossed them over to me and stepped to the passenger door. "I can see why you like this car."

"You said the same thing about my last one," I said.

She laughed. "Don't remind me. All I remember is we almost died."

· · · · • · • · · · ·

Mindy's Lexus was back in the driveway at her house, but I didn't see her sister's Volvo 240. I was afraid the sister would get in the way, so I was relieved to see she wasn't there.

We knocked on the front door and waited at least a good minute before Mindy opened it. She stood on the other side, the look on her face as surprised as she was when we saw each other at the marina.

"Oh, hello," she said, smiling. "Miss me already?"

*An odd comment*, I thought.

Although Mindy's face turned red when she stuck her head further out and realized Alex was standing to the side of the door.

"Hi," Alex said, giving her a crooked grin.

"You have a minute?" I said, looking up the steps at Mindy.

She nodded. "Would you like to come in?"

We didn't have time for chitchat. "We want to ask you a couple of questions. And I'll start with John Mazer. Do you know who he is?"

Mindy stared out at me, not responding right away. But after a handful of seconds, she nodded. "What about him?"

"Is that a yes?" I said.

"Yes, I know John Mazer. Not well, but... I know he's done a lot for the school. He and his wife, Catherine. They're very involved."

"So you know them personally?" Alex said.

Mindy looked at her from inside the doorway, then slowly began to nod. "As soon as their son, Zack, transferred to Barry's school, they became, like I said, very involved. They helped raise a lot of money. Mostly for sports. But they also helped raise money for other things. I don't know how either of them found the time. Barry spoke very highly of John."

"That's interesting," I said. "Did Barry know John had a criminal record?"

Mindy's eyes opened wide. "John Mazer? Are you sure?"

"Yes, we're sure," Alex said.

I said, "Zack Mazer only transferred to the school last school year. It sounds like it didn't take long for Barry and John to get to know each other?"

Mindy shrugged, then nodded. "You could say that. They'd played golf together. And we'd been out to dinner with both John and Catherine. A couple of times."

"But Barry never mentioned anything about John embezzling money from a company he worked for, as CFO, over five years ago?"

"If he knew anything about it, I'm sure he would have mentioned it," Mindy said. "I always thought John was a nice man. But I guess I don't know him as well as I thought."

"Are you surprised?" Alex said.

Mindy nodded. "Yes, of course I am."

I had to think things through for a moment. "Do you think there's a chance Barry could have been involved with something? Possibly with Mr. Mazer?"

"I... I have no idea. I would like to think the answer would be no."

"And you're sure there were never any conversations between them that would cause you to suspect they—"

"I don't know enough about John Mazer or any conversations he may have had with Barry to give you any kind of definitive answer. I already told you all I know."

The three of us stood quiet.

"Do you think it's possible John Mazer would have enough influence on Barry to have Ray Rivers fired?"

Mindy looked at me and slowly shook her head. "I... I don't know. But... why would John Mazer want him fired?"

"I'm simply asking a question," I said. "I'd still love to know why Ray was fired. And what—or who—is behind it. And now that I see John and Barry were buddy-buddy, I'd say there's a strong possibility there was something more to their so-called relationship."

# Chapter 27

ALEX AND I WALKED down the second-floor hall at the school administration building and toward the Financial Services Department. Although Linda Green had requested I call before we showed up, I decided to give it a shot and hope we'd catch her at the right time.

We walked into a quiet office, with the faint sound of music coming from the hall where Linda's office was. I stepped past the photocopier and looked down the hall. "Hello? Anybody here?"

A woman stepped out of the second office on the left, past Linda's office, and came toward us. "Can I help you?"

I recognized her from the last time we were there talking to Linda. I remembered her name. I said, "Jodi, right?"

"Do I know you?"

"Linda told me your name. We were here with her the other day. You were on your way out to lunch."

The look on her face told me she couldn't make the connection.

"Anyway, is Linda here?"

"Linda?" She turned and looked into Linda's office. From where I stood a few feet away, it looked like the lights were off. She said, "She's out today. Is there something I can help you with?"

"Are you expecting her back?"

"I don't think so," Jodi said. "She left a message for me this morning, said she was taking the day off."

Alex stepped forward and stood next to me. "You used to work with Shondra Rivers, is that right?"

Jodi's look turned somber. "Of course. Yes. We'd worked together for quite a few years." She looked down at the floor. "She was a friend of mine." She walked out from the hallway past us and leaned against the copy machine at the front of the office.

I handed her one of my business cards and she looked it over.

I said, "What can you tell us about Shondra being transferred out of here to the HR Department?"

The woman looked from me to Alex before her eyes went toward the doorway as mine did a moment before. She cleared her throat and gestured for me and Alex to follow her.

We walked down the hall again and followed her into an office much smaller than Linda's, enough room for her small desk. What little space was left barely gave me and Alex enough room to stand.

The woman brushed against me to get by and closed the door behind us. She leaned against her desk, facing us with her arms folded. The nameplate next to her, on the desk, said Jodi Congdon.

"I saw you here talking to Linda. But you were here before that, looking for Shondra. Wasn't that you?"

"We were here for a much different reason the first time."

She had her eyes down on the floor for a moment, before raising them to mine. "Shondra didn't do anything wrong," she said. "I don't know why they removed her from her job here. She was a good employee."

"So then, what happened?" I said.

Jodi brushed a strand of hair from her face and tucked it over her ear. She paused a moment before speaking, like she was afraid to talk. "I haven't told anybody else about this. Not even the sheriff's office."

"You already spoke with someone from there?" Alex said.

Jodi nodded.

"So what was it you didn't tell them?" I said.

"I'm not exactly sure what Shondra found," she said. "But it was something, something she wasn't supposed to."

"Something, you mean, in the books? I assume it was accounting related?"

Jodi nodded. "I knew something was going on. When I asked her, she got real nervous. Wanted to know how I knew."

"She didn't tell you?"

She shook her head. "I heard someone talking about it. With Linda."

"And you asked Shondra about it?" I said.

"I did. And she said she'd talk to me when we had some privacy. But then, next thing I know, her office was empty. But she wasn't gone from the building. They transferred her down to the Human Resources Department. And we never spoke again."

"Why wouldn't you speak to her again?" Alex said. "If she was still here, in the building?"

"It wasn't my choice. It was, actually, she who stopped speaking to me. I tried to talk to her. I asked her what happened, why she switched departments. She told me to mind my own business. I couldn't tell if her tone was angry, or if she was warning me."

I said, "And you never said anything to anyone about it?"

Jodi nodded. "Something was wrong."

"Do you think Linda was behind it?" I said. "Behind Shondra being moved out of here, and down to HR?"

She looked behind her, down at her desk. "I don't know if it was her decision or not. She actually came right in my office the same day Shondra had left, asked me if I knew what had happened."

"And what did you tell her?" I said.

"That I didn't know a thing about it. How I hadn't had a chance to talk to Shondra."

"I guess I'm not fully understanding why you wouldn't mention this to the sheriff's office," Alex said. "Don't you think it's all a bit suspicious?"

"I guess I was scared. I mean, at first it was just... I was worried. I can't afford to lose this job. But then, after Shondra was killed, I don't know what to think anymore."

"What about now?" I said. "Are you still worried?"

She shrugged. "I don't know. Linda's been nice to me. She wasn't when she first started. She was kind of mean. But ever since Shondra left..."

I was getting a little claustrophobic in the small office, shifting my stance and moving to find a little more space. "Do you know Shondra's husband, Ray?"

She nodded. "Not that well. But I'd met him a few times. The thing is, Shondra and I were more like work friends. We didn't get involved in each other's personal lives the way some people do. All this time working together, I'd never even been invited to her house."

"I guess I know what you mean," I said, giving Alex a quick look out of the corner of my eye. "Some people keep their work world separate from their personal world."

Jodi nodded. "That was Shondra. We'd go out for drinks once in a while, but that was it."

"Where would you go?" I said.

"Well, different places. But Shondra always wanted to go to Wilmington's, downtown."

"And you'd go there with her?" Alex said.

"We probably went there a handful of times. I think she knew people there. I don't know if I'd call her a regular, but... I know she knew the bartender by name."

I thought about Ray telling me he followed her one night to Wilmington's when he saw Barry Hawkins leaving in his car. But Ray never said anything about her being a regular.

I said, "I'm not sure you're comfortable answering this question, but by any chance are you aware if she was ever involved with another man? Besides her husband?"

Jodi's eyebrows rose, her eyes wide open. Shaking her head, she said, "She never said anything to me about anything like that."

"You sure?" I said.

She looked me in the eye and nodded. "She knew a lot of people. Men and women. She told me once that Ray was always jealous of her relationships with males, even when there was nothing for him to be jealous about. So if Ray's the one who told you..."

"She told you he was jealous of other men?" I said. "Even if they were just friends?"

Jodi shrugged, nodding. But she didn't seem to want to add anything else.

"So her position here in the Financial Services Department... They didn't hire anyone else to replace her?"

"A woman was supposed to be hired. But it fell through because her husband was doing some consulting here. I guess it was a conflict of interest or something."

"You know her name?" I said. "And the husband?"

Without hesitation, Jodi said, "John Mazer, from Mazer Accounting. He was hired to do an audit of the department's financials."

I looked at Alex and she had the same surprised look on her face as I'm sure I did.

"Did Linda hire him?" I said.

Jodi looked from me to Alex. "Why? Do you know him?"

"Can you tell us if Linda's the one who brought him in to do this so-called audit?"

"I don't know. I think so. She seemed to know him, the way they were acting when he was in here."

"Mr. Mazer worked right here, in the office?" I said.

"Only some of the time. I only saw him here once or twice. I think most of what he did took place outside of here. At least, I assumed so since I only saw him that one time."

"And the wife was supposed to work here? At the same time her husband was doing this so-called audit? I could certainly see why that would be a conflict of interest," I said. "Is he still involved? I mean, is the audit ongoing?"

"I haven't heard his name in a few weeks," she said. "I don't know for sure. I try to mind my own business, not ask many questions. Do my job and get out of here."

· · · · ● · ● · · ·

Alex and I walked into Wilmington's restaurant and took a seat at the long dark-wood bar. Most of the stools were empty, although it was barely noon. The lighting inside the restaurant was dim, with a couple of older, white-haired women the only two in the dining room. A grilling smell came from the kitchen. And since Wilmington's was known for their meats, I had a feeling Alex was going to have a tough time finding something to eat off the menu.

She had it open in front of her.

"See anything you'll eat?" I said.

She shrugged, her eyes still down. "I'll find something."

The bartender had a beard with a bit of gray in it, although I wouldn't say he looked old. He came over with two bottled beers and placed them down in front of us. "Ready to order?"

"In a minute," I said. "Would you mind if I asked you about a customer of yours?"

He shrugged. "It depends. I'm not here to get anyone in trouble."

"Well, it's a little late for that," I said, looking him in the eye. "Did you know Shondra Rivers?"

"Shondra?" He nodded. "Yes, I knew Shondra. She was a nice woman. It's sad what happened to her."

"Did she come here often?" I said.

"Often?" He shrugged. "You could say that. Couple times a week, I'd say."

"So you knew her fairly well?"

"I guess you could say that. As well as I could get to know someone like her."

"What's that mean?" I said. "Like her?"

"Oh, well. She was quiet. She didn't talk a lot. She'd come in here, order a drink, just sit quiet at the bar. Sometimes she'd have a book. Or she'd be on her phone."

"Yeah?" I picked up my bottle of beer. "So she kept to herself?"

He nodded, shrugging his shoulders. "I guess so."

"And she normally came alone?" I said.

He looked from me to Alex. "Mind if I ask what this is all about? Are you two with the sheriff's office?"

"No, we're not." I didn't feel the need to go into any further details.

Alex must've felt there was no need to be secretive. "We knew Shondra. And her husband, Ray."

The man raised his eyebrows. "Ray, huh?" He leaned with his hands wide on the bar. "I hope they hang the man, what he did to her."

I wasn't about to get into any of it with him or tell him it was our job to prove Ray didn't kill his wife. Because I knew when someone had made their mind up, there was no need to ruffle any feathers.

"You didn't answer my question," I said. "Did she normally come here alone?"

He gave me a look, like he didn't like the questioning without knowing a little more about who we were. "You sure you're not a cop?"

"I'd tell you if I was," I said. I realized this guy wasn't going to offer us much unless I told him why we were there. I pulled out my business card and tossed it on the bar.

The bartender picked it up, studied it, and placed it back down in front of him. "I assumed it had to do with her murder. I would've never guessed you were private investigators." He smiled. "I actually never met one before. Although I used to watch *Magnum*, as a kid."

Alex pulled out her phone and showed the bartender the photo she had of Barry Hawkins. "You ever see this man in here before?"

He squinted his eyes and leaned closer to Alex's phone. He nodded. "He's been here. Yes. With Shondra. I don't know his name though. He never sat at the bar." His eyes went to the dining room, behind us. "He'd sit at a table. Shondra met him over there a few times."

"You're sure he was with Shondra?"

He ran his tongue inside his cheek and took a moment to answer. "Yeah."

"Just the two of them, together?" Alex said.

"Uh, a couple of times they were alone. But not too long ago they met up here, and someone else came in, sat down with them."

"Male or female?" I said.

"Female."

"Can you tell us what she looked like?"

He gave an exaggerated shrug, held his shoulder in place with his hands out, palms up. "I don't know. So many people come through here."

I said, "Nothing at all you can tell us?"

He dropped his shoulders and shook his head. "She was pretty. Young. In her thirties."

"Blonde? Brunette?" Alex said.

"Brunette, I guess. But seriously, I don't remember. I wouldn't want to steer you in the wrong direction."

"Could you tell if it was *personal*? Or, perhaps, some kind of business meeting?" I said.

The bartender laughed. "I don't pay that much attention. I'm sorry. Especially out in the dining room when I have a full bar to worry about." He looked back and forth. "Twenty-eight stools at this bar... keeps an old guy like me busy."

I turned to Alex. "You have that photo of Linda Green?"

"Why would it be Linda Green?" she said.

"Humor me. Show him the picture."

Alex had her phone out, tapped the screen, and turned it toward the bartender. She showed him the only photo she'd found online of Linda Green. "Any chance it was this woman?"

He shook his head right away. "She looks familiar. Might've been in here at some point, but not with Shondra and that man she was with."

Alex tucked her phone in her pocket and gave me a look, like she wanted to say *Why would it be Linda Green?*

I pulled out my phone and had a picture of Mindy Hawkins, the one where she was dressed in a long gown, much different from the biker-chick look she had when she showed up at my boat. I showed it to the bartender. "This her?"

He looked, studied it for a couple of moments with his eyes squinted. He finally shook his head. "I don't think so. I mean, this woman was younger than her." He looked from the phone. "So who is this woman you're looking for? She have something to do with the case?"

I picked up my beer, looked at him over the top, but didn't answer. I put the bottle down, shaking my head. "I have no idea. Until you mentioned a third wheel, we didn't know who we were looking for."

The bartender walked away and I said, "Two of the three people at that table are dead. We might want to find out who the last one standing is. Before another body shows up."

# Chapter 28

RAY RIVERS STOOD INSIDE the garage at his house, watching me and Alex as we pulled up in his driveway. There was no other car there.

He had a shovel in his hand as Alex and I walked toward him. "Doing some digging?" I said.

Ray looked down at the shovel. "Oh, this?" He shook his head. "I'm just going through some things." He looked back into the garage. "I end up going away for a while, I'm not sure what'll happen to all this stuff." He leaned the shovel up against the wall with the other dozen or so yard tools. "Shondra liked to work out in the yard," he said. "Not me. The only grass I cared about was the one on the football field."

I stopped outside the garage, a few feet from Ray. "Did Wendell call you?"

He nodded. "About Wilmington's? Yeah, he did. Told me what the bartender said." He slowly shook his head. "I knew they were together that night."

I said, "But like I told Wendell, it doesn't mean Shondra and Barry were having an affair. And my gut tells me they were there for another reason, considering someone else was with them." I ducked inside the garage. "You have any idea who it could have been?" I looked up at the garage door opener.

"No idea at all," he said. "Bartender didn't know?"

"I showed him a couple of photos."

The garage was built for two cars, but with what looked like a lot of junk spread all over the place, there was barely room for one. The other side, with the door closed, had boxes piled ten feet high. Some were closed. Some open, including one with golf clubs sticking up out of it. Another had baseball bats and what looked like lacrosse sticks. One of those padded steel sleds used in football training was pushed up against the far wall from where we stood, with more boxes piled around it. "You already cleaning out the store?"

"Huh?" He turned to the other side of the garage. "Oh, that? No, just some things I've stored here over the years."

Alex walked to the other side, looking inside the boxes. She said, "Ray, have you been to your store?"

"No. I don't see the sense in even trying to open right now," he said. "The whole city thinks I killed my wife. I can't imagine there'll be any business for me. At least not until this gets straightened out."

"What about your landlord?" I said. "You talk to him?"

"Not yet. Wendell told me to let him handle it. I gave him a copy of my lease."

"I thought maybe you'd go right over there, make sure he hadn't emptied the place out on you. What about the owner next door... the dry cleaners? You talk to him?"

Again, Ray shook his head. "Honestly, Henry, I have other things to worry about right now. I lose that store"—he shrugged—"maybe it wasn't meant to be. To be honest, the place has been a drain on my money for the past year. And without the income from coaching..."

I hadn't been able to figure out Ray's financial situation but was beginning to wonder if money had become a problem for him. I knew he'd made a decent salary in the NFL. But it's not unheard of for players to go broke following their careers. Especially if that career was short. Although I thought if he had enough to hire Wendell, he must've had something. Even writing a letter to Ray's landlord wasn't going to be cheap. Everything you asked a lawyer to do ends up on your bill. That includes the so-called free coffee and bottled water you get at the office.

"I assume you at least went back to see if anything else was missing?" I said.

"My store?" Ray said.

Alex said, "To see if anything else was taken."

"I don't even have a car to drive over there," Ray said. "The insurance company totaled the Suburban. I can't even drive Shondra's car. It's still at the sheriff's office."

"You can always call one of us," I said, "you need a ride."

Alex and I both looked at each other, and I said to Ray, "We're doing all we can right now, to get this all cleared up. At some point, hopefully you can try to put some of it behind you." I looked down at the garage floor for a moment. I looked him in the eye. "But I need to ask you... Is there anything you haven't told us? Anything, maybe, we should know?"

Ray stared back at me and shrugged. "Like what?"

I leaned with one hand on a wooden workbench covered in empty plastic planters, tools, and bags of soil. "Anything," I said. "Maybe about what happened with your job? Barry? I still find it hard to believe you were fired and didn't demand some kind of explanation."

"What are you asking?" Ray said.

I hesitated. I didn't want to pressure Ray if doing so would take things in the wrong direction. "There's something we're missing. And I hope you're being straight with us."

Ray took off his baseball cap and rubbed the top of his head. After a long pause, he looked from me to Alex, then walked toward the driveway. He stood under the open garage door with his back to us.

"Ray?" I said. "What is it?"

He turned after a couple of moments and looked back at me and Alex. "I stole money."

I was expecting him to say something. I didn't know what it would be. Stealing money wasn't one of my first thoughts. "You want to explain?"

Ray swallowed hard, nodding with his eyes down. "I stole from the school. And somehow Barry found out. He confronted me, told me he couldn't let it slide."

"So all this time, you've been lying about it?" I said.

He raised his eyes. "I regret what I did. But I never thought it would come to this."

I thought for a moment. "Wait. Are you trying to say this could have something to do with Shondra? Did she know about this?"

He shrugged. "I don't know."

"You don't know?" Alex said, her voice showing how upset she was. Maybe because she's been right from the beginning. "How could you not know? Wouldn't she've said something to you?"

Ray didn't answer.

"How much money was stolen?" I said.

Ray walked over to the workbench and leaned back against it, his hands tucked in his pockets. "Just a little over a grand. About thirteen hundred dollars. Maybe a little more."

I looked at Alex, shaking my head. "Ray, what's the story here? Every time we start to think you're being straight with us…" I stepped toward him. "Ray?"

He raised his eyes to mine.

"Did you kill Shondra?"

"No!" he snapped, shaking his head. "You gotta believe me. Why would I kill her?"

"That's what I keep wondering. And, I hate to say it, but I keep finding reasons why it could've been you."

"Because I stole money?"

I had to think about it for a moment. There seemed to be a handful of reasons. And if I were Mike Stone, I'd be feeling pretty good about my case. I wanted to believe Ray was innocent. But he made it a challenge every time I uncovered another lie.

I said, "Can you tell me how you stole this money?"

Ray took a deep breath. "Well…" He looked over toward the boxes on the other side of the garage. "One of the sporting goods wholesalers I know through the store, he came up with a scheme where I'd order equipment for the team, small items—invoices nobody would notice—and he'd never actually deliver anything. He'd give me a cut of the money he was paid from the school."

I looked down at the floor. "Don't invoices like that go through the Financial Services Department?"

Ray nodded. Eventually. But like I said, they were small invoices, so—"

"What if Shondra saw them?" I said. "Is that possible?"

Ray looked confused. He rubbed the back of his neck. "I... I guess that's possible, but—"

"What if Shondra somehow knew?" I said. "What if Barry told her directly?"

Alex looked at me and Ray. "And what if it turns out she was caught trying to cover up your crime?"

"They wouldn't have just transferred her to another department," I said, turning to Ray. "How long has this been going on?"

He cleared his throat, taking his time before he answered. "Uh, about a year. It wasn't all at once either. Just a few hundred here and there. Pocket change, you know? I didn't know how easy it would be."

"Until you got caught," I said.

Ray nodded. "Nobody knew but Barry."

I shook my head. "But Shondra was removed from her position with the Financial Services Department. Her boss, Linda Green, set up some kind of audit with John Mazer."

"Mazer?" Ray said, his head cocked back, surprised.

"I was sure he was up to something there," I said. "But here it is, once again. It turns out, it was you?"

"But how can you say this has anything to do with Shondra's murder? You think it gives me a reason to kill her? For taking thirteen hundred dollars?" Ray shook his head. "And besides, this would have gotten out by now. Shondra would have been fired. I'd probably go to jail."

Alex gave me a look.

Ray was right.

"What if they found something but couldn't figure out exactly what it was?" I said. "Maybe Shondra did just enough to hide the fact her own husband was stealing from the school. But she never expected an outside auditor to show up and—"

Alex said to Ray, "Shondra never mentioned John Mazer's name at any point?"

Ray shook his head in disbelief. "Are you sure it was him?"

I picked up the shovel Ray had leaned against the wall. "Yes, I'm sure. And what's funny is he has something in his past similar to this very situation."

I thought back to the very first time Ray came to see me at Billy's Place. "Somebody knows something about this," I said. "Whoever was harassing you, trying to blame you for Barry's death, knew something about what you did. I'm sure of it."

Alex had her eyes on me, shaking her head. "How can you be sure? None of this makes any sense." She looked over at the piles of boxes and sports equipment on the other side of the garage. "Ray was skimming off the top of invoices. Just like Mazer was doing. Even Billy deals with it—all those bartenders he's fired. It usually doesn't lead to murder."

# Chapter 29

LINDA GREEN HADN'T ANSWERED the cell phone number we had for her, although her message was the generic one, simply stating the number:

*The number you have reached...*

I couldn't be sure it was hers. And the home address Alex found looked to be accurate, although after five minutes of standing outside her apartment door, it was clear she either wasn't home, or wasn't going to answer.

Linda Green had suddenly become hard to find.

We left her apartment building and jumped on Southside Boulevard. I turned my headlights on as we crossed over to Route 202. The sun had started to go down.

Alex had her head turned, staring out the passenger window and staying quiet for a good part of the ride.

I gave her a light backhanded slap on the side of her leg. "Are you going to tell me what's going through your mind?"

She gave me a cold stare. "I didn't like this case from the beginning. And the more Ray lies, the more I want to throw up my hands and face the fact there's a very good chance Mike got this one right."

I wasn't about to tell her she was wrong. She wasn't. But I wasn't ready to throw in the towel either. "Am I supposed to ignore all that's happened? Pretend someone didn't try to take me out with their car?" I pointed at the wound, although healing, was still clearly visible above my nose. "You don't think it's valid to think whoever I ran into in back of Ray's store was likely the person trying to frame Ray for his wife's murder?"

She stared at me, lips pressed together as she nodded, rubbing the back of her neck. "I'm sorry. But it's been frustrating trying to help a man who makes it impossible to believe him. I'm afraid, at this point, it's going to take a bit of luck, hoping we stumble onto something."

I looked at her and smiled. "Nothing wrong with hope and a little luck," I said. "It's not like it hasn't helped us in the past?" I laughed. "Maybe you should go back into law enforcement."

Alex shot me a look. "Is that what you want?"

"Give me a break," I said. "Why would you even think I—"

"I'm serious," she said. "Maybe you're not meant to have a partner. Some people prefer to go it alone."

I wanted to respond but felt maybe it would be better if we just let things hang. Although I knew this case had sucked the life out of Alex, I was afraid the way she was acting—the way both of us were acting—might have all been rooted in what happened between us down in Naples.

· · · · · · · · · · ·

I drove onto Deerwood Drive and into the office park, turning into the parking lot outside John Mazer's office.

Alex and I had both been quiet for the remainder of the ride and stayed that way as we stepped from the car and walked into the building.

I stepped ahead of Alex and through the lobby but was too impatient to wait for the elevator and turned for the door to the stairs. I started up the stairs toward the second floor, Alex coming up behind me.

But I stopped when I got to the top. I was about to reach to pull open the door, but I turned, without much thought, and grabbed Alex. I wrapped my arms around her and we kissed.

It was as if we'd forgotten why we were there.

*What murder investigation?*

We let go of each other and I looked into her eyes. "Don't ever try to tell me I'm better off alone."

I reached around her and pulled open the door, walking ahead of her.

She came up behind me, and somehow we both acted as if nothing had happened.

We continued down the hall and stopped where Mazer Accounting Services was etched in white on a black plastic sign on the door.

I knocked and realized the door was slightly open. Nobody answered. So I pushed it open and stepped into a space I wasn't expecting.

It wasn't a large office with a receptionist and dozens of employees buzzing around, like I'd assumed I'd see. Instead, the dimly lit office was no bigger than a long and narrow walk-in closet, six feet wide at most and maybe ten feet long. It had enough space for the two desks: one on the right wall next to where I stood, and the other farther back, against the wall on the left. There was a window at the far end of the space, overlooking the darkness outside.

The desk closest to the door had a chair pushed under it. Papers were stacked on top, along with a pile of *Accounting Today* magazines. The only light came from the lamp and computer on the desk straight ahead. There was an Atlanta Falcons coffee mug in front of an office phone under the lamp.

I put my hand over the mug. It was still warm. "He's still here, somewhere," I said. I stepped out from the office and looked back and forth along the hall. The entire office building was quiet. There were windows along the hall, overlooking the parking lot down below.

There was a bang when the HVAC system kicked on. Air blew out from the vents on the ceiling above me.

I went back into the office. Alex was in front of the computer on the desk at the other end. "What are you doing?" I said, my voice hushed.

"Just looking," she said, leaning with one hand on her knee, the other on the computer mouse as she studied the screen.

A voice came up from behind me.

"What the hell are you doing in my office?"

I turned and John Mazer stood looking back at me from just outside in the hall, his silly bow tie on his neck. He tried to look past me into his office, where Alex backed away from his computer. "What do you think you're doing?" he said.

I blocked him from getting past me and reached into my pocket. I pulled out the thousand-dollar check he had given me, holding it up. "I wanted to come by to give you this. I don't want your money. I'd hate to be implicated in any way."

He stared at the check but didn't take it from my hand. "Implicated? Implicated in what?"

"I'm not sure yet," I said. "But I know all about your past, up in Georgia," I said. "And it's got me thinking. If Linda Green was somehow involved in your embezzlement scheme up there, who's to say the two of you aren't up to something down here?"

He shoved past me, pushing me out of his way, and walked toward the desk on the other side of his office.

Alex and I both looked at him.

"So what's your scheme now?" I said. Although the truth was, I was making accusations with little to back them up. Sometimes, it's how things worked.

"I have no idea what you're talking about."

"You didn't embezzle money up in Georgia? When you were CFO for—"

"I paid a price for that. What I'm saying is, whatever you've heard, there is nothing illegal going on. And *definitely* not with Linda Green."

"Really? Why would she bring in someone like you to audit their financials? I can't imagine the board would be happy to know she brought in someone with as shady a past as yours."

He shook his head. "I'm not allowed a second chance?"

I laughed. "I don't know. I've run into enough guys like you in my lifetime. I'd guess you can't help yourself. It's all about money. It's your drug."

"You don't know a thing about me," John said. He pointed toward the door. "I want you out of my office. Right now. Before I call the sheriff's office." His voice remained calm, but his face told a different story.

"Call the cops? And tell them what?" I said. "I don't care what you try to tell me. I know something went on at that school with you and Linda. And whatever it is, we're going to figure it out."

John shot me a look like I was the one who was crazy. "You have no reason at all to believe there was anything going on. You don't know what you're talking about." He picked up his phone. "I'm calling the police right now, if you don't leave."

I refused to budge. I had no idea if I was going to come up empty, but there was something in my gut telling me this guy, Mazer, had been up to no good. And the only chance I had was if I could somehow get him to crack.

"Why don't you tell me what happened with Shondra Rivers. Was she just a scapegoat in your scheme? Did she figure out what you were up to? Did she get in the way?"

Every little nudge, the look on Mazer's face told me he was about to snap.

But he just stared back at me, shaking his head with that cocky grin on his face. "You have no idea what you're talking about," he said. "If you're trying to insinuate I've done something wrong, then you'd better tell me what it is. Otherwise, I want the two of you to get the hell out of my office!"

"Why can't you tell me what happened with Shondra Rivers? If you'd found something damaging enough, I don't know how she'd simply be transferred to another department. Wouldn't she've been fired?" I shook my head and took a step toward him. "I'm going to lean toward it being you and Linda. I'm guessing Shondra found whatever it was you were trying to hide."

John turned to his desk and yanked open a drawer, pulling out a .38 revolver. He pointed it toward me and Alex. "Close that door. And make sure it's locked. Then sit your asses down. Keep your hands where I can see them."

Alex closed the door and locked it. We both kept our hands raised.

I gave Alex a look, wondering if she was armed. But she hadn't been carrying her Glock as much lately. Although I wished she had.

"Listen," John said, waving his gun. "Sit down." He nodded toward the chair tucked under the desk next to me and Alex. He grabbed the chair under the desk next to him and rolled it toward me, kicking it with his foot to give it a final shove in my direction. It slammed into my knees. He waved the gun. "I said, sit down!"

Alex pulled out the chair from the desk next to us and sat down. She said to John, "What are you going to do? Shoot us right here in your office?"

I sat down in the chair and looked around, our backs to the closed door. "Listen, I could care less about what kind of scheme you have going on. I don't care who is stealing money. Do what you gotta do. The only thing I want to know is who killed Shondra Rivers."

John shrugged. "If you're trying to imply it was me, what reason would I have to kill her? She seemed to be a nice enough person, to be honest. Smart, too. A lot smarter than her husband, if you ask me. But if you think she's just some innocent victim..." He laughed.

"What's that supposed to mean?" I said.

"Did you know her husband was stealing from the school? Padding his pockets with money meant for sports?"

I didn't respond and wasn't going to admit I already knew.

John had a sly smile on his face. "But that was nothing compared to what his wife and Barry Hawkins had pulled off."

I stared back at him, curious. And maybe confused.

"Why do you think he fired Ray so fast? If Barry had done anything else about it, other than get Ray out of there and keep it quiet, it would have shined a light on the money Barry and his girlfriend were already stealing."

Alex and I both looked at each other.

"What the hell are you talking about?" I said. "Barry Hawkins was stealing money?"

John nodded. "And his girlfriend, Shondra. The two had quite a little scheme going. Looks like Mr. and Mrs. Rivers were broke. But Ray, he was pocketing chump change while Shondra and Barry were taking thousands from the school. It just so happened Linda hired me as a consultant. I won't lie, tell you I didn't need the money. But let's just say, I know how things work. It's like when someone hires a computer hacker to stop the computer hackers. You know what I mean? I know how it works."

"I don't believe you," I said.

"What's not to believe? What good would it do me to lie about it?"

"How much did they take?"

"Since they started?" He looked up toward the ceiling, holding his chin. "Two hundred thousand, seven hundred and fifty dollars."

"From the school?" Alex said.

Barry nodded, his eyebrows raised. "A lot of money, right? It's so tempting when you're responsible for... when you have access to all that money. If you think you're smart enough, as Shondra was, you believe you can get away with it. But, as I learned the hard way, eventually everyone gets caught. Unless you weren't, technically, involved."

"Linda Green?" I said.

He shook his head with a shrug. "I didn't say anything about Linda, did I?" He smirked, let out a slight laugh.

Alex said, "If this is true, then why weren't the police involved? And why would Shondra simply be transferred to another department?"

John smiled, like he was pleased with himself. He leaned back against his desk, the gun still pointing our way. "What do you think was going to happen with all that money she took if we informed the police? Just let it go? Give it back to the school so they could burn through it in the most foolish ways? Like they always have?" He shook his head. "It was the money Ray had stolen that raised the red flag with Linda. It's why she hired me, only to discover all that money. Gone."

"You wanted the money," I said.

John looked me in the eye. "I confronted Shondra. And it didn't take her long to throw Barry under the bus. She placed all the blame on him, like she had nothing to do with it. I got the feeling Barry used her, to make sure his tracks were covered. Especially after he learned Ray was skimming off the top too. Funny thing was, we'd already gotten Barry to confess before we spoke to Shondra. He begged us not to go to the police, that he'd give us a cut of what was left."

Looking at Alex, I could see she was having a hard time believing Mazer was telling the truth.

I said to John, "So, Barry paid you off? Then, what, you killed him?"

He shook his head. "I didn't kill him. He was supposed to get us the money. We were going to meet the evening he was found on the shower floor."

I wasn't sure I believed a word he was saying, and it seemed clear to me Mazer was Barry's killer. "Did you kill Shondra?"

John looked around his office, shaking his head. "I didn't kill anyone. And I still haven't found the money. If I had, you think I'd still be stuck in this crappy little office?"

I nodded at the gun in his hand. "So what's the purpose of holding us here? Sounds to me, at least if I wanted to believe you, you've almost done nothing wrong."

"Well, for one, I thought maybe you could lead me to the money. I was sure you or Ray knew something about it. But apparently, you're not as smart as I'd heard. That means you won't be of much use to me at all, other than opening your mouth to the cops. And I'd hate to think, now that you know there's at least two hundred grand hidden somewhere... I guess it'd be in my best interest to make sure you and your girlfriend don't try to find it for yourselves."

I shook my head. "I'm not interested."

"Maybe not. But if your goal is to find Shondra's killer, I'd have to guess you're looking for the same person I am." He wiped the sweat from his forehead with the back of his hand. "I don't suppose you're interested in making some kind of deal?"

I shook my head. "I don't make deals. Not with someone like you."

"Not even for a share of what's left?" Mazer said.

I narrowed my eyes, staring back at him. "Didn't you hear me? I said no."

He shrugged. "Well, then, you give me no choice. I can't have you and your pretty girlfriend in my way."

I gave Alex a quick glance, saw her looking around for something to help get us out of the situation we found ourselves in.

I turned back to John. "So you're just going to kill us?"

He pulled at his chin, thinking. "Well, I probably don't want to do it right here. This place charges an arm and a leg for cleaning." He stepped from the desk and wiggled the .38 toward us. "Get up," he said. "Both of you. We're going for a ride."

I didn't know if this guy had it in him to pull the trigger. He claimed not to be a killer. But I had a feeling it was all part of his lie. As far as I was concerned, the chances were good he took out both Barry and Shondra. Although I wasn't sure it would do him much good, especially considering one of them had to know where the money was hidden.

Alex and I both stood.

"You," he said, pointing the gun toward Alex. "Open the door."

She stood still, hands up in front of her.

"You heard me," he said. "Open the door. But first, do me a favor; make sure there's nobody out there." He took a step closer. "Turn around."

I did as he asked and he stuck the gun into my back.

Alex unlocked the door and pulled on the knob. She started to open the door, slowly, and I put my hand on top of the desk chair next to me. Without looking back at Mazer, I grabbed the chair with two hands and swung it on its wheels, rolling it hard and fast into his legs.

I hit him hard enough it knocked him back, stumbling into his desk. I turned and jumped at him, grabbing his wrist as we landed on top of his desk—the computer, mug, and lamp crashing to the floor.

I tried to wrestle the gun from his hand, but he was stronger than he looked, especially for a guy who wore a bow tie.

He fired a shot in the air, the bullet penetrating the ceiling.

I had him on his back, finally pinning his gun hand back against the desk. But with his free hand, he grabbed on to my throat, pushing me up off of him.

Alex hurried over and tried to help, but he fired another shot. Alex went down, and for a moment I was sure she'd been shot.

I tried to yell for her, but Mazer squeezed harder on my throat.

I still had his wrist and slammed it harder on the desk, this time knocking the gun out of his hand and onto the floor.

I got a glance of Alex, coming to her feet. I still didn't know if she was all right or if she had the gun.

Mazer drove his elbow into my face and broke free from under me. He rolled off the desk and went after Alex as she tried to reach for the gun. He slammed into her, sending her back into the other desk next to the door. The desk tipped as they crashed into it, drawers falling out with everything inside falling to the floor.

I charged Mazer, but he grabbed a pen from the mess beneath him, came up swinging his arm, holding the pen like a weapon in his hand.

I was close enough to grab him, but he jammed the pen into me, sticking it deep into the meat of my shoulder.

I yelled in pain, ripping the bloody pen from my arm.

Alex rolled on the floor and grabbed the gun, got up on one knee and held it with both hands, pointing it no more than six inches from John's face. "Back away," she said, coming to her feet.

John got up, holding his hands up. "Don't shoot."

She rose to her feet, taking a step back toward the door, the gun still on Mazer. She looked at the blood coming down my arm. "Are you going to live?"

I nodded and pulled out my phone. It was hard to read the screen with the cracks on the front. But I could see the number I was looking for, and dialed Mike Stone's cell.

# Chapter 30

BLUE LIGHTS FILLED THE darkness outside John Mazer's building with the half dozen or so sheriff's vehicles in the parking lot. Mike Stone's Crown Vic had two wheels up on the curb in front of the entrance.

Mike walked out from inside the building ahead of two officers, one holding John Mazer by the arm, his wrists cuffed behind his back.

Alex and I were leaning on the back of the Mustang when Mazer gave us a look as the officer eased him into the back seat of the cruiser.

I grabbed my shoulder and looked at the dried spot of blood surrounding the hole in my shirt where the pen had sunk through.

We had explained most of what we knew to Mike, detailing the alleged scheme Shondra and Barry were involved in and how much money Mazer claimed they stole.

Mike, of course, was skeptical. "Mazer wouldn't talk," he said. "And I don't know about this Linda Green, but we're sending a couple officers over to her apartment now." His eyes were on my shoulder, shaking his head. "Only you would get stabbed with a pen, Walsh." He let out a sigh and rolled his eyes.

"How long can you hold him if he doesn't talk?"

Mike pulled a cigarette from his pack and stuck it in his mouth. "That's a good question," he said. "He claims you're making it all up, said he was only protecting himself when he walked in, found you two in his office."

"You at least have him on assault," Alex said, pointing to my shoulder.

Mike nodded. "We'll come up with a couple of things. False imprisonment is another." He lit his cigarette and took a drag, turning to look toward the building's entrance. After a moment, he turned back, looked from me to Alex. "I hope you understand none of this does much to help Ray Rivers, right?"

"Mazer got a record. Stabbed me with a pen, and"—I thought, looking toward the sheriff's vehicle driving away with Mazer in the back—"I'm pretty sure firing a weapon not five feet from someone could technically be attempted murder, no? And by him admitting he was supposed to get money from Barry, you have to admit the chance his death was an accident is slim."

Mike drew from his cigarette, staring back at me. "How many times do I have to tell you, I don't need some hack to tell me how to do my job?" He started for his car, stopping at the driver-side door. He looked back at me and Alex. "Oh, and make sure your phones are on. I may need you both down the station." He opened the door, ducked inside the Crown Vic, and took off out of the parking lot.

• • • • • • • • •

The lights looked to be turned off at Ray's house when we pulled in the driveway. Even the lamp over the front door was out. I pulled up and parked in front of the garage door to the right. Alex and I got out and stepped through the darkness. The temperature had dropped, with a slight chill hanging in the air.

I pressed the button for the doorbell, but it didn't ring. "I'm not sure why, but it looks like the power's out." I knocked on the door. "Ray? Are you there?" I waited, then knocked again, a little harder. I pulled my phone from my pocket and dialed Ray's number. I heard a ringing on the other side of the door. "You hear that?" I said, turning to Alex.

She stepped next to me and put her ear against the glass. "Sounds to me like he's in there."

"With all the lights off?" I said. I banged on the door. "Ray?" I knocked some more. "Open the door!"

The phone stopped ringing. And Ray still hadn't come to the door.

I pounded on the door. "Ray!"

No response.

I walked down the steps, past Alex, next trying the garage door. But it wouldn't budge, so Alex and I walked around the house and into the backyard. I tried two different doors and numerous windows. Everything was locked.

I took my phone from my pocket and dialed it again, listening for the ring. It was louder from where I stood than it had been at the front door. Looking through the sliding glass, the inside of Ray's house was total darkness.

Alex was at another window a few feet down from me, up on her toes looking in. "I see it," she said. "His phone... it's lighting up. It's inside on the floor."

I hurried to the window where she stood and looked inside, seeing the phone for myself, the screen glowing bright until the ringing stopped. I put my phone up to my ear and listened to Ray's voicemail message come on.

"What if he's in there?" I said. "What if..." I dialed my phone and called Wendell Richards. It took five rings before he finally answered. "Henry?" he said. "Is everything all right?"

"I'm not sure," I said. "I'm at Ray's house. He's not answering his phone. And the place is pitch black inside. Like there's no power."

"Are you sure he's not sleeping?"

"I can see his phone on the floor. I was hoping you knew where he was, but I'm starting to think something happened to him."

"Can't you get inside?" he said.

I looked around the ground for something to either break the window or pry open the door. "When was the last time you talked to him?"

Wendell paused on the other line. "This morning," he said. "Briefly. He said he was going to his store."

"Did he go?" I said.

"I hadn't heard from him since."

"Okay, let me see if I can find him," I said.

"Let me know, all right?"

"Sure." I hung up and turned to Alex. "Ray was supposedly going back to his store this morning. At least according to Wendell."

"What's that mean?" she said.

"I don't know. I was afraid if Ray went there, that kid, Chance, would've changed the locks or something foolish like that. I'd hate to see how Ray would react if that was the case."

I walked toward the edge of the yard. A flowering tree was surrounded by concrete pavers. I dug one up from the soil and picked it up, walking to one of the windows to the left of the sliding glass door. I tapped the glass with the paver and the window shattered. Using the same paver, I tried to clear the jagged edges of glass sticking out from the frame. I cleared what I could and pulled myself up, slid my body through, feet first, and landed on the floor inside Ray's kitchen. The glass crunched under my shoes.

"You all right?" Alex said.

I didn't answer but called for Ray. "Ray? Are you here?" I tried a switch on the wall, but the lights didn't come on. It was almost complete silence in the house, without even a hum from the refrigerator a few feet from where I stood. I walked from the kitchen to the sliding glass door and slid it open for Alex.

"There's definitely no power in here," I said. I tried another light switch without luck and walked back into the kitchen. I opened the refrigerator door and a bad smell hit me in the nose, like whatever was inside had spoiled.

But it wasn't the only bad smell in the house.

Alex shined the flashlight from her phone, moving it around the kitchen.

I pulled my phone out and again dialed Ray's phone. A light came from the hall.

Alex walked past me and bent down to pick up the phone, outside the doorway. She tapped the screen and stopped the call. "It's locked," she said, handing me the phone.

It was no doubt strange his phone was on the floor in his house. "This doesn't look good," I said. I had a pit in my stomach. "Maybe you should call Mike." I activated the flashlight on my phone, but it wasn't very bright. I walked from the kitchen and turned down the hall. I poked my head into the dining room and crouched down to look around the floor and under the table.

Alex had gone in the other direction, toward the front door. I could see the light from her phone shining into another room.

"You see anything?" I said.

She turned the corner and had the light off on her phone. "Nothing."

I looked in the small half bath off the hall. Like the rest of the house, it was empty. "What I'd like to know is why the power's off?" I said.

"Maybe he hasn't paid his bills?"

We continued together toward the front door and stopped at the bottom of the stairs. I looked up and called Ray's name, as if for some reason he'd suddenly answer.

I was afraid of what we might find but headed up the stairs anyway. There was a window high up over the foyer, with moonlight coming through it. Light shined on the very top step and into a portion of the open hall on the second floor.

I walked to the top of the stairs and looked to my right. I already knew it was Ray and Shondra's bedroom. The room where Shondra was killed.

I walked toward the bedroom and stepped past where the railing ended at the wall. It blocked the light from over the foyer so the floor was dark. I had my eyes ahead and tripped over something in front of the doorway to the bedroom. I grabbed the frame on the door and stopped myself from falling.

Alex came up the stairs and stood behind me. "Did you just fall?" She shined the light from her phone toward me, shifting it down toward what I'd tripped over.

And there he was.

Ray was facedown on the floor, blood coming through the back of his gray hooded sweatshirt. "Ray?" I said, dropping to one knee. I turned him over and felt his wrist for a pulse. "Oh no," I said. "No..."

Alex shined the light on us. "Is he..."

I looked up at her, squinting with the light in my face. "Somebody shot him," I said. I turned my eyes back to Ray. "He's dead."

# Chapter 31

I SAT SLUMPED IN my chair on the dock by my boat. With half a bottle of Jack Daniels in my hand, I realized it had only been since noon when I cracked open the bottle. The bottle was half empty. I poured another glass and looked at it from the side. It was half full.

I took a sip and closed my eyes, taking in the warmth from the sun. After the spell of below-normal cold, the heat—on top of the liquor flowing through my veins—made me feel pretty good.

Or at least that's what I tried to tell myself.

I was in no condition to do much of anything else but just sit.

And drink, of course.

It wasn't like I *wanted* to do anything else either.

I called my parents the night before, when I was still somewhat sober, and let them know of my potential plans to come out and see them again. I felt guilty for leaving so fast after Mom fell and, with the investigation falling apart and Ray Rivers dead with a murder charge never fully proven by the sheriff's office—or disproven by me—I wish I'd never left Naples in the first place.

I'd had some cases in the past I considered unsuccessful, but I'd never had one go as poorly as the case of Shondra Rivers.

I hadn't spoken to anyone besides my parents. I had some small talk with fellow live-aboards at the marina, but nothing I actually remembered.

My only concern was I'd run out of Jack. Although my friends who owned the restaurant had already sold me a couple of bottles, since I hadn't been in any condition to drive when I ran out.

Alex had left me four or five messages to call her. But I didn't. It wasn't that I left her hanging. I sent her a text, told her I'd call her when I could. That was how I left it. Other than that text, we hadn't spoken since the night we found Ray's body.

Billy had called more than once, but he wasn't one for leaving messages unless there was some kind of emergency or something urgent. I hadn't called him back either.

I sipped my drink and got up from my chair to get more ice. But the liquor had gotten the best of me as I stumbled with my first step. I grabbed the side of the boat to catch myself and dropped my glass. It didn't break, but bounced off the edge of the dock and splashed in the water.

I pulled myself up the ladder and onto my boat, got a new glass, and filled my ice bucket with enough cubes so I wouldn't have to get up again. As long as they didn't melt.

I plopped back down in my chair with a fresh drink, about to take a sip.

Someone called my name.

With my chair facing the river, I had to make the effort and turn my body, looking over my shoulder toward the parking lot. I didn't see anyone.

I heard my name once more and turned again. This time, I saw who it was. "I thought that was you," I said, my tongue tied. It was the first time words came out of my mouth since the night before.

Billy stepped up onto the dock and put his hand on my shoulder. "Glad to see you're alive?" he said. He scratched the growth on his face, looking at the glass in my hand.

"Are you growing a beard?" I said.

He shrugged, rubbing his face again. "I don't know. Maybe. It gives me something to do with my hands."

I raised my glass. "I like it."

"Hope you don't mind me stopping by," Billy said. "I knew you weren't in the mood for talking but figured I should at least come by, make sure you're not facedown somewhere."

I shrugged, tried to take a sip from my glass but missed my lip. The Jack dripped down my chin and onto my shirt. "What a waste," I said. I tucked my chin and looked down at the spot of Jack Daniels on my shirt.

"How long've you been drinking?"

"In total? I don't know. I guess since I was forced to resign up in Rhode Island." I pushed out a grin.

Billy rolled his eyes. "I'm talking about now," he said. "You look like you've had a few."

I reached for the bottle under my chair and held it up to him. "You want some?"

He laughed. "I've gone this long without a drink. I'm not about to start now."

I shrugged and slid the bottle back under my chair.

Billy climbed up onto my boat and came down with the lawn chair with the yellow-striped webbing. It was the one my mom had always used, although I'd had the webbing replaced a couple of times since. He opened up the chair and placed it down a few feet from me.

We both sat quiet, watching the river.

It seemed like a good ten minutes with neither of us saying a word. It might've been more.

There aren't many people in life you can sit next to in silence without feeling uncomfortable. Billy was one of those people.

He said, "Alex said you haven't called her?"

I rolled my head against the back of my chair to face him. "I'm just hangin' out. Trying to enjoy life."

Billy's eyes went to the bottle under my chair. "You and your buddy Jack Daniels, huh?"

I nodded. "Yup."

He turned to the river again. "So, what's the story? You feeling bad for yourself? Is that what you're doing here?" He looked me in the eye.

I thought for a moment. "I don't know. Not really."

"No? Then what is it?"

It took me a couple of moments to answer. "I just didn't expect it," I said. "Not solving a case is one thing. But you know, the guy died before I could do anything to clear his name. That kind of sucks."

Billy watched me with sad eyes... like he felt bad for me.

"What are you giving me that look for?" I said. I tried to sit up straight on the chair, but again spilled my drink on my shirt.

"So, what are you going to do?" he said.

I shrugged, forcing a tight-lipped smile. "Drink?"

Billy got up from his chair. "I think you're going to have to move on. You have to put it behind you. Let the cops do their job. Hopefully, one day, the truth will come out."

I held my glass up in front of my mouth. "You think the truth just shows up?"

"You don't have to get snippy with me," Billy said.

I put my hand up, like I was giving him a wave. "Was that snippy?" I shrugged, feeling the weight of the alcohol on my brain. "You're right. I'm sorry." I looked back toward the water.

Billy stood, looking out at the water, quiet once again until he said, "So, how long are you going to do this?"

"Do what?"

"This. Sit outside your boat, on a dock, getting drunk every day."

I shrugged. "I got nothing else to do."

"You think every case you ever worked on was going to go the way you wanted it to?"

"What's your point?" I said. I looked up at him. "Sorry, there I am getting snippy again."

"My point is that it's not your fault," he said.

"No? Then whose fault is it?"

"Nobody's. Why do you think there are cases just like it out there. Every police department, every law enforcement official, at one point or another, has to deal with an unsolved case."

"That's because the cops gave up," I said.

"Isn't that what you're doing?" Billy said, looking me right in the eye. "If you're not going to let it go, then I'm not sure how you should sit there, pounding back Jack Daniels. Because, to me, it looks like you think the truth is out there. But you ask me, you've given up."

I finished what was in my glass and placed it down on the dock, beneath my chair. I sat still, my hands folded on my stomach. I closed my eyes and felt the sun on my face. "I'm all washed up," I said. "I'm done. I don't have it anymore."

Billy laughed. "What is this, baseball? You're not some athlete, where you have to keep up with the young kids. You are, the older you get, the wiser you get. You don't lose it in your business. Give me a break. The only reason you'd lose anything is if you decided that's what you wanted to do."

I sat up in my chair. "You don't think I can lose it? Why don't you go talk to my mother, ask her if you can lose it."

Billy shook his head. "Come on, man. I'm not talking about—"

"It's the truth, Billy. There's a very real chance I'm already losing it." I tapped on my head with my finger. "This thing could be falling apart as we speak."

"Yeah, you keep drinking that Jack the way you are..."

I ran both hands over my face and sat forward in the chair, my elbows resting on my knees. "Honestly, I can't tell you why this is bothering me the way it is. It's not like I knew Ray very well. I mean, I should be able to get it out of my mind, right?" I looked up at him. "Alex's the one who always said I need to let things go."

"I'm not telling you to let anything go," he said.

I reached under my chair for the bottle of Jack and my glass. The ice in the bucket I brought down had already melted from the sun. I was about to pour myself a drink but stopped. I put the bottle and glass back underneath and stood up from the chair. "Honestly? Your advice is confusing me. First, you told me to let it go. Now, you're..." I scratched my head. "I don't really know what you're telling me to do."

He stared back at me for a moment, then looked out at the river. "You have to do whatever it is you think you should be doing."

I pushed my hair back on my head and took a deep breath. "I've spent my life... I've regretted leaving a career I loved. It wasn't my choice to walk away. But I did, even though I know I was right, and still let a guilty man walk free because he wore the badge."

"You're lucky you got out of there alive. I remember a customer, had a house down here but spent the summers in Rhode Island. He used to wear a T-shirt that said, Rhode Island, the State of Corruption." Billy again put his hand on my shoulder. "Why don't you go in and take a nap." He reached down and grabbed the bottle from under my chair. "You don't need this anymore."

I stood up but had to hold on to the armrest of the chair to steady myself. "What are you doing? You're taking that? Are you serious?"

Billy turned with my bottle in his hand and stepped off the dock toward the parking lot. "Call me after your nap. Or, better yet, call Alex." He walked to his car and gave me one last glance before he got inside and drove away.

# Chapter 32

I STOOD ON THE porch at Alex's house, waiting after I'd knocked on her door. Raz had his big snout in the window, steaming up the glass, paws on the sill looking out at me. I heard Alex call out for me but wasn't sure where she was. I stepped off the porch and looked up toward her bedroom window.

She had poked her head out, looking down at me. "Hey," she said, smiling. "I'll be right down."

I shielded my eyes with my hand, the sun coming up over the roof. "Did I wake you?"

She shook her head. "Not at all." She closed the window.

I waited a couple of minutes on the porch, Raz staring out at me through the window. He let out a sharp bark every few seconds.

"She knows I'm here, Raz," I said.

The locks on the door clicked. Alex pulled it open, standing in the doorway with shorts and a tank top. She had that old Sharks baseball cap on her head. "Hey," is all she said. She backed away from the door and held it wide open. "Come on in."

I stepped inside and followed her toward the kitchen.

"It's nice to see you," she said, walking to the stove. "I was wondering if I'd ever hear back from you."

I leaned in the doorway, watching her fill a silver teapot. "I know you don't drink tea, but it's all I have... if you want some?"

"Sure," I said. "You have honey?"

She looked at me, smiled and nodded.

"I talked to Billy," she said, placing the pot on the stove. "He told me what you said."

"What did I say?" I said. "Honestly, I did a lot of drinking the past few days. It's all a little foggy."

"He said that too." She leaned against the counter, folding her arms in front of her. "He thinks there's no way you'll get past this without some answers."

I stared back at her, trying to gauge her expression. But it was hard to tell what she was thinking. "I think Billy was making some assumptions."

"Oh yeah? Are you saying it's not true?"

I shrugged. "I needed some time alone. I think I'm okay."

"So you're not mad at me? You're not wishing we were still investigating the case?"

I straightened out from the doorway and looked out the window into the front of Alex's house. "I don't understand why Mike refuses to believe the same person who killed Ray killed Shondra," I said.

Alex took two mugs down from the cabinet next to the stove. "I'm not sure he refused to believe it. But the evidence, he believes, proves beyond a reasonable doubt, Ray killed his wife."

"Are they even looking for Ray's killer?" I said.

"That's a foolish question."

"Is it?" I watched her, waiting. But she didn't respond.

Alex leaned with her hands on the counter. She fixed two mugs with tea bags, then turned back to me. "I have something I need to tell you."

The teapot whistled. Alex pulled it from the burner.

"I'm going up to North Carolina to interview for a position with a sheriff's office... town in Buncombe County."

It wasn't a complete shock to me. I had a pretty good feeling it had been on the table ever since Mike brought it up, like he wanted me to know my time with Alex was limited. I looked down at the floor, not sure what to say, then walked out of the kitchen. I went outside and stood on the porch, looking straight ahead. Raz followed me out.

Alex stepped out behind me. "I'm sorry if you're upset," she said.

I didn't say a word. I couldn't.

"Henry? Please. You have to understand."

I walked down the steps. I wanted to keep going, get in my car and drive away without a word. But there was no need for me to act like a child. Any more than I had already been. "I'm happy for you," I said. "Really."

"I don't believe you."

I had to shield my eyes from the sun again. "I guess the only thing I wonder is if you never wanted to deal with Ray's case because you were afraid it might..." I hesitated. "You were afraid if it went the way it did, how it wouldn't look good, when an opportunity like this came along." I started to walk toward my car.

Alex hurried down the stairs and grabbed my arm. "Henry, you know me better than that. You think I'd hold back from doing what's right?"

I shrugged. "You've got yourself to worry about." I forced a smile. "Your new career. Who could blame you?"

She closed her eyes and took a deep breath, turning to sit on the bottom step. "It's a good opportunity for me," she said. "You even said yourself, you weren't sure how long you'd be hanging around here. And what about your parents? Aren't you..."

"Did I ever say I was ready for us to break this thing apart," I said. "Didn't any of what happened between us matter?"

She kept her stare on me, taking her time before she spoke. "Of course it did."

I looked toward the Mustang. "I think I'm going to take off," I said.

"Why? What, what about your tea?"

I shrugged. "I'll take a rain check. Although I guess I'll have to cash it in soon." I headed for my car, doing all I could to keep it together and not look back. I stepped into my car and slid the key in the ignition. I started the engine and backed out from the driveway. Out of the corner of my eye I saw Alex walking toward me. But I continued into the road and drove away without giving her a chance to stop me.

· · · · · ● · · · · ·

I drove out to Fernandina Beach to clear my head, heading down 1A past the beaches until I turned into my old neighborhood. Most of the homes I grew up around had been remodeled or torn down and rebuilt from the ground up. I drove by my old house, the one I grew up in. I almost didn't recognize it. There was a new addition, increasing the size. And they'd moved the driveway to make it circular. A deck wrapped around from the side to the back of the house.

There was a time I'd regretted not buying the house from my parents, when they first decided to move. It wasn't that I wanted to care for a house. Or that I was even in any kind of financial position to buy it at the time.

I continued my drive and turned down the next road, where my friend Charlie used to live. He was raised there. Bought the house from his parents and sold it when his wife left him. He moved to South Beach about a year after losing his job as chief of Fernandina Beach Police. For someone who was as much a townie as you'd find, even Charlie knew there comes a point everyone has to make a change. Get out of Dodge.

It crossed my mind to call him, tell him I was out in front of his old house. But I wasn't in the mood for conversation.

I drove toward downtown and down Eighth Street past 8 Flags Used Cars, a place a friend of my Dad's used to own. They were one of the few trustworthy used car lots in Northeast Florida, although I wasn't sure if that reputation had changed.

As I drove past, a faded blue Volvo in the lot made me hit the brakes. It was a 240 model. Station wagon, like the yellow one my parents had when I was a kid. I pulled off the street and spotted the sticker on the rear bumper: University of South Carolina.

I was sure it was Mindy's sister's car. Kim had a For Sale sign up in the window when I first saw it. I assumed she'd decided to take the easy road, dump it off at a used car dealer. I pulled the Mustang around to the entrance and entered the lot. It was hard to tell if the place was open; not a soul around.

I stepped out from my car, started toward the Volvo.

A voice called out, "Can I help you, sir?"

I stopped and turned. A man I didn't recognize—certainly not my father's friend—walked toward me. He had a cowboy hat on his head with cowboy boots to match.

"I'm just looking," I said, hoping to cut him off before he started his pitch.

"You don't want help finding the right car?" He shrugged. "We've got plenty of—"

"I'm just looking." I said, my voice stern. You ever let a used-car salesman take control of the conversation, you'll end up driving off with a car you never wanted to buy.

The big smile showing his white-capped teeth left the man's face. He tipped his hat. "Yes, sir. I understand." He turned and nodded toward the trailer on the other side of the lot, the vinyl banner with 8 Flags Used Cars tied with rope hanging in front of it. "You need help, give me a holler."

I nodded. "Thanks." I started toward the Volvo again and pulled on the driver's door, but it was locked. "Sir?" I said, my voice raised enough so he could hear me. "You have a key to this Volvo?"

The smile came back on his face as he walked toward me. "She's a beauty, isn't she? A classic, and in real good condition. I even got a guy, you want to get a nice fresh coat of paint on her."

"Just the key would be great," I said.

He turned from me and ran for the trailer. The door swung closed behind him as he went inside. He was back out a moment later, a set of keys dangling from his finger. He hurried back over to where I stood waiting.

I reached out for the keys. "You mind telling me how long you've had this car?"

"Got it in a couple days ago. I wasn't here when it arrived."

"Any idea who sold it to you?"

He fixed his cowboy hat on his head. "I'm sorry, but we don't normally share that kind of information with our potential buyers. For a number of reasons."

"Oh yeah?" I said. "What if I'm not a potential buyer?" I unlocked the door and stuck my head inside. It stank. Maybe like marijuana. The beige leather seats were cracked, the carpet worn.

The salesman stood over me, by the open door, watching.

"You cleaned it out?" I said, looking up at him.

He nodded. "Not me personally, but it's been cleaned, if that's what you're asking."

I walked around back and looked at the USC bumper sticker. I had no doubt it was Mindy's sister Kim's car. I looked up at the man. "You don't normally remove bumper stickers?"

The man came around to where I stood, looking down. "I'll have to see to it the guy who cleans the cars gets that off of there. Sometimes he's afraid it'll ruin the paint, sticker like that mighta been on there for a good ten or so years."

I walked around the front. I looked at the lights on the driver's side, then stepped to the other front quarter. I kneeled down and looked close at the red plastic cover on one of the front lights. It was cracked, missing a tiny piece of the plastic.

The man walked over toward me, looking down. "Oh, you know... maybe this car wasn't quite ready for the lot. I can get that fixed for you, you'd like."

I ran my hand over the front quarter and could feel the dent. It wasn't very noticeable. But it was there.

The salesman said, "You know, it's not a new car. It's going to have its share of dings and dents. But I assure you—"

"Was there anything left inside the car?"

The man looked at me funny. "Like I said, I wasn't here when it came in. These cars get processed; we hope to have a title in hand but it's not always the case. Man works for us comes in a couple hours a day, cleans the cars, and gets 'em out on the lot. Some cars'll sit for weeks." He nodded at the Volvo. "Car like this one, people like these old Swedish vehicles." He put his hand on the hood. "Be gone in a day or two. So if you're interested, you might wanna act fast. Maybe we can talk some kind of deal."

I opened the passenger door again and sat inside. I opened the glove box and found nothing. I looked in the back seat, then stepped out and felt around under the seats.

The salesman stood outside the passenger door. "You mind me asking what exactly it is you're looking for?"

I stepped out, about to close the door. But I decided to get a better look under the seats. I crouched down and started with the passenger seat, got my head inside and looked underneath. There was something under the seat. I reached under it but the first thing I grabbed was an old pen that had exploded. Although the ink was dry. I looked under again and grabbed a small plastic box. When I pulled it out, I saw what it was:

The remote to a garage door opener.

# Chapter 33

I PULLED OFF TO the side of the road before the sign to the marina, not more than twenty feet from where I was hit. I stopped and parked outside the entrance, up next to the chain-link fence.

The grass along the fence was tall and thick. I wasn't sure of the exact spot where I was hit or where I'd landed. So I walked along the road, back and forth more than quite a few times, my eyes down.

I thought about that night and how dark it was. Probably too dark for me to be walking after quite a few drinks. But it happened so fast. I was never able to get a good look at the car; not with the headlights blinding me from behind every time I tried to see who was following me.

I remembered the next morning, being woken by the old man who drove me to my boat. But if I saw him today, I don't think I'd recognize him.

I continued my walk along the road, my eyes shifting from the grass to the pavement. Too much time had gone by; I knew there was a good chance I wasn't going to find what I was looking for.

When I thought it was finally time to give up, I walked back to my car and stood with the door open. I rested my elbow on the roof, looking toward the water beyond the parking lot of the marina. I finally ducked into the driver's seat. And as I started to pull the door closed, something reflected in the sun from the other side of the road.

I got out and ran to where the grass met the pavement. Sitting on top of the dirt was a small, red piece of plastic.

I picked it up and slipped it into a plastic ziplock bag and started the engine, heading out to 8 Flags Used Cars. I slammed down the pedal and squealed the tires for no other reason than I felt luck had finally tapped me on the shoulder.

It seemed like a long time coming.

· · · · ● · ● · · · ·

Billy was outside the restaurant when I pulled into the parking lot. He stood watching a delivery being unloaded from the back of a box truck, a clipboard in his hand.

He smiled and gave me a nod. "You look better than last time I saw you. Like a new man."

I didn't have time for small talk. "Be right back." I ran up the stairs and opened the office door. The lights were off and it was warm inside. The whole office was cleaner than normal, especially Alex's desk—completely cleared off. Her laptop was gone. Her mug was gone.

I stood still for a moment looking around the empty, quiet space. It was Alex who'd first persuaded me to get my private investigator's license after we solved Lance Moreau's murder when we were both still working for the Sharks. Then she helped me turn Walsh Investigations into a real business.

I was surprised to see she'd come by and cleaned the office, in preparation for her imminent departure not only from our business, but maybe from my life.

I didn't like the thought of it at all.

I opened my laptop and searched for Kim Cox. I found what I could on the database, including numerous addresses over the past five years: two in Georgia, one in Jacksonville, and three in Miami. I looked further back in her life, and twenty years earlier, her only other address was in Piney Bluff, Georgia.

It appeared that's where she came from. I assumed it was the same for Mindy. We'd already run a background search on Mindy, but I hadn't realized she and her sister were both born and raised up in Georgia.

I found plenty of photos of Kim online. She seemed to be fairly active on social media, including a professional profile on LinkedIn: Freelance IT Consultant.

I thought about the post on Twitter.

I sent the photos to my phone but printed out the most recent one I'd found of Kim. I took the printout down to my car, on my way to Wilmington's.

Billy was still outside dealing with the delivery. "Everything all right?" he said.

"I think it is," I said as I continued across the lot. "I'll fill you in later. I have to go." I stopped before I got to my car and remembered Billy had mentioned the different women Barry Hawkins had gone into Billy's Place with. I walked back and handed him the printed photo of Kim Cox. "You recognize her?"

Billy took the photo and looked it over, raising his eyes to mine. "Should I?"

"I wasn't sure if she'd been one of the women in here with Barry Hawkins."

Billy shook his head. "I don't think so." He looked up from the photo. "Who is she? She's pretty."

I took the paper back. "Barry Hawkins' sister-in-law." I started back toward my car.

He yelled as I opened the door to my car, "You're not going to tell me what's going on?"

I didn't have time to go into it, but Billy was my friend. And his mind was always something he'd put to good use. I could credit his thinking for more than half of the cases I'd solved. I left my door open and walked back to him. I pulled him aside so the delivery man couldn't hear. "She's the one who hit me with her car. But she also killed Shondra Rivers."

· · · ● · ● · · · ·

It was good to see the same bartender behind the bar when I first walked through the front door at Wilmington's. The place was fairly empty, as it had been last time I was there, with Frank Sinatra coming from the speakers on the ceiling.

I walked up to the bar and put the photo down as the bartender stepped over. "Is this the woman who was here with Shondra, when she was here with Barry Hawkins?"

He took the printed photo from my hand and nodded without hesitation. "Yes, that's her," he said. He leaned with one elbow down on the bar and handed it back to me. "I'm sure of it."

"Thank you," I said.

He asked if I wanted a drink. I shook my head and walked out.

⋯⋯•⋅•⋯⋯

My heart raced as I drove toward Ray and Shondra's house. If my assumption was right, I'd have enough to feel comfortable getting the sheriff's office involved.

There was already a For Sale sign up on the front lawn of the Rivers' house when I pulled up into the driveway. I was surprised to see it was listed so fast, but it turned out Ray and Shondra had not only fallen behind on their electric bills but also their mortgage.

I reached for the garage door remote next to me, a bit hesitant about pressing the button. The remote was the evidence I needed to prove Kim Cox had access to Ray and Shondra's house. If the door *didn't* open with the remote, I'd be back to square one. Or close to it.

I stepped out of my car and stood outside the driver's side with the door open, holding the remote in my hand. After a moment, I pointed it at the garage and clicked the button.

Nothing happened.

"No," I said, shaking my head. I clicked the button again. Still, nothing happened. Frustrated, I tossed the remote onto the passenger seat. I ducked back into the driver's seat and sat staring straight toward the house. I slammed both hands against the steering wheel in frustration.

I slapped the shifter into reverse and started to quickly back out of the driveway. But for one reason or another I put my foot on the brake and picked up the remote. I pointed it toward the garage and pressed the button with a little extra pressure, holding my thumb on it for a handful of seconds.

This time, the garage door opened.

• • • • • • • • • • •

I called Alex on my way to Mindy Hawkins' house to find Kim. But Alex wouldn't give me a chance to talk.

"Henry, I'm sorry," she said as soon as she answered. "I know you're mad, and I just need you to understand that—"

"Quiet," I said. "Listen for a minute. We can talk about all that later. I've figured it out. I know who killed Shondra Rivers."

First, there was silence. "What do you mean you know who killed Shondra?" she said.

"It was Mindy Hawkins' sister. Kim Cox."

"What?" she said, like she wasn't sure she believed me. "What makes you... what evidence do you have? Where are you?"

"I'm in my car," I said. "On my way to Mindy's. All I can tell you right now is I got lucky," I said. "There's no other way to explain it. I mean, we both knew she acted strange. I knew there was something about her from the moment we met."

I went on to tell her everything I knew. At least at that moment. Although the one thing I hadn't been able to put my finger on was why she would kill him. What was her motive?

"She was at Wilmington's with Barry and Shondra," I said. "So, she was somehow involved in whatever scheme they had going on. I don't have all the answers. But I have enough."

"It sounds like you're making some assumptions," she said.

"Is there something wrong with assumptions?" I said. "I still have evidence."

Alex said, "But don't you find it kind of strange, she brings her car to a used car lot, not far from here, the next day after she tried to take you out?"

"I told you, I don't have all the answers. She must've been in a hurry to get rid of it. Who knows what she was thinking."

"And left the garage door remote in the car?"

"It was way under the passenger seat," I said. "Maybe she thought she got rid of it."

Alex was quiet on the other end for a moment. "I think you should call Mike," she said.

"Not before I go to Mindy's house. I want the answers."

"It's not your job to corner the suspect. Let it go. Let the sheriff's office, let Mike handle it from here."

"No," I said. "And don't call him until you hear back from me. By the time I go through everything with him, he deals with all the red tape, who knows? Maybe she's already left the area."

# Chapter 34

I RANG THE DOORBELL a couple of times before Mindy's sister, Kim, opened the door.

Although I had been hoping she was there, I was also surprised to see her. I looked back toward the driveway. "Where's your Volvo?"

She stared back at me, appearing hesitant before she answered, "It was stolen."

"Stolen?" I said. I wanted to laugh. It crossed my mind to come right out and call her a liar, but I held my tongue. I knew I had to play her game. "I assume you reported it to the sheriff's office?"

She nodded, looking at me like I had two heads. "Of course I did." She squinted her eyes and looked out toward my car. "Where's your partner?"

"It's just me today," I said. "I wanted to ask you some questions, thought maybe the two of us, one-on-one."

She gave me a curious look, her eyes narrowed. "Mindy's not here, if you—"

"You're the one I'm here to talk to," I said.

She smiled. "Okay. Then would you like to come inside?"

She appeared to be a little too welcoming and more pleasant than she'd been the other times we'd met. Although, of course, I knew she had something to cover up. And I couldn't imagine how she'd know what I knew.

She pushed the door open and backed out of my way. "Come on in," she said.

I stepped past her and into the house. The place was warm. It smelled sweet, like someone had been baking.

I looked into the first room on the left, just inside the front door. With an upright piano and two chairs perfectly placed in front of a bookcase, the room looked to be one that went untouched. A room like the one I remembered my grandmother had, where I was never allowed to step into it.

I followed her into the kitchen, past the dining room where Alex and I had first sat down with Mindy. The piles of papers and folders stacked on the table and floor had all been removed. The room was spotless.

"I'm sorry the way I was the other day, when you came here. I hope you understand; I was looking out for my sister." She looked back at me over her shoulder. "Mindy's been through a lot."

"I understand," I said. I looked up toward the stairs and wondered if someone else could've been up there. Perhaps hiding. Something didn't seem right. I felt like I was being lured into a trap of some sort.

She stopped at the island in the kitchen and turned to me from the other side. I stood opposite her.

"So," she said. "How can I help?"

I looked her straight in the eye. "Why don't you start by telling me what really happened to the Volvo."

"What really happened?" She shrugged, tucking her hair behind her ear. "I woke yesterday and it was gone. Which is kind of odd, because this isn't the kind of neighborhood where something like this happens. Although it is a vintage vehicle." Kim frowned. "I've had that car since I graduated college."

"University of South Carolina?" I said.

"Yes."

I hesitated, not sure I should come right out with it or continue playing the game. But there was no sense in waiting any longer. "I know your car wasn't stolen."

Kim cocked her head back. "It wasn't stolen?" She laughed. "I... I don't understand. If it wasn't stolen, then—"

"Did you leave the keys in it?" I said.

She shook her head. "Why would I have left the keys in it?"

"Because whoever allegedly stole it, included a set of keys when it was sold to the used car lot in Fernandina Beach."

Her eyebrows tightened over her eyes. "Why would I bring my car to a used car lot in Fernandina Beach?"

"Well," I said. "I assume you foolishly believed you could bring it out there and nobody would see it. A way to get rid of any evidence."

"Evidence?" she said. "Evidence about what? What are you trying to insinuate? I'm sorry. I thought maybe you were a nice guy. But I'm starting to think you have a couple of screws loose." Kim pointed toward the door. "I want you to leave."

I didn't budge. "I saw the Volvo up there. And I know it's yours." I held out the piece of plastic from the Volvo's front light. "And this piece of plastic just happens to fit the cracked light cover on the right front of the car, I picked it up where

I was hit on Trout River Drive. I know it was your car. And I can only assume *you* were the one behind the wheel."

She stared back at me, shaking her head. "You think I tried to kill you? Are you nuts?"

"No. But I have a feeling you might be." I pulled the remote control from my pocket. "Recognize this?"

She looked down at my hand, holding the remote. With a shrug, she said, "It looks like a garage door remote."

I laughed. "The one you mistakenly left under the passenger seat inside your Volvo. And it just happens to open the garage door at the Rivers' house. I assume, in your haste to get rid of the car, you forgot to get rid of it."

Her eyes seemed to fill with tears. "You... you think I tried to hit you with my car? And... that I killed Shondra Rivers? Is that what you're trying to say? I swear to you, none of what you're saying is true. I never brought my car to some random used car lot. Why in the world would I do that?" She walked from the kitchen, and I followed her down the hall, unsure what exactly she was up to.

She walked into a bedroom, and I stood out in the hall, watching her. She opened a drawer on the dresser on the right.

"Don't even think about it," I said, only assuming she was about to pull out a gun.

"She fished through the drawer and turned to me with a piece of paper in her hand. "Here," she said, stepping toward me. She handed me the paper.

"What's this?" I said, taking it from her hand.

"The police report. My stolen vehicle report."

I ran my eyes up and down it, with KIM COX typed on top. The report had Mindy's address, where the alleged theft had occurred. It described the blue 1984 Volvo 240 station wagon with faded paint, a University of South Carolina sticker on the back, stolen between the hours of 9:00 p.m. and 8:00 a.m.

I looked up from the report. "This doesn't tell me anything. Other than you reported your car was stolen."

"But why would I bring it to a car dealer to try and sell it? Why wouldn't I try to hide it if I had a reason to do so?"

"It's not that easy to hide a car," I said. "I thought it was pretty smart of you, actually. Although once whoever purchased it realized it was stolen…"

She shook her head. "I'm telling you the truth. Did whoever you talk to tell you I was the one who brought it there? How do you know whoever stole it didn't bring it there?"

I shook my head. "The man I spoke with didn't know who dropped it off. He was supposed to let me know. I couldn't wait any longer, figured I'd get it right from the horse's mouth."

"You have to believe me," she said, placing her hand on my forearm. A tear came down her cheek. "I didn't do anything."

"I'm sorry," I said. "I don't believe you." I pulled my arm from her grasp. "It's not just the car." I held up the garage door opener. "Or this," I said. "Because I also know you had met with Shondra and Barry, at Wilmington's, downtown. Are you going to deny that too?"

"Shondra and Barry?" She shook her head. "Barry is the one who introduced me to Shondra. She was going to try and get me some contract work with the school system. It's been hard for me lately. And Barry thought she could help me. But after we met, Shondra wouldn't take my calls. She wouldn't call me back. And then, when Barry died, I've been out of work."

"You're trying to tell me you met in a fancy restaurant with Barry and Shondra about a job?" I laughed, shaking my head. "I'm sorry. Either you're quick on your feet, a good liar, or—"

"I have no reason to lie," she said. "You can ask Mindy. She knows I met with them."

I looked at my watch. "Where is Mindy?"

"I… I don't know. She was gone when I woke up this morning. I haven't heard from her."

"The thing is, to me, Mindy seems to be a little naïve. I could see how someone like you, a little manipulative, could easily pull the wool over her eyes. In fact, Barry had thrown her the line about how he didn't like Shondra. I knew it wasn't true. But your sister seemed to believe it. And when I found out he and Shondra had been meeting… and turns out you were there with them?" I shook my head. "I don't buy it," I said. "You expect me to believe you met with them about work?"

"It's the truth," Kim said.

I looked her in the eye. "I hate to be the one to tell you this, but I'm going to the cops with everything I know at this point. I don't have the time or the money to keep dealing with it. I've done my part."

I started for the door and she again grabbed me by the arm. "No!" she cried. "I swear to you, you have it all wrong. I didn't do it!"

I reached for the door but stopped, looking back at her. "Then tell me who did it. Because no matter what you've got baking in there, it doesn't cover up the smell of a liar."

She looked down toward the floor. Tears were flowing from her eyes now as she shook her head. "It wasn't me," she said.

"Then tell me the truth."

She raised her eyes to mine, shaking her head again. "I... I can't."

"What do you mean you can't? I told you, I'm done with this." I held up my cell phone. "Start talking. Or I'm calling the cops."

# Chapter 35

I WAS IN THE driveway leaning on the hood of the Mustang when Mindy Hawkins finally came home. I'd parked up near the garage, where she'd normally parked her Lexus.

"Henry?" she said, stepping out from her car. She looked around the yard. "What are you doing here?" She looked toward her front door. "Where's Kim?"

I had my arms folded in front of me, not giving her any answers until she was close enough I could look right into her eyes. "How about first you tell me where I can find Kevin?"

She stopped mid-step. "Excuse me?"

"Kevin? You know, your old high school sweetheart?"

Her mouth started to move, but she stood there, frozen.

"Where should I begin?" I said. I stepped away from the car. "With Barry?"

Mindy shook her head, shifting the purse she had hung on her shoulder so it was toward the front of her body. "I don't know what you're talking about."

"What I find crazy is that Barry had no idea Kevin was your old high school sweetheart when he hired him before the school year started."

I watched her move her hand, placing it on top of her purse.

"I'd think twice before you reach in there," I said. "You missed me with Kim's car. I assure you, you'll miss again. Don't think I'm alone this time. You reach in for that gun, I promise you won't have a chance to get off a shot."

She scanned around the yard as if looking for a sign of someone else there with us. "What do you want?" she said. "You don't have a client anymore. You're not a cop. What does any of this matter to you?"

"What do I want? The truth. And I guess we can start with you telling me what happened to Barry."

She reached into her purse and removed a small 9mm pistol, pointing it toward me. "You didn't have to stay involved in any of this."

"Maybe not," I said. "But here we are. So you might as well tell me the truth."

Mindy stared into my eyes without a response.

"What's the difference now?" I said. "You're going down for murdering Ray and Shondra Rivers. Although... I still haven't figured out how you killed Barry."

She shook her head. "I didn't kill him!" She closed her eyes and took a deep breath. "Shondra and Barry were together outside the school that morning. The only reason I knew is because Kevin saw them. They were in her car."

"Shondra and Barry? They were in her car? You mean—"

Mindy nodded. "You're a grown man," she said. "I don't think I have to explain what I mean."

"Yeah, but I didn't know grown men went parking, like teenagers in a school parking lot."

"When they're cheating on their wives they do," she said.

"And Kevin saw them? He told you?"

"Of course he told me. He was more than happy to have proof Barry was cheating on me. He'd been trying to tell me that for months, so I'd leave Barry."

"And be with Kevin?" I said.

"Oh, I don't know. We'd messed around a little here and there over the past few months. But it was more for, I don't know, old times' sake. At the time, I couldn't see myself with a man who drives a Harley, sweeps floors at a high school." She shrugged. "But he grew on me, like when we were kids."

She was dressed like the last time I saw her, with the black boots and tight black jeans. She even had the black leather vest over her white, long-sleeved T-shirt.

I said, "So, what happened? Did Kevin kill Barry?"

She shook her head. "Nobody killed Barry. Although Kevin was worried someone was going to point the finger at him. That's when we decided to try and turn it toward Ray."

"But what did he do after he saw them?"

"Kevin? He left, went and got a coffee. He didn't want them to see him. Although, he had his Harley. Of course, they must've heard it. But I can't tell you what happened after he left. He got back; Shondra's car was gone. He went inside and found Barry. He was already dead."

"So you killed Shondra because of their affair?"

Mindy kept the pistol pointed toward me. "She had my money." She looked over her shoulder, toward the street.

"Your money?" I said. "You mean the money they stole from the school?"

"Why should she've gotten to keep his half? He was my husband. That money belonged to me."

"But it was stolen," I said.

She laughed, shaking her head. "Money's money. But what a selfish, foolish woman Shondra was. All she had to do was give me my share. And none of us would be in this position."

"So you just killed her?"

Mindy squinted her eyes, like she was thinking it through. "It wasn't my intention. Not initially. But I was mad. If she thought I was going to walk away without getting it, she had another thing coming."

"So am I right, that she let you in the house?"

"The first time, she did. I tried to have a civil conversation with her. Woman to woman. But she was very hostile toward me. To think, I'm the one who was cheated on, and she's the one treating me like I'm wrong for wanting what's mine?" She laughed.

"I'm going to go ahead and assume that's when you took the garage door opener? On the way out?"

She stared back at me, a slight tilt to her head. She finally nodded. "I decided I'd go back when she was asleep. But I needed help. So I called Kevin. At first, he didn't want anything to do with it. But I promised him we could be together. I promised him we'd get all the money from Shondra. The full two hundred grand." She grinned. "Some people may turn down love, but few turn their back on the green stuff."

"So he helped you kill her?" I said.

"Kevin?" She shook her head. "I didn't tell him I was going to kill her. In fact, I still hadn't made up my mind. But he's smarter than he looks. It was actually his idea to plant Ray's earring at the scene."

"So you went in through the garage. But she didn't hear it open? When she was in bed?"

"I went in before she got home. And I waited, hiding in that mess in their garage." She laughed. "I thought she'd never go to bed."

I closed my eyes, picturing Mindy sneaking up the stairs to Shondra's bedroom, the knife in her hand. "I still don't understand why you went out of your way to set Ray up? You sounded like you liked the man, but you were intent on taking him down."

She shrugged. "I had a feeling he knew more than he'd let on. Honestly, I thought he knew where the money was."

"So you killed him?"

"Well, with the two of you out of the picture, nobody would be able to figure it out. I've never hit anybody with a car before. It's not as easy as you'd think." She nodded her chin toward me. "Hitting you with that nine-iron, I should have taken care of you then."

I reached for the wound, although somewhat healed, above my nose. "That was you in the back of the store?"

She smiled. "I used to play a lot of golf when I was younger. The game had gotten so expensive, I really hadn't been able to afford to play. But it sure felt good gripping the club, taking those swings."

At that point it was easy for me to figure out Mindy was more than just a woman after stolen money. And as I looked at the muzzle pointed my way, I started to wonder if backup was going to show.

"So where's the money?" I said.

The sly smile dropped from her face. She shook her head. "I wish I knew. Kevin disappeared with it."

"I don't believe that."

"It's the truth," she said, nodding her head. "He said we had to get the Volvo out of here, after I told him I tried to kill you with it. He knew of that place up in Fernandina Beach. But then we'd have to get Kim involved more than she already was. It was my idea to tell her it was stolen. But I waited for Kevin to come back." She shook her head. "I haven't heard from him since."

"What makes you think he has the money?"

She didn't respond, her eyes going past me toward her house. "What have you done with my sister?" she said.

"She's safe," I said. "Away from you."

She sighed. "Kim was always the good one. Even my parents liked her the best. But I tried to keep her out of it. She couldn't mind her own business. Wouldn't stop asking questions. I know she tried to help. That stupid Twitter post... like that did any good." She sighed again. "I should've known I couldn't trust her."

"You couldn't trust her? That's funny, coming from someone who used her sister's vehicle to commit crimes. And you weren't even smart enough to pick up the remote from under the seat."

"Well, of course, it would've raised suspicion, if anyone saw my car out there. And Kevin's Harley makes so much damn noise."

Mindy kept the gun pointed and stepped backward, facing me, slowly moving toward her car. "You seem like a nice enough person, Henry. I hate that I have to kill you too."

I looked around for cover, but all I saw were bushes and the corner of the house. I was worried she wasn't buying my initial warning and was clearly calling my bluff. "I told you I'm not alone. You can shoot me if you want, but I promise you won't make it out of the driveway."

She shook her head. "You seem honest. But at this time, I'm going to have to believe you're lying." She looked around. "There's nobody else here. And the way that cranky detective spoke of you, I can't see him showing up to save you."

I stared back at her, wondering where everyone was.

Mindy stared back at me, raising her free hand toward the gun. She held it with both hands, pointed straight at me. "I'm sorry, Henry." But she looked toward the street when the yellow Jeep came flying around the corner and into the driveway.

Alex was behind the wheel, smashing into the rear end of Mindy's Lexus and sending it straight toward me. I dove out of the way of the car.

Mindy was on the ground, the gun a few feet from her. Her face was bloodied from the fall, but she quickly crawled toward the gun. She grabbed it and fired a shot in my direction, trying to get to her feet. She was up on one knee, the gun raised toward me as she tried for another shot. This time she looked to be taking better aim.

I raised my hands in front of my face and another shot rang out.

I squeezed my eyes shut, expecting the explosion of pain. If I was lucky enough to feel it. But I looked myself over and knew I hadn't been hit. I shifted my eyes back to Mindy.

She dropped her gun and fell to the ground.

Alex walked up behind her, the Glock in her hand still pointed at Mindy.

"Is she dead?" I said, pushing myself up from the driveway.

Mindy had blood on her shoulder, but she was up on all fours. She crawled for her gun a few feet away and had it in her hand before Alex or I could get to her. She turned over, pointing it toward Alex.

But Alex swung her foot through the air and knocked it from Mindy's hand. The gun flew past the driveway and dropped in the grass.

I hurried over and picked up Mindy's gun. "Thanks for coming," I said, wiping the dirt off my arms. "You didn't call Mike?"

She nodded and looked toward the street as the maroon Crown Vic turned the corner, the tires squealing as Mike cut the wheel and pulled into the driveway. He slammed on the brakes and stopped inches from Alex's Jeep.

Three sheriff's vehicles showed up behind him and pulled onto the grass. The officers jumped from the cars, guns drawn.

# Chapter 36

I sat on my chair on the dock outside my boat with a bottle of beer I'd hardly made a dent in. I followed Wendell Richards with my eyes as he walked across the lot and onto the dock. He was dressed in a beige suit, no tie, suspenders stretched to either side of his round stomach, showing from under his suit jacket.

He reached his hand out as I stood from my chair. "I'll be honest with you," he said, shaking my hand. "I was far from convinced Ray was innocent," he said. "Glad you proved my initial instincts wrong."

I nodded with a grin. "To be honest, I wasn't either. And I'm not convinced I would've ever figured it out if I didn't get a little lucky."

"Seems to me it was more than just luck," he said. "Persistence doesn't hurt either. I imagine in your business, it's a big part of your success. Am I right?"

Out of the corner of my eye, I saw Billy's Lexus pull into the parking lot. Alex was in the passenger seat, her Jeep being repaired for the damage. I nodded toward them and said to Wendell, "It doesn't hurt to have friends on your side."

Wendell tucked his thumbs inside his suspenders, had his eyes toward Alex and Billy stepping out from the car. "I hear you and Alex won't be working together anymore? Is that true?"

"Well," I said. "It's not a done deal yet. But I'm pretty sure it will be soon. She's taking a job up in North Carolina."

"You don't look happy about that," he said.

I laughed, shaking my head. "Should I be?" I shrugged and sipped my beer. "She's a good detective. It'll be good for her, get back out there. I guess I'd have to say it's where she belongs."

Wendell reached inside his jacket, came out with an envelope. "This is for you and Alex."

I looked it over but didn't open it. Both sides were blank. "What is it?"

"The money for your work on Ray's case. You think you weren't going to get paid?"

I folded it over and tucked it in my back pocket. "I assumed when the client's killed..."

"Well, he wasn't your client, Henry," Wendell said. "He was mine. Remember? I'm the one who hired you to do a job. And you did it."

I shook his hand one more time. "Thank you, Wendell."

We both turned to Alex and Billy as they stepped up onto the dock.

"Good work," Wendell said, reaching out to shake Alex's hand. "And good luck with the new job, Detective."

She smiled with a shrug. "It's not official yet. Still have to go through a few steps."

Wendell gave her a nod. "Well, you need a good word from a small-town lawyer…" He started to walk away and stopped before he stepped off the dock. "Henry, I may have something coming up, right around the corner. If you're interested in more work." He stood, waiting for my response.

"I'm going to take a little break. I'm heading down to Naples to visit my parents. I'll probably stay down there for a couple of months. But you have my number. You can call me whenever something comes up. You never know."

Wendell nodded then headed across the parking lot without another word.

I reached into my back pocket and handed the envelope to Alex. "He gave us this. Payment for the work."

"Wendell?" she said, looking confused. "He paid us the rest?"

"That's what I just said."

"But he must not've been paid, right? You sure we should—"

"I wondered the same thing. It's fine." I leaned down and reached under my chair. I pulled out the small canvas cooler with a couple of beers on ice inside. I took one out and held it out for Alex. "You want one?"

She shook her head and waved it off. "Not tonight."

I put it back in the cooler and looked at the beer in my hand I'd been drinking. I didn't really want it.

Billy had gone up onto the boat and came down with two more lawn chairs. "So, are you serious about not wanting the office anymore?" He unfolded the two chairs.

Alex sat down in one of them, next to me.

Billy didn't sit. "A couple of local insurance agents are interested in renting the space. Husband-and-wife team. They sat at the bar last night, happened to ask about the space. I told them I'd have to let them know. I won't feel obligated to cut them the deal I gave you these last couple of years. So maybe now I can make some decent money off the place." He laughed.

"With Alex leaving," I said, "I just don't see what I need it for." I looked at my boat. "I can get away with working here. Or sit at your bar, same way I always have."

Billy looked out toward the river. "You can sit at my bar anytime," he said. "But I'm not sure how often I'll be there over the next few months." He turned back to me. "I hired a bartender I'll be training to take my place. We're not getting any younger. And, for me, running around behind that bar every night, trying to run a restaurant..." He shook his head. "It's too much. I need a break."

"I hope you're not thinking about selling?" I said.

He shook his head. "No. But I'm tired." He sat down in the chair across from me and Alex. "I've talked to Chloe already. She's going to have more responsibility. Help manage the place. With Jake's help, of course. If I can get it to a point I can trust everyone to keep the place running smoothly, I'd like to do some traveling."

"Seriously?" I said, looking from Billy to Alex. "Why are you both leaving me?" I picked up my bottle of beer from under my chair and held it because I felt I should take a sip. But I didn't.

"You told Wendell you were going to Naples," Billy said. "And it didn't sound like you'd be in a hurry to get back."

I thought for a moment. "I don't think I'm staying down there forever, but"—I faced Alex—"but I might have to travel up to North Carolina once in a while, see if Detective Jepson'll need a hand."

Alex smiled, tight lipped, and put her hand on my shoulder. "You'd better visit." Her phone rang. "Sorry. One minute." She stood up and stepped away, facing the parking lot, with her back to us. "Hey, Mike," she said, the phone up to her ear. She looked at me, nodding. "Yeah, he's right here." She turned back to the parking lot. "You're here? At the marina? Henry's marina?"

I stood up as Mike walked toward us and stepped up onto the dock. "I figured you'd all be here," he said. He gave Billy a nod and looked at Alex. "I thought I'd come out, thank you both." He reached out and shook my hand. "You're not a bad PI, Walsh." He cleared his throat. "We tracked Kevin Smith down, up in Georgia. He's confessed to his role helping Mindy, but claims he didn't kill anyone... was just trying to help his old girlfriend. Although he's still being hit with plenty of charges. We still haven't located the missing two hundred thousand, although John Mazer's cooperating with us. He says it's all in cash, which I was surprised to hear. Linda Green is still missing, and Mindy Hawkins claims she has nothing to do with her disappearance. But with her suddenly missing along with all that cash, I can't tell you I'm confident she'll be located anytime soon."

I reached down and grabbed a beer from the cooler for Mike. "Thirsty?"

He shook his head. "I am. But I'm trying to quit smoking. I have a beer, the next thing you know I'm burning through another pack of cigarettes."

The four of us stood quiet, like nobody knew what else to say.

Mike gave Alex a nod. "I'm sure I'm going to see you, before you leave. Right?"

She stepped forward and gave him a hug. It was hard to tell, but I thought she had tears in her eyes. Even though it was dusk, she kept her sunglasses on her face.

Mike started for the parking lot.

"Thanks for helping her get that job," I said. "But now who's going to be there to get between us when we don't see eye to eye?"

Mike stopped, turning to me. "Who knows how long either of us is going to be around doing this stuff. All I know is right now I'm going home, get a good three hours of sleep. I'll worry about tomorrow when I wake up." He continued across the parking lot toward his car. He stepped into the Crown Vic, closed the door, and took off toward Trout River Drive.

I stepped to the edge of the dock and tipped my bottle of beer, emptying it into the river. I looked out at the orange sky above where the sun had slipped below the horizon.

• • • • • • • • • •

Thank you for reading *Dead Luck*. If you enjoyed the story, please leave a review on our store or wherever you purchased it. If you're ready for more, the adventure continues with the next book in the series, *A Shot in the Dark*. Find out more by visiting: GregoryPayette.com

Sign up for the newsletter on my website:

**GregoryPayette.com**

Once or twice a month I'll send you updates and news. Plus, you'll be the first to hear about new releases with special prices. If you'd like to receive the Henry Walsh prequel (for free) use the sign-up form here:

**GregoryPayette.com/crossroad**